These Golden Days

'*These Golden Days* seem limpid. This sequel to *One and Last Love* takes his narrator ahead several years into an autumnal happiness he celebrates in a lyrical tone that is touching, not sentimental . . . his exactness is bathed (not shrouded) in light, a sunshine of fulfilment that transforms whatever he deals with' *Financial Times*

'Utterly believable' *Good Housekeeping*

'An absorbing, lucid . . . account of an individual struggle to make good an independent life style and nurture a relationship free of exploitation, that must find an echo among many embattled spirits' *Time Out*

'John Braine has lost nothing of his ability to write clear, tense and evocative English' *Yorkshire Post*

JOHN BRAINE

These
Golden Days

A Methuen Paperback

A Methuen Paperback

THESE GOLDEN DAYS

British Library Cataloguing in Publication Data

Braine, John
    These golden days.
    I. Title
    823′.914[F]   PR6052.R265
    ISBN 0-413-15490-4

First published in Great Britain 1985
by Methuen London Ltd
This edition published 1987
by Methuen London Ltd
11 New Fetter Lane, London EC4P 4EE
Copyright © 1985 John Braine

Printed and bound in Great Britain
by Richard Clay Ltd, Bungay, Suffolk

This book is sold subject to the condition
that it shall not, by way of trade or otherwise,
be lent, resold, hired out, or otherwise circulated
without the publisher's prior consent in any form of
binding or cover other than that in which it is
published and without a similar condition
including this condition being imposed
on the subsequent purchaser.

'Love has never been a question of age. I shall never be so old as to forget what love is.'

Colette

One

First of all you have to see Vivien Canvey, the great love of my life. *Great love of my life* isn't the sort of phrase I'm given to using, but in this case it's absolutely accurate: I met Vivien eight years ago, when I was fifty-two and she was forty-four, and we've been lovers for seven years.

She doesn't look her age, nor does she give a damn about it. She has black hair and hazel eyes and strongly marked eyebrows, not bushy, always properly trimmed, but real eyebrows. And her skin is creamy rather than sallow, warm and glowing but essentially fair, essentially English. Her face is what I call Regency, with a high-bridged nose, always responsive, always alive, never afraid. I've never seen even the faintest blemish on her skin, and she has very few lines. Not that it matters: neither of us cares about age.

It was different before I met her. Then it was a matter of pride with me to go about with very much younger women, even thirty years younger. There is a stage in their life when young women prefer older men, particularly successful writers, whose professions have glamour and who have the advantage of a Name. It's not much of a name in comparison with show business Names, but these things count. What's always helped with me, too, is the fact that I actually like women. Many Englishmen don't really like women. It isn't that they're homosexual. They prefer the company of men, just as some absolutely heterosexual women prefer the company of women. I, however, enjoy the company of women, just as Vivien enjoys the company of men.

I see this all clearly now and don't confuse simply enjoying the company of women with being a champion swordsman. I can be friendly with women now with absolutely no sexual intrusions. More and more it strikes me, particularly since coming to Hampstead some eighteen months ago, that men and women have much more to give each other than ever they're asked for. What they have to give each other is simple happiness, though I should of course define it more precisely. What I'm talking about with Vivien is a positive peace, a lively quietude. There is no more loneliness, even when she's not with me. I talk to her often when she's not here, though not aloud. I save up things to tell her about, I give her descriptions of anything of interest or amusement that's happened to me just as I give her flowers and little presents, the presents always gift-wrapped. The gift-wrapping and the ribbon add to the festivity of life.

Of course our relationship is based upon absolute fidelity. Nothing else would be good enough. We live in a place where people are in favour of special arrangements, where it makes one's head ache to sort out who was married to whom, which children are natural and which children stepchildren – and who right now is sleeping with whom or sometimes, even more astoundingly, who is not sleeping with whom.

But we are a couple and briefly you'd better see me. My name is Tim Harnforth, I am a professional writer like Vivien, and I am sixty. I don't feel it, I think that there's been some mistake, but there it is. Some people think that

8

I look younger, but recently at places like cinemas and libraries I've been asked if I wasn't paying too much – with the best of intentions, the cashier or library assistant has thought I was entitled to an old-age pensioner's reduction or didn't have to pay a fine. However, I still have my hair, and it's mostly brown, with only a few touches of grey.

My eyes are blue, a shade darker than light. I haven't too many wrinkles, though there are the telltale deep lines at each side of the mouth, which are the result of biting the bullet. There's an interesting book about human faces, and I like to think that I've got a Lion face, like Robert Redford, but suspect that at the best I've got an Earth face, like Henry the Eighth. My body is an Irish navvy's body, a Regimental Sergeant-Major's body, built more for endurance than for speed. It isn't in terribly good shape, but it works in all the essential ways. And, finally, what is perhaps more important for a man than a woman, I'm two inches under six foot.

Now you can see me. When Vivien talks about my personal appearance, as she does do, she sees me with the eyes of love. So that's not quite enough for a personal description, though indeed you might be able to make your own personal deductions.

Now to the place where I've been living for nearly two years: a little courtyard off the lower end of Heath Street, below the Hampstead Tube Station, on the same side as the Three Horseshoes. There are only three houses in the courtyard, all on three storeys and painted white, and with window-boxes on the upper windows. They're solid, no-nonsense mid-Victorian houses with large square windows and all, curiously enough, have bright pink doors. I don't know the reason for this uniformity, because only the one I live in is rented. And the rule in this part of London is that everyone does their own thing, even to the point of eccentricity. The whole appeal of the Village is its glorious mix of styles and exterior paintwork. But in this instance the uniformity works; don't ask me why. And the courtyard is cobbled. The entrance is off an alley off another alley, and though the traffic in Heath Street is so near, the sound is always muted there. It's not almost moribund, not too silent, as it used to be in the part of the Surrey town of Boxley where once I lived, but somehow the noise from outside is soft-pedalled. And inside my flat it's soft-pedalled too though not strangled, not cut off, which is worse than the worst of noises, because one isn't in touch with the life of the streets.

There is in my flat a large living-room with the sink, a gas cooker, a rubbish bin, and open shelves behind a hinged partition. There's a three-seater sofa in dark green moquette, a beechwood rocking chair with tie-on cushions, a let-down beech table with four dining-chairs in steel and black plastic, a large circular coffee table and a beech writing-bureau. Above the partition there are two very large cupboards. Only the bottom sections are much use for storage unless one has the use of a step-ladder. It doesn't matter to me; since coming here I've made the rule of travelling light, of accumulating no personal possessions except absolute necessities, of throwing away or selling anything which I don't use.

This is all part of the action which Vivien and I take against what we term the Brent Cross Syndrome – visit the Brent Cross Shopping Centre on a Saturday and you'll see what we mean. It isn't that we don't prefer seeing well-fed and cheerful people driving to such places in nice shiny cars and spending like mad, to seeing people starving in wretched stinking hovels in hellholes like Calcutta – or for that matter on the road as refugees or confined in camps behind barbed wire. But for ourselves, in the time we've got left upon this earth, we don't want to waste any energy upon acquiring any more consumer goods, whether durable or otherwise. So there's nothing of mine in my flat beyond books and clothes and a large old pine chest full of manuscripts, and my radio-cassette tape recorder. There are magazines and papers on top of the chest. The TV and video recorder are rented. I have thought of buying a new refrigerator (there's one in the cupboard left of the sink, together with the gas heater), but it's too much trouble.

There are, of course, the three oil paintings I have – all large, all of urban *trompe-l'oeil* effect – but I've grown increasingly fond of them over the years, and they're very easy to transport; they don't clutter my life. I often take consolation in reflecting that if the worst comes to the worst and I'm made bankrupt there's nothing anyone can take from me – I no longer own property or furniture or indeed any valuable consumer durables, and, when I come to think of it, even the radio-cassette tape recorder and my books are the tools of my trade.

The conducted tour of my flat is soon concluded. A small bedroom with a single bed and a bedside cabinet and a bookcase and a small wardrobe and a beech chest-of-drawers. There's a large red wool tartan rug in there which Vivien gave me, but if the bailiffs ever come, I'll tell them it's an essential part of the bed-clothes.

There's nothing else to tell you. The walls are stippled cream, dark grey above the picture rail. The paintwork is cream and in fair condition. The rooms are lofty. In the living-room and bedroom there's dark-brown fitted carpeting. I bought the bathroom mats and the sheepskin bedside rug, but if the bailiffs do come, how are they to know that they're mine?

When Vivien and I first became lovers some years ago she taught me how to love for the first time. I don't mean only how to love a woman; indeed, she taught me that, indeed she taught me how much a woman has to give a man.

This doesn't mean that what we have didn't start from sexual attraction, a sort of *coup de foudre*, some eight years ago at a weekend conference of the Radical Association at Bratton Manor in Hertfordshire. What I felt upon seeing that vivid face for the first time I still feel in precisely the same way. Her face still astounds me with delight. And making love to her is always as if for the first time. Both of us were descended upon by Eros. He can be a cruel god, and wrecks more lives than he enhances, but he has been kind to us, he has shown with us what he can do when he puts his mind to it.

Friendship is an integral part of what Vivien and I have between us, and had she been a man she still would have been my friend. We don't have any language problems; whether or not we agree with each other or not, we always understand each other. And even when we've had real quarrels, even when she's made me have the sensation of the top of my head opening and shutting, even when she's made me feel quite literally sick and tired, it hasn't destroyed the friendship. And there's always been decency, there's always been humanity, there's always been honour. Not very often and not for very long there's been war between us, but it's been an old-fashioned war, war according to the rules.

But there is no question of romance dwindling, of Eros ever being absent. There's much to be said for settling for affection and friendship, and an easy-going and matter-of-fact cooperation, enlivened by healthy and straightforward animal desire. There's much to be said simply for each partner considering their own best interests. I don't always see eye-to-eye with Christ but, like him, commend the Unjust Steward inasmuch as he was wise in his own generation. I would have thought myself lucky if my ex-wife Val had quite coolly and selfishly considered what was the best for her.

There is so much to say to you that I run ahead of myself – so much has happened to me that I want to tell you about that I scarcely know where to begin. (And who is *you*? The Victorians would have had no qualms about it. *Reader*, they would have said. *Reader, I married him*, is the classic Victorian statement.) What I've told you so far is absolutely real. I exist, Vivien exists. And it's easy enough to get to Hampstead, wherever you may live. Or, come to that, to Casterley in the West Riding of Yorkshire. It's just over two hours from King's Cross to Leeds by the Inter-City, just over thirty minutes by road to Casterley. And there has been another important place in my life, which is Boxley in Surrey, but that's not much more than forty minutes from Waterloo.

There are other people and other places in my story, but what matters to you is Vivien and me, Hampstead and Boxley and Casterley. I know what I want from novels. I want to be surprised and delighted. I want the unexpected to keep on happening, I want an ending which brings all the threads together, which establishes a totally satisfying and harmonious shape, yet which leaves you with the feeling of having been spectators at one battle of a war which still continues. Where this novel will end will be the right and proper end, but if the action doesn't continue beyond it, if you're no longer interested in what happens to Vivien and me beyond it, then it has failed.

I capture what I know about, what I've seen, heard, touched, smelled, tasted. At this very moment in June, just past midsummer, I talk to you, my reader, about the

Midsummer Party of the World Writers in Chelsea. It's been a buffet supper, but with places reserved at three long tables. All for the price of six pounds there's been unlimited red and white wine, both French but, of course, not vintage. The white wine, though naturally it didn't keep chilled enough throughout the evening, was neither too acid nor too sweet. I can't tell you anything about the red wine, because I never drink red wine unless of Château-neuf du Pape standard, but I could see people who know more about wine than I do drinking it and coming back for more.

This evening I actually sat out in the patio adjoining the bar, a large courtyard with a rockery and a high stone wall and a green-painted gate adjoining the street. The bar is a long narrow lofty room with signed photographs of authors of the standing of John O'Hara and William Saroyan and Sinclair Lewis, and framed cartoons and drawings from a period when writers were actually of as much importance to the media as politicians and pop and sports stars are now. This evening I've enjoyed myself. Outside on the street, surprisingly, the chestnuts have not yet cast their flambeaux; the Alpine aster and the rockrose and the edelweiss and the pansies are in full bloom in the rockery; and Vivien and I were entirely happy eating chicken and ham and roast beef, beetroot salad and tomato-and-onion salad and mixed salad and wholemeal rolls with our best friends of all, Tibor and Ruth Bachony. Tibor and Ruth are in their forties, both very alike, short with sleek black hair and round cheerful faces.

And the evening has been perfect for midsummer, cool not cold, with a hint of sadness, and a twilight which seemed longer than most midsummer twilights, like a dancer knowing she's fully captured her audience, unwilling to leave the stage, ready to give any number of encores.

14

That's how it's been this evening. And people have drifted from room to room, glasses in their hands, not drunk and silly and boring, but beyond themselves, and have come to our table and talked to us and drifted away, the occasion a real occasion, relaxed and spontaneous, but having a shape.

And the best of it all, my reader, is that Vivien and I were always together – we came together and we left together – but always were also fully together with other people. We began the evening in the bar, met people we knew and went away to them, came back together, somehow ended up on the patio with Tibor and Ruth. At a real party everyone mixes. One of the worst sins is for two people to go to a party and stay with each other all the time. But what's even worse is for one of the couple to be a solo turn and latch on to someone else, singular or plural, and totally to forget who he or she came with. And worst of all is for one to get pissed and treat the other as a minder, the muggins who'll hold them up when they're spewing and make the apologies and drive them home or pour them into a taxi.

It hasn't been like that with Vivien and me. What I've learned since I came to live in Hampstead nearly two years ago, is not to be greedy. It's not just a question of not being too greedy for food or for drink or for notice. (In what I often feel is a country which is not merely tepid but torpid there's not much danger of men, in particular, being too greedy for sex.) It's a question of wanting to possess too much, it's a question again of the Brent Cross Syndrome. Greed, the desire to possess things, spreads out into the desire to possess human beings. And greed is always bound up with hurry, the desire to gulp rather than sip; greed is the desire to possess quickly and immediately, to possess it all so that no-one else will get any.

Greed this evening at World Writers would have been in me getting sloshed quickly, in making a beeline for the nearest attractive woman who showed any interest in me, in taking 'phone numbers, in making luncheon engagements which I'd no intention of keeping, in showing off – or rather, in trying to show off. Greed might also have been rather more subtle: gulping my white wine, I might well have talked mainly to one person who, one way or another, would have seemed to offer me something to improve my material circumstances or build up my ego. And Vivien would have taken me to Waterloo as she used to in the old days and, even if I'd not had a hangover, the next day would have ended in tears.

Tomorrow will not end in tears, and we shall be in Hampstead together. All of this day has been happy, but happy because ruled by order and tranquillity. And tomorrow I shall remember it all, I'll remember what everyone looked like and all that they said and how they said it. And there will be nothing I don't want to remember. True love has spread through the whole of my life and I see now that, when I was living at what I jestingly described as my home in Surrey, I was being hurt every day. There is nothing more painful than living under the same roof with a person who doesn't love you; there is nothing more souring than not wanting to go home. And because now I want to remember each day, it's almost as if I had stopped time. No longer am I afraid of time's passing: it's as if I stand outside it. No longer do I have a sense of time being spent to no purpose, no longer is any of it lost. Nothing is lost now, and I no longer dread old age.

I can remember many nights when I hoped, on going to sleep, that I wouldn't wake up. And, paradoxically, often I'd think of death and be afraid. I look forward each night now to waking up and I'm never afraid of death now, I see it as part of the pattern. It's a pattern which only has one flaw: selfishly I hope that I die before Vivien, because I wouldn't want to live in a world without her.

Two

And now it's the morning after: eight o'clock and the June sun pouring in through the net curtains. I'm reading the paper and listening to the radio. The music is pleasant and undemanding. I'm never sad in the morning. Even if yesterday has been lousy, there's always a chance that today will be better. Easy for me to say, of course: I'm getting back on my feet financially, the work is going well, and for a professional writer there's always the chance of a sudden influx of big money. No doubt I'd feel differently this morning if I were an unemployed steelworker in Scunthorpe or, come to that, an unemployed executive in Weybridge with a mortgage and two children at private schools and absolutely no prospect of another job.

So I enjoy my breakfast of a large orange and Jordan's muesli (sweetened with raw sugar and with no additives, a genuine high-fibre food) with extra seedless raisins and a banana added to it. This isn't a working day; it's Friday, when Vivien comes at three and we go to bed together after a cup of tea and then have a leisurely supper and watch TV or listen to music or, more often than not, just talk. We always have plenty to talk about.

I finish my breakfast, then rinse the breakfast things and put them in the drying-rack. I clear up as I go along. Without being obsessively fussy, I'm lace-curtain Irish my mother's side and lace-curtain English my father's side, *petit bourgeois* through and through. What I aim at is a military and masculine neatness: I know exactly where everything is. Every day I throw out all the papers and magazines I don't want to keep, every six weeks or so I get rid of all the books I absolutely don't want to read again. And I set the table for breakfast last thing at night, no matter how tired I am.

That's how I want my life to be: no mess, no disorder, no dirt, moving as a crack regiment moves into battle. This flat is both my home and my place of work: once I let rubbish accumulate, it won't function as either. There is only room for one to live here, though I suppose that in case of necessity someone could bed down on the sofa. Only room for one to live here? Put it another way: the flat was meant for one person, meant for one person who most of the time needs solitude. Solitude means being by oneself through choice; loneliness is having no choice in the matter. Vivien and I share our lives and are absolutely emotionally and spiritually committed to each other, but we don't share a home. She needs solitude too, and not only because we have the same profession. She needs space in her life, as I do; she needs to be still and to let things come to her.

Things? Not, of course, material objects. But experiences, true feelings, true thoughts, true thoughts not in the abstract, true thoughts which aren't mere juggling with jargon. Think of a little child or a dog or a cat meeting someone for the first time. Move towards them and they'll run away. Stay still and calm and relaxed – relaxed not frozen – and slowly they'll come to you. And that's why Vivien and I need solitude.

I brew myself another mug of tea – which I'll leave in the pot so that it gets really strong – and light a cigarette and lie down on the sofa, pulling the coffee-table alongside me.

I'm quite happy for the moment simply to exist. I don't think of anything in particular; I taste the tea and the tobacco, and I take them both slowly. Real smokers, the dedicated ones, always say that I don't smoke cigarettes, I waste them; often they go out because I take so few puffs. When I've finished the tea and two cigarettes I move to the table and write six letters and send off two cheques and I'm still full of energy and I'm thinking of finishing the notes for the synopsis of the radio play which I promised, and then suddenly it's happened and I've run out of steam, the energy has drained away suddenly and I have to lie on the sofa and I close my eyes and drift off but then see Val's face, white and bitter, and hear her words: *We all hate you, we wish you'd go, we're only happy without you* . . .

And then I'm not really resting but struck prostrate and wounded and even if I could sleep I'd fight against sleeping, because I know what sort of dreams I'd have. I'm back in the house at Boxley in Surrey, the comfortable Twenties house with a third of an acre of well-kept gardens but it's grown bigger and grander, with domed rooms, impossibly lofty, and it's full of people I don't know, all misshapen, all grotesque, all hating me and all laughing at me, and I'm looking for my children and am always catching a glimpse of them and I'm running after them but everyone's in the way, all laughing. And there's always the great sense of loss – I have lost it now, lost most of the things which I worked to build up, and that's why I'll always in future travel light. And I shall love as the pagans love, I'll only love those who love me.

And, reader, I'll not be unhappy. There will have to be some unhappiness in my story; I am forced to remember things I'd rather forget. That's how it happened – my life started to become unbearable some four years ago and grew steadily more unbearable until only anti-depressants and alcohol and seeing Vivien once a week saved my sanity. I always see sex, when desired equally by two people, as being both godlike and serenely and cosily amoral. I've never been sad after love, as all humans are supposed to be. Even when I've made love to the wrong woman, I've always been jocund, like cocks and lions. When dressed and leaving a warm bed to go home I have, of course, been aware that I was heading for trouble and have ceased to be jocund. The imminent trouble, though, is what has made me sad, not making love. The wages Eros pays are always the highest, but often they're fairy gold.

And now I'm rested and I'm out in the cobbled court-yard and the sun's dazzling and it's very warm, but there's still a cool breeze. I emerge as Cressida from next door scurries out with a black executive briefcase, looking every inch the rising media producer in dark glasses and her blonde hair short in a style which I term 'NW3 Punk,' spiky but not outrageous, just spiky enough to show that she's absolutely with it. And her linen trouser suit isn't a track suit but somehow informs one that she's fit enough to jog if she really wanted to. She's very slim and her jacket is amply cut but I'm aware of pert little breasts under the linen. There's a red patterned handkerchief round her neck which will, of course, be silk and she wears a very large watch with at least six buttons, digital and analogue functions, and no doubt at least a dozen others, and waterproof up to 300 metres. But I once saw her going out to dinner in the evening, and she was wearing a wafer-thin gold watch with diamonds for numerals.

She's the sort of person one sees around here, and simply

21

to see her cheers me up. For she has genuine glamour, there's no drabness about her. And she means nothing to me in one sense and everything in another; for what we have got is simple casual friendship. And I'll never forget that last spring, when I was just about beginning to recover from the traumatic events of the winter before, she sent me a birthday card, because she'd seen my birthday on the list in the paper. And this moved me to tears.

So, as she half-runs off into the other direction towards Heath Street, she yells 'See you soon!' and I yell back 'The sooner the better, young woman!' and that's fine, I've been given a boost. We don't have to be chums or to have a meaningful relationship. I don't think that either of us is really interested in residential associations or, indeed, doing good to anyone.

In the meantime the brief encounter nourishes me. It nourishes me all the more since it is so extremely pleasant simply to be friendly with an attractive, intelligent young woman in the region of thirty and not to feel that I have to do anything about it.

Vivien said to me when I first got this flat in Hampstead that now I'd get to know who I was. And she was right, dear reader. If I address you as 'dear reader', it's not merely me being smart, but feeling free enough at my age to talk to you. And what I'm here for is to take you with me now, twice left, once right, and then into Perrins Lane and under the verandah outside the Coffee Cup on Hampstead High Street. There are two young men and two young women sitting there. I take my seat and the waitress finishes serving the four young people, smiles at me, and goes into the café. She appears a moment later with a mug of cappuccino and hands it to me. She knows what I want. This is one of the minor pleasures of living here: one never feels anonymous, merely a consumer unit.

I'm absolutely content sitting there in the sunshine, smoking a Dunhill Luxury Length and noting with amusement that the two young men and one of the young women are smoking also, that all the Government propaganda hasn't made a blind bit of difference. I note with amusement also that all of the young people have sweaters, tied by the arms round their necks. One young man actually has a polo-neck sweater under his sweatshirt: I wonder at this passion for woollies on a fine day in midsummer. Can it be a longing for security?

Not that any of them seems insecure. And they have clear skin, white teeth, bright eyes: they seem intelligent and alert. I wouldn't be anywhere else, sitting here with my coffee. The High Street is a live street, the main street of a village and yet metropolitan, a place where all the action is. The trees are now so luxuriant in foliage that they meet to form a sort of green tunnel, to give a little shade. The foliage is even more luxuriant on Rosslyn Hill. Trees make the dullest of streets interesting, and the High Street, with its mixture of styles, is never dull. And even new buildings like the Laura Ashley shop fit in; jerry-built glass-and-concrete monstrosities aren't allowed.

I want to share all this with you, because I know it all has to be paid for. I can only pay for it by sharing. I've had more than most people – most people can't sit outside in the sunshine in mid-morning drinking coffee; most people have routine jobs and, quite understandably, only begin to live when they finish the day's work. I am working now because essentially my work is what Yeats called the solitary impulse of delight. I want that delight not to be solitary, I want you all to experience it.

I can't tell you everything all at once, but now I have at least set the scene and told you something of the two main characters in the story. Vivien and I are living the story

23

now; we make the story as we go along, we aren't being manipulated. It's a story I have to get right now, because there isn't all that much time at the age of sixty.

I pay my bill and give the waitress ten pence and stroll down to the Post Office to post my letters. A bearded young man comes up to me, smiling. 'You must be Tim Harnforth.'

'None other,' I say, returning his smile.

'I've just read *The Fall of Night*,' he says, naming my last book. He shakes my hand. 'I just want to tell you how much it meant to me. You're a marvellous writer. Really marvellous.'

'Thank you very much,' I say, feeling the words inadequate. 'That really does me good. It really is encouraging –'

'I'm so glad you're living here in Hampstead,' the young man says. 'We must have a drink sometime.'

'I look forward to it,' I say sincerely, and the young man walks away briskly towards Rosslyn Hill.

I go into the Community Centre market and buy a bunch of Sweet William for Vivien. The deep rich pink and the fragrance of the flowers add to my elation. There's never been a time when I've been out here without either being recognised or being greeted by someone I know. It isn't conceit which elates me, but the feeling of not being a stranger, of being part of a community.

Now I'm back home and, though I've enjoyed my small outing, glad to be there. I've never felt quite like this about anywhere I've ever lived. It's only a small rented flat and the furniture and decorations aren't my choice, but it's mine. I have the feeling I can't be got at and that the cliché is true and this is my castle. I've had lunch – an

24

orange and Cheddar cheese sandwiches of wholemeal bread – and am drinking tea, lying down on the sofa. It's very quiet but I'm aware that life is going on outside. This is Friday, and Vivien is coming very soon. I'm not thinking very deeply, I'm completely relaxed, there still is the taste of the orange in my mouth and the taste of the Cheddar and the wholemeal bread, none of the tastes quarrelling with each other or with the tea, which is exactly as I like it, strong but not too astringent. And I realise with gratitude that the nervous dyspepsia which once plagued me now plagues me no longer. And I am not alienated, as I was in Surrey increasingly for those two terrible years before I came here.

And I have had the best of mornings and have made it so from the simplest materials. My life now has the proper shape and I'm growing into the person I always should have been. It's like the wedding feast at Cana: the best wine has been kept to the last. And soon Vivien will be here and nothing more will be needed and I have flowers to give her and I have a new cassette of Elgar's Violin Concerto. There will be flowers and music and love, and now I'll await her arrival with serenity. Impatience is the same thing as greed. The best wine must be sipped slowly.

Three

I'm nearly asleep when the bell rings, and at the door is Vivien in a red linen jacket and skirt, a white linen blouse and a green and tawny-brown silk handkerchief which matches but doesn't try to duplicate the colour of her eyes, which are a warm hazel. Her tights are brown with a tinge of red, her shoes are Cuban-heeled, a darker red than her skirt and jacket. She's properly dressed for the weather and the occasion, but, as always, she's well dressed, spontaneously and cheerfully *soignée*: clothes for Vivien are fun.

'How lovely to see your pretty face, queen of my heart.' I say it and mean it, and I kiss her and take her into the living-room and settle her in the rocking-chair and slide the partition open and put on the kettle.

'Tea, my darling?'

'I'd love some.' She catches sight of the flowers. 'Are these for me?'

'For you and for no-one else, my darling. A tiny present. It'll be orchids when my ship comes home.' I put out the brown earthenware teapot and matching milk jug and the green flowered teacups and saucers from Liberty's. 'Mind you, I think that the bloody ship's lost with all hands.'

'Sweet William – they're lovely! And a marvellous scent.' She moves across to me and kisses me. 'You're filling my study with flowers and nice little presents. Neil drifts in from time to time and looks around glumly. Never says a word, but he knows where all the flowers and pretty things come from.'

Neil is her husband and he's a freelance TV director and two years younger than me. 'Do you think me giving you things makes him jealous? Not that the bugger has any right to be.'

'I don't think that he's exactly jealous, but he's not pleased either. Deep down in him I don't really think he approves of me having a lover. If he has a mistress, that's different.'

'I've learned not to be surprised by anything about Neil. When he was made they broke the mould.'

'He's been odder than usual lately. He told me about it this morning. Tracy's giving him a rough time. He wept into his Scotch.'

'Mistresses young enough to be their lover's daughter generally do just that,' I said. 'Particularly if they're successful actresses.'

'He doesn't do badly himself.'

'He's not in her league. Neil's reliable, Neil knows everybody. Neil gets on with people. He never throws fits of temperament, he saves that for his home circle. He'll never be out of work. But he'll never be a name to conjure with. I wonder why Tracy bothers with him.'

She shrugs. 'He's become a habit, I suppose.'

The red light shows on the kettle – it's very quick – and I make the tea and bring it to the table. 'I'll let it mash, as we say in Yorkshire.' I touch her hair gently: it's very soft and clean and very springy and she keeps it short – it's almost what used to be called an urchin cut – and it's black and lustrous, but not the Mediterranean blue-black. The tinge somehow is reddish; she has Irish blood. I feel absolutely eupeptic because of the simple pleasure of giving her tea in my own home, my place and nobody else's.

'He's been asking her to marry him again.' Vivien smiles. 'Of course she refused. He told me with tears in his eyes.'

'Silly devil!' I stir the tea in the pot and push the teabags down to make it brew more quickly. 'I bet he'd run a mile if she did accept him.'

'You know the old story. She can't live with him, she can't live without him.'

I'm melted by her. My day has been so full and so happy, and at last, for the first time since the days in Casterley before my first marriage, I feel free. I move over to her and kiss her knee gently and stroke it, feeling through the whole of my body warmth and smoothness.

I'd want better than that for us. And there is no hurry, but already I'm feeling a stirring. Understand this, reader. I'm not telling you about a man of years – as my grandmother would have put it – entertaining his bit of stuff, his fancy piece, at his own pad. I'm telling you about a grown man and a grown woman, who have given without stint and who have always done their duty. We're not portentous about it. But for Vivien Canvey and Tim Harnforth, bearing in mind our age-group, every time we make love is important. Even to be naked in the presence of another is important. It isn't a light matter. The young and the lithe and the boundingly fit, with the smooth unblemished skins and the firm breasts and the flat bellies and the rippling muscles, those who don't weary or have anyone laugh at them or feel sorry for them, can couple as casually as animals. Whatever you do when you're young and fit, it isn't ugly. In a way, the young are public people. Vivien and I are private people.

So now I tell you what is the great joy of our special day

Friday (and, with luck, Saturday and Sunday). We take it easy, we take it slowly, we are never greedy. I don't see her as a sex object. And in this respect the new women have got it right: no human being is a thing, no woman is a receptacle, just a hole, as my wife Val once put it, something for sperm to be poured into. And – don't forget this – no man is just a prick either. Otherwise why worry? Let the women have vibrators, which are tireless. Let the men have Japanese inflatable dolls. Let there be no personal demands and no conversation, let there be no involvement, no vulnerability, no poetry, no memories, no love.

But that isn't good enough for Vivien and me. The gesture of kissing her knee – like our kiss when she came to the flat, like me stroking her hair – has enormous significance. Our bodies, increasingly as we grow older, become private. I have my secrets, even from Vivien, as she has from me – harmless secrets, secrets which are part of being human and ageing, secrets which are thought of by the mature as being comic and endearing, but nevertheless secrets which are revealed only to the doctor and the dentist. We all grow old, barring war and accidents. And as we grow old, the body increasingly matters. We can't take it for granted, we need sticks and corsets and, if we're very unlucky, all sorts of appliances. Don't let us go into it any more closely.

If it came to it, if we were ill or helpless, there is no service which we wouldn't give each other, and give each other cheerfully. We know all the facts of life and the facts of death too; we have no illusions about the human body. But this is a romance, this is a love story. The dark side of life will enter it, for this is a true story. But squalor, mean and petty ugliness, and unfeeling coarseness will not be here.

The tea is exactly right now and we take our first sips in companionable silence. This is another great bonus of our relationship. We both of us are the sort of people who can feel absolutely fulfilled simply being alive, sitting quietly, not even drinking or eating, not reading or listening to the radio or looking at TV or knitting or playing Patience: we both can sit in silence, content to be alive and in a pleasant place. We don't always have to do something, we never are bored, we never have to kill time. The Victorians knew about this: Tennyson used to ask his friends to come over and sit with him. He wanted simply the pleasure of their company; they didn't have to do anything, they didn't have to put up any sort of performance.

'It's lovely being here with you.' Vivien smiles at me. 'I keep thinking how different you are from Neil. He wanders round the house like a ghost, puffing those little cheroots and sighing.'

'Hasn't he any work to do?'

'Albion TV gave him a script to look at and he's looked at it.' She gives the writer's name and I grimace.

'All about the sodding working classes suffering in some hellhole in the North?'

'That's it roughly.'

'Sooner him than me. That bugger's been rewriting the same play for twenty years now. He still gets good reviews because of his gritty realism. Much he knows about the working classes. Not that he sees much of them in Frognal.'

'You know him, don't you?'

'He pops into the Flask from time to time. Introduced himself to me. These idiot journalists always link us. But I never wrote about the working classes. Only about people getting the hell out of the working classes. I suppose Neil admires him.'

'He used to. Now he's rather depressed at the prospect

of being involved with him. He says he's never asked to do anything exciting, and his whole life is over.'

'The time to complain is when you're *not* asked to do anything.'

She grins. 'Don't worry. Neil never turns any offer down. He'll direct the play, grumbling like mad about it and everyone in it, and he'll be perfectly charming to everyone, absolutely the public school gentleman – but he won't be happy about it.' Bitterness creeps into her voice. 'Maybe he keeps the happy side of his nature for Tracy.'

I shrug. 'The more some people get, the more they grumble. The more I gave to Val, the nastier she became. Who cares? We're happy.'

'Yes, we're happy.' There's a catch in her voice. 'I never grow used to it. You're always so pleased to see me.'

'What else should I be, seeing such a beautiful young woman?' The stirring in my loins increases. 'Darling, I think that you need a rest.' I get to my feet, noting wryly that after sitting for even a short while, my joints aren't exactly supple: it's not a painful effort to get up, but it is an effort.

She raises her eyebrows. 'I can't think what you mean.'

'It's only you I'm thinking of. You've been working very hard recently. As always, I'm being unselfish. I just want you to relax totally. I won't bother you at all.'

'You won't break your promise?'

She gets up and takes a bottle from the carrier bag she has brought. 'I'll just put the wine in the fridge. You've put the meat on, haven't you?'

'Yes, darling, half an hour ago.'

I smile at her and go into the bedroom. I undress quickly in the way that Gillian taught me in Casterley in Yorkshire a long time ago: shirt off first, then socks and shoes, then trousers and underpants in one movement and leave them on the floor. A gentleman when about to make love doesn't fold his trousers neatly and put them on a hanger. Nor does he ever let himself be seen clad only in shirt and socks.

I lie in bed naked, feeling calm and free. Actually I have no narcissistic feelings about my own body – it functions with very little trouble, it's not beautiful but I have no hang-ups about it. Its nakedness is for Vivien as her nakedness is for me. I lie in bed completely tranquil: there never is any question with the two of us of any sensation being expected as of right, of there being any obligations enforced upon either of us. As the saying goes, we play it by ear, we never worry and we never hurry. This is complete relaxation with the cool sheets against me, and no rough male kiss of blankets, thank you very much.

Vivien enters the bedroom, smiles at me, and begins to undress. This is a reversal of the usual order, but this is the way it generally happens. We don't have to worry about what is usual and unusual, we are consenting heterosexual adults in private and we please ourselves entirely. Her jacket comes off first, then the skirt; she, being a woman, is right to drape the jacket on the chair and fold the skirt neatly. Women have a different relationship to their clothes than men. The white slip comes off next, then the white bra. And what must be understood here is that every stage of the divestiture is important; every stage is a gift to be treasured, a token of trust. I'm only the second man in Vivien's life: for her to undress in front of me is enormously important. We are neither of us pretentious about it – shared laughter for us is never very far away. The point is that we're neither of us casual and prosaic about it – to take it all for granted means the end of love and the debasement of Eros.

And now she's taken off her pants and tights, and is

shaking out the tights again and folding them over the back of the chair. And it's always, always as it was the first time seven years ago. And more than that, it's even better; for the first time, though not a disappointment, had an element of tension, of unspoken questions being asked. Now we know each other, we're in harmony, we unhurriedly and delightedly explore each other's bodies. And, if either of us were unresponsive, if either of us were tired or ill, we'd settle down happily in each other's arms, there'd be comfort and cuddles. But now we're building up pleasure and now she's above me, smiling, her eyes bright. This is what I like the best, the Roman way, but we have no rules, we use whatever posture our instincts urge us to use, but always we're grateful to each other, always we put the other's pleasure before our own. And in so doing increase our pleasure, in so doing lose ourselves.

And we tell each other we love each other, we're crying out our love for each other now as she drives herself down upon me and once again I'm struck with wonderment at being so much at one with a woman and wanting it never to end and yet moving towards culmination, and then we're both crying out and then there's absolute peace.

'Oh God, you're so wonderful, darling! You look so young.'

I smile at her. 'You gave me my youth back, darling. I do love you.'

'I love you too,' she says, settling beside me. 'It's nice to hear those words. I can never hear them often enough.'

'I'm the same, darling. I never heard them at Boxley. Only requests for money. It's not meanness – Christ, I don't give a damn about money. It's just being seen as a source of money, not a human being. You've no idea how much it hurts.'

'I do, darling.' She puts her arms around me. 'Lie still and rest now. You won't see Val again.'

I remember Val's white face, contorted with rage – *We all hate you, why don't you go?* And even though I'm happy, happy in the right place with the right woman, for a moment an arid sadness overwhelms me, a huge sense of waste. It still hurts sometimes, it still can come between me and my sleep.

She holds me tightly. 'Let go, darling, let go. It won't stop hurting for a bit yet, not after even twenty years.'

'I did my best, I gave her everything a woman could ask for. God knows, I gave. There's nothing she couldn't have had. . . .'

'Relax, darling. It's all over. No one will hurt you here.'

'No-one ever hurts me here. You never have.' Sleep is now descending suddenly upon me.

'Let go, darling, let go. The bad days are all over.' She strokes my hair again and I close my eyes; she settles into my arms with a sigh of contentment and I slide into sleep. I let go, I lay down my armour.

The bed is a single divan with a headboard which isn't actually a contradiction in terms, since the headboard seems an afterthought and has a gap at the bottom through which pillows have a way of falling down. It's big enough to make love in and big enough for sleep after love, but not big enough for two to sleep all night. This flat is the home of one person, the archetypal bachelor's pad. Once Val said to me that I was a married bachelor and I think now, remembering this, that perhaps she was right and that's why I'm so much at home here. I drift off to sleep and again I'm younger and I'm at the seaside but not at the seaside in any place I've ever known and my daughters Penelope and Vanessa are little and I've lost them and I feel a terrible desolation as I run through the narrow streets of the strange town and all the faces hostile and a storm brewing and a sense of unmerited punishment soon to be imposed on me and the streets closing in then lengthening and Val's face suddenly there triumphant and I'm awake and clutching Vivien, who's now sleeping peacefully.

I take a pack of Dunhill Luxury Length and a Cricket lighter from the drawer of the white bedside cabinet, thinking for the thousandth time that I ought to give the habit up. But the Second World War generation is like the First World War generation: just as my father was hooked on the Western Front, so was I in Normandy. And, occasionally, lighting a cigarette, I remember that smell of corpses, animal and human, and worst of all the sharp smell of apples. I'm back in the real world now with the faint sound of voices outside and the reassuring sense, never felt at the flat off Shaftesbury Avenue which we once had, that outside it's civilised and humane, that there are no predators or deadbeats or junkies, that most of the people are young and bright and clean and about to do great things, that there are no drudges or nonentities out there and no-one who'll be hostile towards me.

I look at my watch and finish my cigarette and get out of bed – a little stiffly again, I note ruefully – and put on my pants and trousers and socks and shoes and shirt and go into the bathroom to sluice my face with cold water and brush my hair and gargle with Listerine. Then I go into the living-room and make a pot of tea, let it brew for five minutes, pour out two mugfuls, and take it into the bedroom. I can smell the meat cooking and suddenly feel very hungry. But it's not as it once was. Before I left what I, for want of a better word, call my home in Boxley I used to be almost ill, I had hunger pains at about six-thirty. Now I'm hungry in a healthy, wolfish way, almost in a young man's way.

I put one mug of tea on the bedside table and move the chair to the chest-of-drawers and make a space there amongst all the colognes and after-shave lotions and talcs and hair conditioners and hair lotions – nothing greasy, only Eau de Portugal and bay rum – and evening primrose and kelp and brewers yeast tablets and the whole gamut of vitamin tablets. I touch Vivien's hair softly. 'Time for tea, young woman.'

She awakes, smiling. 'How lovely. You're becoming very good recently.'

'I'm mellowing. Each day of living in Hampstead has made me kinder and kinder.'

She drinks her tea. 'Perfect, darling. . . . I've noticed you become less nervy. You're still rather outrageous.'

'It's my *métier*. I bet I still shock Neil.' This is another of the good moments after love, built up into a ritual over the years: we sleep after love and then on awakening drink tea and chat casually: and all of it is important, all of it is to cherish, all of it is sacred, all of it helps to maintain the high and impregnable ramparts which protect us from the barbarians, from all those who have used us, from all those who wouldn't care if they destroyed us.

'Shock Neil? He's never really got over finding out we were lovers.'

She's sitting up in bed as real naked women sit, the full breasts with the large nipples revealed, not as women do in films and TV with the bedclothes hiding the nipples. They are full breasts, the breasts of a mature woman who has had children: they droop with their own weight but they don't sag, they're not pendulous. I'm free of immediate physical desire now, but I take pleasure in looking at them and at her vivid face – and how rightly is she named Vivien, a genuine poetic name, not a saint's name, Tennyson's inspiration – and I understand her.

36

And now tears are coming to my eyes: I keep on remembering how it was when I was driven from the house I'd paid for some two years ago, with the book half-finished, the money run out, the Inland Revenue and the Customs and Excise and all the bureaucratic vultures baying for money, and the feeling of total defeat and nowhere to go and not wanting to eat and always the desire for oblivion and the gnawing pain in my belly and the feeling of waste, of great riches having been squandered. But not by me. Never by me, and that was the worst of it, that and ending up at the Post House Hotel at Belsize Park with only the fact that I'd paid up my American Express card to carry me through.

None of it matters at this moment, dear reader. What matters is that a man and a woman have had the great joy of having made love; and I use that phrase deliberately. Certainly we should be joyful, even frivolous and laughing about it. And certainly for Vivien and me it is an unalloyed pleasure: since we first became lovers there's been no-one else; and since her hysterectomy she can't have a child, so sex for us is quite simply joy with no distressing conse-quences. Vivien and I don't worry – since for us faithfulness is totally mandatory, the horrors attendant upon promis-cuity can never come near us.

And now there is more talk, and finishing the tea. I will not detail all the talk, because there isn't all that much time. My story is more than a story. It is an urgent message. Young or old, no matter who you are or where you live, listen to my message. As Vivien and I live, so you can live. Live now, take it now, live to the fullest. Now, the moment you read this, is all that you have. You're entitled to no more than my father's generation was, led out in all innocence towards the slaughterhouse.

You're entitled to no more than my generation was, growing up in an era of mass unemployment, knowing that we'd end up in uniform fighting in a war exactly like the war in which my father fought. It didn't in fact turn out exactly like that; but we did end up in uniform, scared out of our minds and most of us somehow surviving.

Vivien would understand all this. Neither my first wife, Shirley, or my second wife Val would even begin to understand it. But you will, dear reader, before I finish, particularly if you're a woman. And you'll understand how important it is that, after talking a little more together and after enjoying talking, Vivien and I find ourselves both dressed in the living-room, sitting on the sofa having each a bone-dry Martini with a great deal of ice and with lime – a bonus of living in Hampstead being that fresh limes are always obtainable. Limes aren't the correct thing for dry Martinis, but they're what we like. And we take them very slowly. The glow is gentle and doesn't shock the stomach, and one can taste the juniper in the gin and the herbs in the vermouth, and the sharp freshness of the lime, sharp without any of the mouth-puckering sourness of lemon.

We eat at the table off the large plain white plates which were here when I took over the tenancy. The meat is fillet of lamb, cut from the neck; one doesn't come across it very often and it's as expensive as prime steak, but you haven't tasted lamb until you have tasted it; there's no bone, or inedible fat, and it's so tender and juicy that it really deserves the name of lamb. With it we each have new potatoes with butter – to hell with the dangers of animal fat, for what are boiled potatoes without butter? – and peas. We don't insult the meat with mint sauce. We drink Liebfraumilch: neither of us likes red wine, so once again we don't care what is correct, only what we enjoy. But

Vivien only has one glass, because she's driving. Then we each have a fresh peach: I bought them yesterday, and now they're properly ripe, with no hint of softness but no hint of toughness, and with their superb sweetness which goes beyond sweetness, a flavour which is delicate yet full, as much a scent as a flavour.

We move to the sofa to each have a cup of coffee with just enough milk to colour it and with no sugar. I've never drunk tea with sugar but it was Vivien who taught me that it doesn't go with coffee either, not because of all that old rubbish about it being sweet, white and deadly, but because it spoils the taste. We take our coffee slowly too, and I have a cigarette. And then I put on the Elgar Violin Concerto, and we sit listening to it hand in hand, being filled by it completely, not analysing, not dissecting, not comparing it with other performances but giving ourselves to it, not trying to find a meaning, but helped along by it towards a deeper knowledge, a knowledge beyond words. We don't, of course, talk – how can one talk and listen to music? We each listen individually but because we listen together, because we share, there's an enhancement of the experience, a further strengthening of our love. We don't think this consciously, but the music is as much part of this afternoon and evening together as was making love.

When the music has finished Vivien and I sit in a trance for a moment.

'It seems to make sense out of life, doesn't it?'

'One doesn't often have that feeling any more. Not from any of the arts – '

I check myself. I'm so happy at this time, but every now and again there is the helpless feeling, a feeling Elgar wouldn't have had in 1910, of the world being ruled by evil idiots, of an irresistible tide of violence approaching (how long before the IRA plants a bomb in Hampstead High Street?).

'What were you going to say, darling?'

'Nothing. It's been a perfect day. The meal was marvellous.' I kiss her. 'But bread and cheese and tea would be a banquet in your company.'

'You always say such nice things to me.' Her eyes moisten for a moment. 'I'll never get used to it.'

I move to the table and pour myself a glass of wine. The sunlight is ebbing now, there are shadows in the room which weren't there half an hour ago – friendly shadows, shadows without menace, but still the precursors of night.

'I'm still not used to being loved. And being asked for nothing but myself.'

'That's a great deal to ask, my darling. You have more to give than most men.' She glances at her watch. 'I've got this bloody article to finish.' We get up and we take the plates and cutlery away from the table, scrape the plates into the wastebin and wash up. We do the job very quickly: even in this small matter we are as one.

'You're looking tired, Tim.'

'I'll be all right. I'm a damned sight better than I was when I came here. Thanks to you.' I squeeze her hand. But she's quite right; suddenly at nine o'clock, having slept well the night before and having only exerted myself pleasurably, my strength has leaked away. I'm not ill, but I have no energy.

'You are looking tired.' She turns to the door. 'Don't come out with me, darling. I can see myself to the car. It's only at New End.'

'The walk will do me good.'

'I won't argue with you, my sweetheart.' She picks up her handbag and the Sainsbury's shopping bag. 'Have you got your keys? And are you sure you won't need a jacket? It's turning a bit cooler.'

I check my trouser pockets and show her the keys, two of them on a key-ring with a small penknife attached, a small present, a being-in-love present, which she gave me some two years ago. When I was a house-owner and a married man, I had a dozen keys and a set of car keys: now there are only these two, and two will be enough for the rest of my life.

It is turning cooler now as we leave the house and the sky is flecked with pink. Somehow or other, as we thread our way through the narrow alleyway which leads to Heath Street, there is not only a sense of privacy, of hidden corners and strangeness, but a sense of space, of a higher sky. And because it's cooler, because there's a cool breeze, because here the carbon monoxide fumes don't settle, I feel a little less tired and, as we cross Hampstead High Street by the Tube Station, I reflect with gratitude that when I first came here nearly two years ago even the climb from the Tube Station to New End left me breathless; I couldn't manage without a stick. I couldn't run up it now, and I don't walk as briskly as I used to not so very long ago, but it doesn't present any problem.

Heath Street is full of people, most of them young, and there's a queue outside the Milk Churn. And the Horse and Groom and the Nag's Head and the Coach and Horses will be crowded, as will be the Pizza Hut and the rest of them. But the reason why I'm happy simply walking up Heath Street, narrow and curving sharply just beyond the Baptist Church, isn't just its mixture of styles, its human dimensions, the fact that its name doesn't lie and it does actually lead to the Heath, but that, like Hampstead High Street, it doesn't become a tomb at half past five. There is a street life here and more than one supermarket open in the High Street and Rosslyn Hill from half past eight to eleven at night. They're all far from being cheap, but everything has its price. If I didn't want to go to a pub or restaurant in Boxley at night, there was nowhere to go, even presuming I had wanted to go to a pub or restaurant in Boxley. Boxley was dominated by the new shopping centre, which wasn't merely dead, but never had been alive.

'What I like about this,' I say to Vivien, returning the wave of a middle-aged man, a school inspector, who introduced himself to me at the Flask one evening, 'is that it won't change. Casterley was a bit like this once – my God, even places like Wetherford and Bradford were.'

'They didn't have a large well-heeled articulate middle-class,' Vivien said. 'Nothing here is going to change.'

'I'm tired of change,' I said. 'I'm damned if I've seen any changes for the better.'

'*We* won't change,' she says, as we pass the Baptist Church, a Victorian Gothic building which is generally described as undistinguished, but which I always enjoy looking at because it looks like a place of worship, and not a small computer factory or gymnasium. Only the words of the Wayside Pulpit jar, Jesus saying *I shall live for ever and ever* – the words of a child – and *I have authority over death*, as if He were some kind of local government functionary and death a department of local government like housing or finance. I personally hate and despise any other translation than the Authorised Version, but as I don't go to church any longer – not in fact since my first marriage broke up – it doesn't really matter.

Vivien's Mini-Traveller is parked on the right of New End, just below the hospital entrance. The terrace of the Duke of Hamilton is full again, mostly of young people.

There are lights in the window of the hospital. It's redbrick, nicely mellowed, with unusually restrained white stone-work and a facade which has real dignity without being intimidating, built early in the 19th century first as a workhouse – I wonder, as always, how it was that once all public buildings, if not all beautiful, were at least not offensive, and were also soundly built.

I kiss Vivien goodbye at the car. 'Another happy day, darling. I'll see you tomorrow.'

'I love you,' she says, and winkles the car out of a narrow space with practised dexterity.

I walk up New End towards Heath Street and home, resisting the temptation to have a drink at the Duke of Hamilton, as I'll resist the temptation to have a drink at any of the other pubs I pass. Nothing is perfect: I know that at pubs in the village I almost always find congenial company, enjoy myself by becoming legless, but now I'm aware of my age and glad that my walk now is all downhill and eager to get home.

And once home I undress quickly and take a glass and a bottle of milk and a packet of Garibaldi buscuits to the bedroom. I pull the coverlet down from the pillows, but lie on top of it, with the red rug that Vivien gave me over it. I think of reading for a while but decide against it: my eyes are already beginning to close. I say an Act of Contrition quickly; it's a free and instant insurance of which I'd be a fool not to take advantage. I reflect that in one sense I haven't much left, living in rented accommodation at the age of sixty, my health better than it was but still not as good as it could be, the Inland Revenue growing increasingly restive, scenting the chance of destroying me, the new novel not flowing: I'm still, in a sense, one of the walking wounded.

But I'm not frightened and this place, more so than anywhere I've lived, is my home. And Vivien is still with me, and what enables me to fall asleep with startling but pleasurable speed is that during the whole of the day I can't remember one bad moment, and our meal together has been a sacrament. She would understand this; her face wouldn't go blank, her eyes slide away when I explained it to her. I wouldn't have to explain it to her.

And what I remember now and must never forget is how many nights at Boxley I honestly wished not to wake up in the morning. I'm going to sleep now: there's gin and vermouth and brandy and whisky and lager and a bottle and a quarter of wine in the flat, but I don't need alcohol, and I don't need sleeping pills. And if I awake with a slight twinge of pain in my stomach, I'll nibble a biscuit and sip a little milk and the twinge will disappear. These days I don't ever need antacids or even aspirin. I'm beginning to be the person I was meant to be, my wounds are healing, and I look forward to waking up in the morning.

Four

No, I wasn't a mother's boy. But I was the firstborn, and I was my mother's favourite, and if Freud was right about nothing else, he was right about that: the male firstborn who is his mother's favourite has unshakeable self-confidence. My mother assured me, as soon as I was old enough to understand, that I was handsome, irresistibly charming, and a genuis. The world soon disillusioned me – my little chums at primary school, for a start, gave me many a thumping. And I was a bright boy, bright enough to realise that I wasn't quite as wonderful as she had told me – but this was merely conscious thinking, this was in the front half of my brain (the left half as it's believed nowadays). In the deeper half, in the instinctive half, there was the absolute faith that my mother was right, that nothing could stop me, that I was a special person, one of the lords of creation.

And on top of it all I was breast-fed – I think now that this is the reason why I've always been physically spontaneous, have never had any hang-ups about expressing physical affection, have always felt tenderness towards women's bodies, have never felt that breasts ought to be any specific size, that they ought to stick straight out like flying buttresses, that they ought not to droop with their own weight – which is part of their richness, which is what

45

makes them life-giving. Only the other day I came across a film review in which is quoted with approval the words of a boozy poet as a middle-aged woman takes off her bra for him: 'Released from their support, her breasts drooped like hanged men.' And what was his body like then, since he was a middle-aged boozer? Middle-aged male boozers have pot bellies and bloodshot eyes and little red broken veins on their faces and – as can be observed on any beach – often need bras too. And into the bargain – which is always what has prevented me from being a truly dedicated drinker – as often as not they have brewer's droop. And that's a different kind of droop, that's total humiliation, the one humiliation no man can endure. The centre of a woman's body, the place of pleasure and the place of the travail of birth, cannot droop, no would-be clever words can affect it. It may be earthy, it may be comic, but it has elemental power.

What my mother gave me was not only self-confidence, the most precious gift of all, but an actual liking for women, not far from awe-struck fascination. I've paid dearly for it with two disastrous marriages. I'm here now at the age of sixty, living in a rented flat, the Inland Revenue still hounding me and, though not yet in the shadows, not as resoundingly and resplendently in the public eye as once I was. But I'm still undefeated, I won't, as some writers I've known have done, die in my lifetime. The start I got from infancy, the push in the back, the bugle call forcing me into the heart of the battle – this is always with me. I can't give up. 'Wealth lost, something lost; honour lost, much lost; courage lost, all lost,' Goethe said. I shan't lose my courage. It's just that I get tired more frequently than I used to, that I want no more struggling and rebuilding, that I want an easy quiet life.

On my mother's side – she was born Maureen Cloneen, granddaughter of Thaddeus Cloneen, a drunken horse-dealer who came over to the West Riding of Yorkshire in the 1850s – they were all Irish. On my father's side, they were all English, mostly millworkers, though there were some small farmers amongst them. Of all of my English relations the one I liked best was my cousin Vera, tall and decisive and severe at first sight, but with gentle brown eyes, the eyes of her father, my Aunt Ethel's husband (Aunt Ethel was my father's sister). Vera was five years older than me, an academic high-flier, a scholarship-winner. She moved away to Northumberland when she was twelve – her father got a job at an engineering factory there – and eventually got an Honours Degree in History and a lecturer's post at King's College, as it was then. Remembering her now, I still miss her – she married late in life to another lecturer and still lives in Durham. I remember how much I missed her when she went away – at seven one doesn't think to any great purpose about love, but somehow I'm sure that I would have felt somehow that one of the reasons for human love being so imperfect is that no-one stays – one and all they die or they go away.

And I have been going away from people for a long time, I've been losing touch; for a long time I lost touch with Vera. I've never quite lost touch with Casterley and there constantly in my mind's eye is the terrace-house I was born in and lived in until I was six, a stone-built terrace steeply sloping up to a footpath leading to Casterley Moors. And there in my mind's eye is my mother, small, plump and black-haired with blue eyes, a shade darker than light, which I have inherited. Once a journalist said that my eyes were friendly but full of a devouring curiosity, taking everything in, and I more and more feel these days that I'd like to switch off for a bit, just be the human being

47

I was once in Casterley, simply a person, living and not recording, living in a small town with the river and the canal running almost parallel through it and hills and trees and the moors around it. In Casterley I could always look up to the hills, and I expect that's why I've found the right place now, in a hill town.

Some six months after I'd been driven from my house in Surrey, Vera somehow heard about it and wrote to me. And I told her what had happened, and how long my marriage had been a marriage in name only. I hadn't told her before. I had in fact told only four people, one of them, of course, Vivien. I had also told my lawyer, but for me lawyers don't count as people. I'd kept it to myself, I hadn't complained. And when Vera wrote back, she told me why I had kept it to myself. 'When you were little,' she wrote, 'you fell and hurt yourself. There didn't seem to be anything broken, but you burst your nose and you were bleeding badly. I was rushing to pick you up and your mother stopped me. "Don't worry about Tim," she said. "He's tough." I've never forgotten that.'

I had myself forgotten it; but since Vera told me I can't get it out of my mind. Yes, there was that unstinted support. Yes, I was my mother's favourite – to adapt Cyril Connolly, supercharged like a tiny Alfa Romeo for the Brooklands of life. Yes, there was the breast-feeding, and when I was a baby there would have been an unstudied animal closeness: if I actually like women and children, I owe that to her. But as for being tough – at my age I'd like to be weak and human. I'd like to rest behind the lines, I'd like to give way, I'd like to cry when I'm hurt.

After the First Battle of the Wilderness during the American Civil War, a terrible battle in thick woods during which the gunsmoke smothered the daylight and the trees

48

and the undergrowth caught fire and roasted the wounded alive, the Union troops were ordered to cease fire and marched out of the Wilderness to a crossroads where Ulysses Grant sat on his horse waiting, absolutely immobile. If my memory serves me, the troops might even have managed a cheer. Although he was never economical with their lives, they had a notion that he knew what he was doing, that he was a winner. Humane and compassionate generals are all very well, but victorious generals are better – the sooner the war is won, the sooner the troops go home. However that may be, Grant with one gesture directed them back the way they'd come, and back they went into the Wilderness and the gunsmoke and the stink of roasting flesh.

And thinking of what my cousin Vera told me, I can, as they say, identify with these troops. And I'm becoming mutinous, I'm fed up with my mother ordering me back into battle. I want to be safe and sound. I don't want to be a hero.

And yet I still love my mother. There's hardly a day goes by when I don't remember her; she's in my dreams very often, and I wish to God the dead would come back. Since growing up I've never been frightened of ghosts – the dead have never done me any harm. I have always to be grateful to her. The world I grew up in was a hard one; I had to get on or get under, and knew in my bones from my boyhood that I'd end up in uniform like my father, who was conscripted in 1916. My mother taught me never to expect justice and, although she herself had a great talent for happiness, not to expect happiness either. The way of living she taught me has dignity: a man has to be brave and strong, she said, in order to protect and cherish women and children; a man has to look after those weaker than himself. Yes, she programmed me.

But last Spring, when things were much worse with me than they are now, when Val's lawyers and the Inland Revenue were demanding huge sums of money, when worry about money prevented me from doing the work which would earn money, I fell ill with a new illness, a violent grinding pain in the pit of the stomach and, grotesquely and humilatingly, an inability to urinate. And that seemed the final blow, worse even than blindness or deafness, the failure of the prostate, the pathetic ailment of the old man, the end of sex.

I 'phoned Vivien and she took me to the Royal Free, and I went in there with Vivien supporting me by one arm and a young nurse by the other. And this is what is difficult to tell you, dear reader: I burst into tears, I gave way. I'm not ashamed of crying: I cry at sad things, I cry in particular when children suffer. I cry at what is beautiful, particularly soldiers marching with a band. But I cried at the Royal Free that day because I felt defeated, because I'd given up. I was weeping for myself, and not for other people. And I still feel ashamed of myself for it.

This story is a romance, a love story. It's about the great happiness a man and a woman can give each other. Vivien and I in the end will be like Philemon and Baucis, the old couple who asked Zeus that, just as they had not been separated in life, so they should not be separated in death. There were two trees by the door of their cottage, one each side of the door. After their death the two trees intertwined their branches and became one. My theme is the realisation of the truth of that legend. But before the two trees can become one, I must learn to accept defeat, to lean upon others, not to be ashamed of crying for myself.

Five

It's mid-July now and I'm back in Wetherford in the West Riding of Yorkshire, walking along Whitegate to the home of my Grandfather and Grandmother Cloneen in Inkerman Terrace opposite St Bridget's Church, where my grandfather is the verger and caretaker of the school. I use the present tense: he died in 1946 and my grandmother died the year after. But now they are alive and I want to see them; at the age of sixty I need them even more than I needed them as a child. I need their calm, I need their gentleness, I need to be in the living-room of that old stone terrace-house, where the nuns once lived when St Bridget's was built, which would have been at the time of the first great wave of Irish immigrants, the refugees from the Great Famine.

Whitegate starts from the city centre, a broad straight road bordered by high buildings, almost a boulevard. There's a maze of narrow terraced streets running off each side, with small shops which keep open to all hours. The Textile Hall, a wonderfully ornate Victorian building with stained glass on the ground floor, is there, and a fishing-tackle and gun shop and two bespoke tailors that everyone says are better than Savile Row. And there's an exclusive milliners and an exclusive shoe shop: Whitegate is – I still use the present tense – what is called a prime shopping area. Nearer Inkerman Terrace and the old Royal Infirmary the shops become smaller. It still has distinction, it isn't run-down, the doorsteps of the little terrace-houses will be yellow-stoned and the pavements scrubbed. And always it's alive, always there are people on the streets, always there's a street life. And always there are children playing, always the sound of children's voices. It isn't a beautiful quarter, and Wetherford isn't a beautiful city. But it's a place of human habitation; those small terrace-houses are homes and not machines for living.

And I am happy going along Whitegate to my grandparents' home. I am who I am, I'm sixty and badly battered, one of the walking wounded, one of those who won't be sent home but will be patched up behind the lines, within earshot of the guns. My grandparents will be there in that comfortably shabby room, that quiet safe room with the grandfather clock ticking, with the battered leather three-piece suite and the large mahogany table and the set of oak dining-chairs and the crammed bookcase on the wall and the flowered wallpaper which was once predominately pink but now has become, like the once red Axminster carpet, a not unpleasant tobacco shade.

My grandfather is balding, with gentle blue eyes but a bold nose; a handsome, commanding aquiline nose of the kind one doesn't see very often these days. (Each era has its own facial features; faces are as much a matter of fashion and of choice as are clothes.) My grandfather has a cavalry moustache, more flowing than the Pilot Officer Prune moustache but equally dashing. I remember it always as grey, though once it was black. He'll be drinking mild-and-bitter, which he'll have brought in from the little off-licence shop in the next street in a blue jug with a pattern of fleur-de-lys. He'll be smoking his pipe, a straight-stemmed briar with the stem mended with string a long time ago. The string is quite black now. His expression isn't phlegmatic or stupid, but it's the expression of someone who accepts with gratitude whatever reasonable and proper pleasure life offers him.

'Everybody in the parish knows your grandad,' my mother often told me. 'And everybody's always glad to see him.' He had warmth, he was always friendly, everyone liked him, but he never went in for flashy Mick charm, the old win-the-birds-off-the-bushes approach. He was easy-going, he never lost his temper.

No, he is easy-going, he never loses his temper. In my dream it's the present tense. I wouldn't be going along Whitegate now if my grandparents weren't there, if their house wasn't the field hospital, if I weren't at the end of my tether. I need my grandfather's gentleness, I need his warmth. And yet he wasn't soft.

'He never hit us,' my mother told me. 'But if we were naughty he'd be really sorrowful. *You've hurt me*, he'd say, *you've really disappointed me*. He'd make us cry. But he couldn't hit a child, any more than he could hit a woman.'

And I'm reminded now of Admiral Collingwood, who could never bear to have a man flogged. He felt there to be a contradiction between flogging and the message of love preached at Divine Service on Sunday. Instead, with absolute sincerity, he would say to offenders much the same things as my grandfather told his children: that he was disappointed in them, that they'd let him down, that they'd hurt him. And the sailors used to say that this hurt them more than being flogged; but this, I suppose, was one of the reasons that they loved him.

Collingwood was a noble spirit. I don't think of him in my dream but in my dream I do think that I'm going into a world where phrases like *a noble spirit* are valid currency. Whitegate, which means not only the thoroughfare but the district around St Bridget's, is scarcely a select residential area; it has more than its share of poverty and suffering, but it isn't unclean. It can be a brutal world – get on or get under – but it's clean. My Uncle Desmond's name is on the war memorial outside St Bridget's, a large tablet let into the wall. Yes, I'm aware of the horror and futility of the First World War. But the sacrifice which all these names represent, is one of the reasons why Whitegate can't be dirty; this is one of the reasons why I'm so eager to get to my grandparents' home. I haven't got very much time; it's too long since I've seen them, it's too long since I've seen Wetherford, they'll be overjoyed to see me, only disappointed that I haven't brought the children. And then I see my daughters, Penelope and Vanessa, Penelope fair-haired and slimmer than Vanessa, who is black-haired like my mother. And they're little girls now, three or four, old enough to be highly mobile, but not old enough to have any sense, and they're running away now, their bright dresses fluttering, but I know they're going to my grandparents.

My grandmother's hair was black when she was young, but turned grey early. She has neater features than my grandfather, with a clear skin, almost unlined except for the harsh lines from the nose to the corners of the mouth. She has the gift of sitting quite still, simply being peaceful, peaceful without being phlegmatic. She doesn't work at it, she doesn't strive for effect, but she has enormous natural dignity. Penelope and Vanessa can't be lost if she's there, and no-one gets lost in Whitegate, everyone knows everyone in Whitegate. They'll be in that living-room in different shades of tobacco brown, with its smell of roast beef and tapers and my grandfather's pipe. He has his own special mixture made up for him at Cliftons, the little tobacconist near the Wool Exchange, where not only are special mixtures made up to the customer's specification, but special cigarettes with the customer's initials. My grandfather's mixture is more than usually pungent and aromatic, with a high proportion of latakia. This, and the evening mild-and-bitter and in winter hot rum-and-peppermint, are my grandfather's chief luxuries. He isn't rich, and his house is, of course, rented, but he and my grandmother are careful and, with his wages as caretaker and various honorariums from being verger, he and my grandmother get along very well. They worry about money less than I do.

I want to be there, I want to be in that fortress. I want to be with Penelope and Vanessa. Lately I'm always looking for them. I'm always losing them. I never lose my sons, Simon and Kevin, I don't dream about them when they were little. Kevin is my son by my first wife Shirley; she ran away with him to her lover when he was very small. Maybe I did lose him – but I don't dream of losing him and I don't dream of losing Simon. I don't work this out, there is no reasoning in dreams, but only raw emotion.

And now my grandparents' home is no nearer, and now it's all desolation. Every shop is boarded up, there is no traffic and there are no people. The glass in all the windows of the little houses is broken but the bells of St Bridget's are ringing. Whitegate elongates itself into desolation. The words are, in my mind now, *dies irae, dies illa – Day of wrath, O dreadful day* – and Penelope and Vanessa are lost, the bright fluttering dresses are out of sight. I have lost everything – and now suddenly I'm at my grandparents' home in Inkerman Terrace. But Inkerman Terrace is razed to the ground and behind the remains of the walls – a line of stones about a foot high – is an eruption of gravestones and crosses and vaults – stone angels, stone wreaths, stone shields and swords, stone urns and stone laurel wreaths, but never a flower. And I wake up sweating and now in my mind are the words of David on hearing of the death of Absalom: *O my son Absalom, my son, my son Absalom! would God I had died for thee, O Absalom, my son my son!*

It is Penelope and Vanessa I've lost, but these are the words which come to me. The words make me cry, and crying makes me feel better. I switch the bedside light on, and I'm awake on a hot July night in Hampstead in my small bedroom lying on the bed which is bigger than the average single, but emphatically not a double bed. And now – though I'm certain it won't last – I don't like my flat, I don't want to be here. I don't want to be with my wife Val anywhere, but I do want to be in a proper house again, with a separate kitchen and an upstairs floor and more than one large bedroom and plenty of space for my books. The bookcase in my bedroom is overflowing now, and soon I'll have to sell some books. And I want a garden – not to do any gardening in, but to sit in when it's fine weather.

I want a house like my house at Boxley, sold now to pay off the second mortgage – which meant in effect to pay off the Inland Revenue. My wife has a house now, a smaller house, paid for in cash, near her parents' home. She's still in Boxley but the big Ford estate car has gone now, replaced by a Citroën 2-CV. She wanted the Charleston model with the fancy seat coverings and the special paint-work, and I let her have it. I don't care about that – I won't bother to own a car again. But what haunts me now is the sense of waste, of something having been built up over a lifetime and having been squandered.

I get up and put on my purple Paisley-pattern light-weight silk dressing-gown, and go into the living-room. I'm tempted for a moment by the prospect of a stiff whisky or a can of Carlsberg Export Lager or a glass of white wine (the bottle may as well be finished). Aware of what alcohol will lead to – since I shall be wanting it because I'm unhappy, which is the worst possible reason – I fill the electric kettle and switch it on. A cup of tea no doubt won't make me sleep any the better, but I shan't at least wake up tomorrow morning with a sense of remorse and of impending doom. I ask myself what I want, ask myself at ten minutes past midnight alone at sixty in a rented flat, not quite poverty-stricken, not quite drained of energy, but drawing heavily upon my last reserves.

'I want normality,' I say to Vivien. I don't say it aloud, and neither do I think that at this moment I'm sending telepathic messages to her home in Downshire Hill; but I am nevertheless talking to her and she is answering me.

'That's all either of us has ever wanted. For people not to be miseries. Do you know what I hate most about Neil? Nothing ever makes him happy. I don't ever seem to see him really cheerful.'

'Val used to hate it when I was bright and breezy in the morning. She's always horrible first thing – as if she had a hangover. Not that she's ever had one.'

'Neil's like that. Grumpy, and that's an understatement. But it's rather an improvement when he does have a hangover. When he has a hangover, at least the bastard doesn't speak. He sits there, shaking in every limb, drinking black coffee and trying to give an impression of unjustified suffering.' She laughs. 'It's rather as if he'd been dragged off the night before and had booze forcibly administered.'

'I know. Nothing is ever his fault. It's a funny thing. I've only ever met the bugger twice, but he has no secrets from me. I know him inside out.'

'You're very much on his mind lately. He was sorrowing about the striking miners and I said they ought to get back to work. He got quite peeved. Said I'd obviously been indoctrinated.'

Now it's my turn to laugh. 'I wish I could, darling. You're always going to be an old-fashioned Social Democrat – a real one, one of the sort who's been butchered all over Europe. I'm a counter-revolutionary. Mind you, I don't think that Neil is about to join his comrades on the picket lines or empty his pockets to send the miners' wives and children food either.'

'That's all too true, darling. Neil hangs on to his money. He hides the *Financial Times* in his study like other men hide hard porn. He studies the share index every day. He's becoming more and more obsessive about money. God knows why. He's not millionaire, but he won't be destitute in his old age.'

'The English side of my family is a bit that way.' Then, the dream still setting up reactions, I add an afterthought. 'But they had to be careful with their money. And no-one ever left them anything.'

'You don't talk much about the English side of your family.'

'No. That's what is beginning to occur to me, a bit late in the day. Not that the English side was ever anything but nice to me. But the Micks took over. They're more pushy. Everyone on the Mick side is horribly pushy. Even when they're ghastly inferior shits, they think they're wonderful. And they're always in there with that irresistible bubbling Mick charm.'

'I've seen you use that same charm yourself from time to time,' she says drily.

'When I'm pissed, perhaps, and when someone seems to understand one out of every ten words I use. But I'm growing out of it. These days I'm just nice to those who are nice to me.'

'Like loving as the pagans love.' She sounds a little sad.

'I tried to love the other way for long enough. Now I love only those who love me.'

'We both know what it's like pouring out love and getting none back.' There is no self-pity in her voice; she is stating a fact.

We're sitting beside each other on the sofa; I squeeze her hand. 'It won't happen again. Those who don't love us are losing their power to hurt us. But why the hell did they ever want to hurt us? We didn't want to hurt them.'

This, dear reader, is a real conversation, past midnight in July in the living-room of my flat in Hampstead. It doesn't matter that Vivien is asleep in her house off Downshire Hill: she is here with me. It's very quiet in the living-room and very quiet outside. Quiet, but not dead. There's some traffic but nothing thundering and heavy, and still a few people about. There's the odd drinking club and disco in the vicinity but no real violence; the Village hasn't been dirtied. What makes the difference is that here in the centre people have their homes. There's always this current of life running through Hampstead, it doesn't die after half past five. And there are people here who, like me, often keep late hours. They don't seem to draw their curtains in Hampstead; going along Well Road in winter, I've more than once seen people writing late at night, alone with their vocation.

I feel this life all around me and feel part of it. It supports me, it strengthens me. And I do dare now to say this: I feel part of a community, I'm among friends. It's what I grew up with, it's my birthright. There were two important places in my life, Wetherford and Casterley; Wetherford the city where my grandparents, Irish and English, lived, and Casterley the town where I was born and where I lived (with an interval in France and Germany during the War) until my first marriage broke up. And in both these places I was at home, I was a citizen as St Paul was a citizen of Tarsus. Casterley will come later. I now talk to you, dear reader, about Whitegate. It has been dirtied and desolated now, as indeed Wetherford has. But some things haven't been spoiled. Conservation happened just in time, so there's still the splendid Gothic Town Hall and the Wool Exchange and the Thompson Art Gallery and Museum in Thompson Park, and the Leeds and Liverpool Canal and the moors and the hills and the solid houses in local stone. I think that if the evil lunatics who began the publicly funded vandalisation described as redevelopment in the late Fifties could possibly have destroyed every old building and filled in the canal and have crammed the moors with high rise jerry-built tower blocks, they would have done so. With the best will in the world, they couldn't; and now the properties which could once have been bought for a song are climbing up in price and Wetherford in the centre and in selected areas is, like Bradford, a tourist centre.

A tourist centre? I'm breaking my rules again, dear reader. I'm not keeping faith with you. *A tourist centre*: that's telling you, not showing you. My justification has to be the pressure of time, the necessity to get it down quickly. I remember a long time ago deliberately choosing first person narration for my first book. For what I wanted was this: not to tell you how important I was, but to show you what excited me, to share with you. I actually over a quarter of a century ago saw what was under my nose, I saw that the fields nearby were the greenest. Greenest? Every colour of the spectrum and colours which haven't yet been discovered. At the age of sixty, still with all sorts of horrendous problems, I can be transfigured looking at colour. Green isn't a colour of the spectrum: it is yellow and blue. Think about that, dear reader. Take nothing for granted: there's not much time for any of us.

I leave a space now to denote a shift, to make plain to you that Vivien and I are still here together. I am always talking to her. If I'm ever going to marry anyone again – and I think two marriages are enough – it will be to her. But both of us want space for ourselves. We are both of us writers. She's a better and stronger and saner person than I am. And that's another thing to talk to you about. My first wife, Shirley, my second wife, Val, weren't either of them persons whom I could look up to. I don't mean that I regard Vivien as a stern authorative figure driving me on. She is a warm and loving woman, a real woman, a proper woman. I don't mean a doormat, I mean a woman to respect. As I respected my Grandmother Cloneen. There was always about her that dignity and that quality of endurance. My Uncle Desmond died at Passchendaele. My Uncle Michael died at forty, a hopeless drunk. He did have one high ambition at least, as my mother told me: from the age of eighteen it was his intention to drink Tetley's brewery dry. He failed; but, by God, he did his best.

There were more sorrows than that, if that wasn't enough. She had two sons, Matthew and Gerard, who died at two and four. And two daughters, Mildred and Sarah, who died at fifteen and four.

That's enough, I won't go into it. I have said it before, and you understand me, dear reader. Though I'm no hero, Tim is tough. Not just tough – I'm rather like an Old English Sheepdog. Or, come to think of it, a Maremmar sheepdog, or a Rhodesian Ridgeback, bred to fight lions.

I've been programmed: I look after women and children. Vivien understands this. She looks after children, this goes without saying. But she looks after this selfish shit Neil, just as I'm still looking after Val and my children by her.

But now we're not talking about Neil and Val: we do in fact discuss them less and less. They're moving away from our world, they're becoming ghostlike. I haven't in fact seen or spoken or even written to Val since she drove me out of my home almost two years ago. Drove me in two senses of the word: she gave me a lift to Boxley station. When she said goodbye to me I said in a loud clear voice: 'I won't ever see you or speak to you again.' I don't think she heard me. In what was to be the final year of our marriage I don't think that she ever listened to me. Even if I were saying something innocuous and, I hoped, reasonably interesting, her eyes would slide away from me. We didn't exchange ideas, we didn't really communicate. There was no real conversation: what words were exchanged were almost always about personal matters, and this boiled down to a statement of her wants and the children's wants, which were all, it seemed to me, material and which, however much I paid out, I never seemed able fully to satisfy. There were times when I had the feeling of my whole life being dominated by expensive and, I always felt, useless and hideous artifacts.

Now I'm telling Vivien about my dream, because it's important that I understand its message. No, it's important that we understand its message; we're no longer alone. And the dream is so deeply disturbing that we must go to the root of it.

She listens with all her attention, her eyes fixed on mine. Her eyes never slide away from me, she always listens. 'You've lost your way somehow,' she says. 'You've had dreams like this before, and that's what it always comes down to. But you haven't lost your children. You miss them, that's all.'

'They seem to take her side,' I say bitterly. 'That I have any feelings isn't recognised.'

'That's always so, my darling. But you do see them, and you'll come closer and closer to them. They'll need you more and more, and not just for money.'

'I never go inside St Bridget's in any of my dreams. That's the strange thing. You'd think I'd want to go there, that I'd feel it was some sort of sanctuary. It still is there. I don't know where the congregation comes from, because most of the houses in Whitegate have been knocked down. I suppose they've all got cars now. It was a real church. Rather grim and bleak on the outside, nothing fancy. But dim inside, with stained glass windows and lots of gilt and glittering brass and always lots of flowers and always the smell of incense. . . .'

'I've never heard you talk about it with such longing before.'

'I haven't been inside a church for long enough, except for funerals and weddings. But what I remember best about St Bridget's is that it always seemed full of old women. I expect most of them had had a pretty hard life. They all seemed to wear dark clothes and sensible shoes and lisle stockings. Sometimes they'd be saying the Rosary, sometimes they'd be praying, sometimes they'd just be sitting. They seemed to me to look very tired. I expect they just wanted quiet, and the feeling they couldn't be got at. . . .'

'Perhaps you should go to church sometime,' she says. 'You're still under stress, you know. You need some sort of sanctuary.'

'This is my sanctuary.' I look round the living-room. 'It's not much to show for sixty years, though.'

'You'll have a property of your own very soon,' she says reasuringly.

'I'll start again, you mean. The trouble is that I get tired so easily. Those old women were tired. I remember their faces now. And the way they walked – as if some spring had been broken.'

'They're in your mind a lot these days. You'll have to think it through, you'll have to face it.'

'Religion is the heart of the heartless world, the hope of hopeless conditions; it is the opium of the people. That's what Marx said, and he didn't say it in *Das Kapital*. He said it when he was young, in a philosophical essay. He thought of himself as a poet then.'

'Heart of the heartless world – that's beautiful. You are beginning to know yourself here, aren't you?' Her tone is loving and understanding and suddenly the room is beautiful and I'm proud of the row of my books on the bookshelves to the left of me. The quotation is one of my favourites, it's so deep and compassionate, it has true greatness. When I quoted it to Val once, of course her eyes slid away from me – I think that what was in her mind at the time was a new dishwasher. Vivien understands: as always with her, I feel myself growing.

'Perhaps it doesn't matter about knowing myself, but knowing other people. And deciding whose side I'm on. I want to be on the same side as those old women. Not quite defeated, but doing one's duty. Like the epitaph for Leonidas' men at Thermopolae: *Stranger who passes us lying here, go tell the Spartans we obeyed their orders*. It was all a long time ago, and when they were dead, would they care about their epitaph? But I'd rather have been on their side than on the side of the Persians. And it's like the notice the British found above the trench full of the Devonshire dead at the First Battle of the Somme. *The Devonshires held this trench. The Devonshires hold it still.*

There are tears in her eyes. Vivien's father was a Lieutenant-Commander in the Royal Navy, on active service throughout the War, mostly in the Mediterranean. And she's a Medway Town girl, born and bred in Chatham. And that's another bond between us: like all sane persons, we hate war, but being professional writers, being as much concerned with the facts of death as with the facts of life, we are also fascinated by it. But Vivien and I have heard the trumpets at Roncevalles, we worship courage and we love and honour all those who died in our country's battles.

We move away now, not leaving each other, but giving each other space, deliberately chosen solitude, not loneliness. We shall be together whenever either of us needs each other, we are on each other's side. She loves the Medway Towns as I love the West Riding, loves them all the more because now they're out of the mainstream, now they're running down, now they're forgotten, a little shabby, and down at heel. They're not pushy and plastic but comfortably English, secretive and clannish but not uncaring.

And I'm in my bedroom and soon I shall sleep. I have begun to think my dream through and I am hearing my mother describing the Wetherford Pals marching off to war along Whitegate. 'All those fine young men, all volunteers, and the band playing, all smiling and happy. And everyone cheering, but I was crying.' She got it right. Of course my war in Normandy wasn't like the 1914 War because we didn't have any illusions – nobody cheered us any more than they cheer dustmen, and I don't remember my time in Normandy, only that smell of rotting bodies,

65

animal and human, and the smell of ripe apples which in an odd way was worse.

There was that storm of sorrow which swept Wetherford, there are all those names on the memorial tablet at St Bridget's. There was always the sense in Wetherford and throughout the West Riding of young eager men being absent who should have been there, of there having been happy smiling faces once, and a feeling of adventure. There was always that sadness, as if a great feast had been arranged and as if none of the guests one had most loved and wanted had been able to come. But still, as I put out the bedside lamp, I have a feeling of marching, of being part of a regiment; I'm dressed in scarlet and my boots and equipment are gleaming and the band is playing and the sun is shining.

Six

It's the morning after and another bright day; there hasn't
been a summer like it since 1976. I've had my large orange,
as large as a grapefruit, sweet but not cloying, its juiciness
almost effervescent, stingingly fresh, almost as if vodka
had been injected into it. And now for a change it isn't
muesli but bread and butter and home-made lemon cheese
that I bought at the Community Centre Market in High
Street. The bread is malt-and-bran loaf from Rumbolds in
Flask Walk, with a very full and nutty flavour, the fullness
again almost alcoholic, as if there were beer in it somewhere, not the pale gassy kind but the strong dark sweet
kind. And I've smeared the butter on thickly – it's unsalted
Normandy butter – and smeared the lemon cheese on
thickly too. I enjoy the clean richness of the butter and the
tang – a mellow tang – of the lemon cheese. The lemon
cheese is utterly different from the usual commercial stuff,
which to me tastes like billposter's paste flavoured with
citric acid. I eat four slices, probably taking in enough
cholesterol to give a whole regiment massive coronaries.

But this is a day when I don't care, when I know that
the butter and lemon cheese is doing me good, when I'm
listening to my body, and my body is telling me that it
needs animal fats. And I make myself tea in my pint mug,
using two teabags, and giving it time to brew. This is my

third pint of tea today and I must in consequence have absorbed rather too much caffeine, not to mention tannin. Once more I don't care, any more than I care when I light a cigarette. And I remember my Uncle Jerry Fitzgerald, a wiry cheeful little man who lived with his brother Dan in a back-to-back house off Bradford Road, a long road southwards of Whitegate. Uncle Jerry never married, and neither did Dan.

I see them both now. Uncle Dan was taller and bulkier than Uncle Jerry and slower-moving. Uncle Jerry bounced; Uncle Dan was inclined to shamble. And I'm in the living-room of their little house, a living-room which also is the kitchen, with an old-fashioned cast-iron range. It's winter and there's a roaring fire. The heavy maroon velvet curtains are drawn. There's fawn linoleum on the floor; in these days we called it oilcloth. It actually does look like oilcloth with a curiously glistening texture. There are two large rag rugs, warmly coloured in, if I remember rightly, mainly red and green and orange. The oilcloth shows them off to the best advantage, though I don't suppose my uncle's planned it. I'm there with my father and mother and my two sisters Christine and Josephine. I am seven, Christine is four, Josephine six. Tea has just finished; it must be about six. Tea wasn't afternoon tea, but a stand pie and boiled ham and brawn from Charles Brown's in Northgate, a narrow steep street in the centre of Wetherford. Charles Brown's of course used to be Karl Braun's before the War; but my mother told me that everyone liked Karl, a fat jolly man who came over from Bavaria when only a child. There was no pork butcher in Wetherford to equal Karl: I can still taste that pork pie.

And there was tinned salmon and pickled walnuts and pickled onions and bright yellow home-made piccalilli and HP Sauce and mounds of white bread and brown bread and currant teacake and Bakewell tarts and Eccles cakes and home-made raspberry jam and blackberry jam and lemon cheese. Lemon cheese? Yes, That's what has brought this back. And there were tinned pineapples and tinned cream. Now in Hampstead I reflect that it's a long time since I've eaten tinned fruit of any kind; but at breakfast this bright July morning I taste the pineapple and cream as I tasted it when I was seven. I couldn't eat tinned cream now; when I was seven I couldn't eat fresh cream. A child's palate isn't really unsophisticated, but sophisticated in a naïve sort of way: I found fresh cream too sweet and preferred the faint bitterness of the tinned. And of course I liked the pineapple syrup as much as the pineapples themselves.

Uncle Dan and Uncle Jerry weren't in fact my mother's brothers but the sons of her first cousin Thomas on her mother's side. My mother often would talk about her family, using the word in its widest sense: all I know now is that I seem to be related to a great many people in the Wetherford district, taking into account the Irish side alone. They will no doubt have all gone away now, both the Irish and the English side. They've all gone away; Wetherford's just a place to make money in, not a place to be loved. But when I was seven they hadn't gone away, each district of Wetherford had its own personality and its share of resident personalities too. My mother talked of Wetherford as my father talked of Casterley: she knew it through and through, it was her home.

I shall not let what has been done to Wetherford hurt me. I can escape, I need not be bound by time, I can remember and be back safe and warm there in the living-room of that little terrace house, pleasantly replete and a little sleepy, knowing that my uncles will give us each a shilling. And my mother will say, 'Really, Dan, it's too much! Really, Jerry, it's too much! You spoil them.'

And they'll both say almost in unison: 'Nay, they're nobbut bairns – it doesn't last long. . . .'

It doesn't last long: my childhood did. And there were always all those relations and all the feeling of hands reaching out to help, always the feeling of there being somewhere to go to. *Home is the place where, when you've nowhere else to go, they've got to take you.*

Even when I was a young man, there was more than one place where I could take it for granted that they'd got to take me. There is nowhere now. My father died last year, my stepmother has her unmarried sister to live with her. My stepmother and I have always agreed well enough, but she doesn't have to take me. My sisters, Christine and Josephine and I have always agreed well enough, too, but they don't have to take me either. Christine is married to a doctor in Leeds, Josephine to a textile designer in Burley-in-Wharfedale: both of them are progressive ecumenical Catholics, always getting their knickers in a twist about racism and the Third World and the H-bomb, but not progressive about divorce. Due for a second divorce now (after a second marriage in a registry office) I don't feel that they exactly approve of me.

And all those relations have moved away. My parents' generation stayed where they were. And where they were was Wetherford and the Wetherford district. I have now, thinking of all this two hundred miles away, thinking of this on a bright summer morning, a feeling of a cold wind blowing, a feeling of darkness, a feeling of loss.

The words come back to me:

> *It's dark about the country I remember*
> *There are the mountains where I lived. The path*

Is slushed with cattle-tracks and fallen timber,
The stumps are twisted by the tempest's wrath.
But that I knew these places are my own.
I'd ask how came such wretchedness to cumber
The earth, and I to people it alone.
It rains across the country I remember.

It rains across the country I remember? I've always had a photographic memory. It has been my blessing and my curse. I remember as if they had just happened things I wish to forget, like seeing Tommy White on D-Day catching a burst of machine-gun fire in his balls and going down screaming. What made it worse was that I'd always thought him a very boring person, a little draughtsman from Pontefract and a pious Methodist.

But that's not the worst of my memories. Back again in my house at Boxley in Surrey, I hear Val's voice. It's over two years ago and I hear every word. I'm in that nice kitchen, that Homes and Gardens kitchen with positively every appliance that the heart of a true housewife could desire, and I hear Val's voice, not an unpleasant voice normally, but now almost a scream. No, not a scream: it's discordant, like a wet finger rubbing across glass. The texture is wrong, it sets the teeth on edge.

'You come home again in the small hours pissed up and I'll lock the door on you! And you can sleep in your bloody office! Or go to your mistress, go to that whore in Hampstead, that rotten Communist whore!'

'She's not a whore. She insists on going Dutch.'

'A likely story. She's the reason why you're always complaining about money – don't think I don't know.' She lights a cigarette and my stomach turns – she always inhales with a sort of little grunt, like a baby at the nipple.

'You don't know anything. Except how to smoke sixty fags a day and drink the good old red vino.'

There's a sort of muted scream. 'I'm your *wife*! Not that bloody Vivien.'

'You haven't been my wife for over six years. You cut all that off.'

'Do you want me to *die*! You know the trouble I had. You pig! I'll *kill* you – '

Now I'm feeling ill. I already have a hangover, the sense of remorse and impending doom, and it's ten in the morning on a bright spring day and she's just returned from taking the kids to school.

'You *are* killing me. You'll kill the goose that laid the golden egg if you don't watch out.'

Now her face is actually not flushing but turning white with hatred. 'Don't you talk to me like that! I'm not nobody and nothing! You watch your step. *You watch your step*. I'll throw you out like Judy Smithers threw her husband out. See how you like that!'

And it's all here with me, just how it was, even me rising at that moment and hostilities being suspended whilst I poured myself another cup of tea. My answer would have been delivered in amongst pouring tea and lighting another cigarette and rooting around in the cupboard for a glass and the bottle of soluble aspirins. 'See how you like it when I stop paying the mortgage. You lock me out and the first thing in the morning I cancel the standing order.' And I remember this: my first wife Shirley was a rotten greedy bitch, but never this rotten. And I remember thinking, with a sort of odd pleasure, here I have a concrete example of a termagant, now I really know what the word means. And I'm once again delivering the message. 'I just have to stop the standing order. You'll be out without a roof over your head. It won't take very long.'

'You'd do that to your children! You're the most utterly selfish person I've ever met!'

'Who pays? What am I getting out of it?' I make a gesture which covers the kitchen and by implication the whole house and her personal car and her two wardrobes full of *couturier* clothes and the children's school fees and a mountain of material benefits besides. 'Who pays? Who's earning the money?'

'We all hate you! The children hate you! We'll be glad when you're gone!'

Now the poison is out. That's what she said in the house that I had paid for. No, now some of the poison is out. I've told you, dear reader, and I've told Vivien. Whatever I tell you, I tell her. There is more. What I'm telling you is this. I remember it. I remember it exactly in the way that it happened. I could describe to you the surroundings, the colour of the sunlight, I can remember which mug (not cup, when I come to think of it) I used – but that isn't what matters. Nor does the quarrel which ensued when I told her that if she locked me out, I'd cancel the standing order for the mortgage. What matters is this: I asked her what she expected me to do if she cut off sex. She looked at me with an expression of absolute bewilderment. It was as if I were speaking in a foreign language.

'Get whores,' she said. 'Get whores. There are plenty going. I needn't tell you where to find them.'

And this is what hurts me even now. It's making sex dirty. It's making the root of my being, the root of all of our beings, dirty. I hate whores. And I hate all the people around them. If there were only the choice between whores and chastity, I'd choose chastity. I was of course programmed by my mother. Uncle Dan worked as a porter at the old Wetherford Royal Infirmary opposite Inkerman Terrace. When I was twelve, my mother told me: 'When they're too far gone with syphilis do you know what they do at the WRI? There's these big strapping male nurses and they smother them with pillows. No point in keeping them alive. Uncle Dan said it was heartbreaking to see all these fine young men raving, out of their minds, eaten up with sores. . . .'

And when Val tells me to go with whores, I remember that. It's right that I should remember it. I don't suppose that it was true – Uncle Dan, like Uncle Jerry, was given to embroidering the truth. And I suppose that it wasn't what the sex education experts today would recommend for a twelve-year-old boy. It gave me bad dreams for a long time, and I don't even now like thinking of it. The old Wetherford Royal Infirmary was a huge barrack-like building in smoke-blackened local stone, almost its only decoration being a lofty pillared portico and a massive parapet. To me, it was a place of pain and despair. My mother brought me up to think of it in that way. Her story probably was enough to make a sensitive boy impotent for life – in actual fact it quite simply had the effect of putting me off whores. And that's why I now have the desire to hit Val and hit her again and again: she has dirtied me, she has insulted me, she has profaned me.

I don't hit her: I've never hit a woman in my life. This was another way in which my mother programmed me. She never had any doubts about moral values, she never for one moment was interested in understanding wrong-doers. 'The man who hits a woman is the lowest of the low. *Not fit to live.* A woman's body is sacred. Remember that. Men have to protect women. Your grandfather always said that the best man in the world wasn't worthy of a good woman. . . .'

So Val is safe. 'You make me sick,' I say. 'You make me sick.'

'Why don't you go to work then? Why don't you go to your rotten office to write another dirty book? Get on with it – I don't want you here.' She lights another cigarette, puffing noisily.

I leave without a word, then at the door am doubled up with a violent stomach pain and only just make it to the cloakroom to actually throw up. I'm left shaken and empty and dizzy: I sit on the WC seat, my head in my hands, wondering how I came to this at the age of fifty-seven, not able to see any escape, with no hope left. That morning there has been a final demand from the Inland Revenue for an enormous amount I haven't got and a polite but firm letter from my bank manager pointing out that my overdraft has exceeded its limit.

There's a knock on the door. 'I'm going out now. Can I give you a lift?' There's no trace of anger in her voice now, it's as if all the ugliness of scarcely ten minutes ago had never happened. I would prefer it if she kept on being angry: there's something almost schizophrenic about this ability of hers to switch anger off and on.

'No, I need the walk.' I sold my Bug convertible six months ago: it was tax-deductible, but I still had to find the money to run it. Val keeps the Ford estate car. I was fond of the Bug, but I don't think that I have the strength to drive any more. I can't cope with split-second decisions. I'm becoming too frightened of accidents. The month before I got rid of the Bug I nearly killed a motor-cyclist when I turned out to the right into the main road without properly checking: he came up at sixty from the left and missed me by inches. He wouldn't have been much more than eighteen: If I'd killed him, would I ever have got over it, would I ever have forgiven myself?

I brush my teeth and gargle with Listerine, still feeling dizzy but a least with my mouth clean. I go into the kitchen and make myself a mug of tea and light a cigarette. It's very quiet in the kitchen and now I'm recovering. The house is fine as long as she's not in it, it's marvellous when she's not in it, it comes into its own because there's no-one here to hurt me.

I'm back with my Uncle Jerry and my Uncle Dan, but it isn't clear any more. Only one thing is clear: my Uncle Jerry saying, 'Only one thing to remember: *A Hail Mary each day and keep tha bowels oppen*. . . .' This is his favourite saying, it comes back to me often. And often there comes back to me what he said about the atom bomb: 'Someone's bahn to get lamed with that thing.' And what's in my mind now at this moment in high summer in Hampstead is that I never was hurt by Uncle Jerry or Uncle Dan or any of my relations. No-one in the family was a saint, but they weren't interested in hurting people. I wouldn't say that anyone on the Irish side was unduly demonstrative: oddly enough it was the English side that was the most effusive, the most given to hugging and kissing. But *effusive* is the wrong word; they had less guile than the Irish side, they had no trace of the sardonic, they were simpler and more straightforward, they belonged to the Nonconformist tradition. My father of course, like most of his generation, ceased to believe in organised religion after his service on the Western Front. 'Gentle Loving Jesus be damned,' he'd say to me when I was a boy. 'I never saw Him when I needed Him. He wasn't there when my mates were hanging on the old barbed wire, though they called His name out often enough. . . .' But this sort of thing he'd only say to me occasionally when my mother wasn't there: he wasn't in the least frightened of her, but he hated argument. 'Find out the facts, Tim,' he'd say to me. 'Argument's daft. Find out the facts, and then there's a chance you'll find out what to do.' And as I grow older I more and more live by this. I only care about what is and not what should be.

I never saw my Grandfather Harnforth; he died of a heart attack before I was born. He was a woolsorter, whose job was to sort the raw wool by colour and texture and, some in the trade would say, even by smell. The woolsorter is the key man in textiles, just as the reader is in publishing; though I'm sure that neither ever has been rewarded commensurately. In a photo of him I remember large blunt features, a square beard and rather puzzled eyes. He was a great reader, my father would say, a great walker and someone who knew all about birds and flowers and trees and insects. My father spoke of him always with love. Grandfather Harnforth was a pious Methodist too, a lay preacher. He was, of course, a lifelong teetotaller. Teetotalism was as essential a part of Nonconformism in his day as the doctrine of redemption through works.

My mother used to be very scornful about Nonconformists. I can hear her now, sitting comfortably by the living-room fire in our home in Parker Terrace, a stonebuilt terrace only some two hundred yards away from the smaller terrace-house where I was born. I can see her now, smoking a Woodbine with great enjoyment, silver paper wrapped round her first two fingers so that they wouldn't be nicotine-stained. She was very proud of her hands: they were small with long tapering fingers and filbert-shaped nails. I don't inherit them: mine are large and square, workmen's hands, makers' hands. (It's a strange thing, but these are the sort of hands most writers have.)

'They're all of them such fanatics about drink,' she is saying. 'Some of them won't even have sherry in trifle. Though your Uncle Thaddeus says that if only booze was free they'd never be sober. . . .'

My Uncle Thaddeus was her younger brother, and I think her favourite. He was in the Army Service Corps as a mechanic in 1918: he saw the Kaiser's Battle, the last German push in 1918, though from the sidelines, his job not being to fight but to keep the transport operational. He stayed on in the British Army of Occupation in Cologne after the War, and ended up with a rather perverse admiration for the Germans: they were rotten bastards, he said, but they were better than the bloody Frogs any day. That's another story. Uncle Thaddeus was small but broad-shouldered, with his father's aquiline nose, and light on his feet; a dressy man whom I always seem to remember in his Sunday best, a chalk-striped mid-blue suit with padded shoulders, and always with gleaming shoes, so pointed that I used to wonder how any human feet could ever get into them. He was a sardonic man, too sardonic for his own good, not a respecter of persons; he wasn't a charmer and never tried to be.

The house in Parker Terrace had bay windows on the ground and first floor and a dormer window in the attic. There was a decent-sized living-room, a small kitchen with a gas cooker, and a parlour, always described as the Best Room. My bedroom from the age of twelve was the attic room from where I had a view of the top of the road, which rose steeply and then levelled out briefly to rise again to Casterley Moors. There was a stile at the top of the road from where a narrow stony path rose steeply again. The reason why I remember, the reason why it's so important to remember, is that this view was one of the privileges I was born to. I couldn't feel hemmed-in by bricks and mortar, there were the fields and the moors and the blue distance, there were trees and the sound of running water. And, like Whitegate, it was clean, but in a different way – the air was clean here, there wasn't the smoke. I liked the view, especially in rough weather: I liked it in driving rain with a high wind, I liked it best of all in the snow, looking at that steep path from the dormer window, warm and safe, but somehow adventurous, somehow voyaging, somehow moving, like the captain on a ship's bridge.

I knew where the steep narrow path led to, having walked on it often enough. But always I'd have the sense that one day it would take me somewhere I hadn't been before, some new place where there'd be adventure. Thinking of it now, I know what there will be there. For Parker Terrace is still there. Casterley isn't big enough to be worth redeveloping on a big scale, and these terrace-houses now are prime property. There's been some new residential building, but very little public building and that, though scarcely beautiful, isn't in crumbling, stained concrete, isn't at least a positively savage insult to the human eye and the human spirit.

What the path leads to is what I call The Real Place. The Real Place is more than a fantasy, it has houses and shops and pubs and a police station and a fire station and offices and mills and factories and Friday is pay-day and Saturday night is for dancing and feasting and on Sunday morning the church bells ring. It is not Paradise, the place where all the tears will be wiped away. But it is a place where everyone knows each other, where everyone is kind, it's a place which is easy-going and English, it's a place which never changes. And it's a place which no-one ever goes away from, because there no-one is ever lonely and no-one is ever greedy or cruel.

This picture has established itself with me more and more lately as I've grown nearer to Vivien. No natural laws are suspended in the Real Place: there is death, there is illness, there is accident and bankruptcy and crime. But here the burdens can be laid down, here one is safe, here one isn't being flogged on to increasingly unremitting effort, here time runs slowly. Yes, death is here, and the dead are remembered. But there's nothing to be frightened of – in the Real Place there is no fear and no worry, people belong together and live together; it is, in a spontaneous and untidy and English way, the *Civitas Dei*, the City of God.

When I was younger the Real Place would have been for adventures – fighting with sword and spear and perhaps fighting with dragons and trolls and ogres and warlocks. And in adolescence I would have outgrown any desire to fight (the real fighting drawing uncomfortably nearer from my fifteenth birthday onwards), but would have found in the Real Place the flesh-and-blood passionate female fulfilment of all my dreams, better even than Hedy Lamarr or Claudette Colbert or Jean Arthur or Marlene Dietrich, better because they would be actual women, three-dimensional persons whom I'd see every day or maybe whom I knew well enough to have occasionally a word with.

But now at this moment in Hampstead in mid-July it's not adventures or sex that I long for, but refuge. And what I see now is that any sort of residence in the Real Place is costly. It's not enough to desire to live there, it's not enough even to need it desperately. Those are, naturally, vital qualifications – the Real Place isn't a tourist attraction or a sort of tax-avoider's haven. But these are the preliminary hurdles, the first steps towards being on the short list. Next there has to be understanding, one has to know the history of its place and its purpose. And it has no written history and there are no words to express its purpose. Maybe music might explain it (in Elgar's Violin Concerto I seem to come near) but I'm not a musician and music is a pure art: if you imagine that any piece of music says anything you haven't listened to it.

The answer to how one becomes a citizen of the Real Place is simple and brutal: one has to be prepared to pay the price. And the bill isn't presented immediately and, one need hardly say, isn't a matter of money, though not to care about money might well be one of the items. The price of citizenship in the Real Place is to be forced to take action one never expected to be asked to take, rather like Abraham being asked to sacrifice Isaac. Whatever the action is, the moment it is asked for will be the wrong moment; however strong one is, the action will be beyond one's strength. And the old women I used to see praying at St Bridget's, the old women who went into church to lay down their burdens, and the men who died at the Somme, and the men who died at Thermopylae. Didn't they pay the price, didn't they pay it in the proper way at the proper time, pay it to the last penny?

Yes, they did; and it's in the light of this knowledge, knowledge acquired in the hard way since being driven from my house in Boxley, that I remember my mother's story about my Grandfather Harnforth now, and remember the new pink and orange and pale green wallpaper now and remember the gleaming cream paint, which were all too new and made the leather three-piece suite and the dark green carpet look rather shabby, comfortable but rather seedy. My father was a great home decorator, a quite accomplished handyman, though maddeningly slow; my mother was of a more impatient and slapdash temperament, but gave him his way with redecoration because sooner or later it meant new furniture and fittings to live up to the decorations. At the time when my mother told me about Uncle Thaddeus and my Grandfather Harnforth at her wedding, the leather three-piece suite and the dark green carpet had not long to go.

'Of course, there was everything to drink you can think of,' she's saying. 'It was at the old Royalty Hotel – your grandfather knew the owner and got it reduced price. He was a grand man, the owner, old Jim O'Hara. He lived at the hotel, so really St Bridget's was his parish. A big fine man he was, though he never had but the one son. . . .' She inhales her Woodbine with enjoyment. 'Funny fellow the son was, never took to the catering business . . . I think he sold insurance eventually – mind you, he did very well. . . .'

My mother's a great one for digression – though digression is the wrong word. It's simply that she seemed to know every member of St Bridget's parish, that in the non-stop drama which is her life there are no walk-on parts. I wouldn't be at all surprised to have her give me character sketches of each waiter and waitress at the wedding – for when I come to think of it, she seemed to know everyone in Wetherford also.

She looks into the fire as if to focus her memories. 'Everyone was very jolly. Not drunk mind you: the Canon was there, old Canon Hofstein, and he liked his drink but he'd stand no nonsense. But everyone had just what they wanted – wine, beer, spirits, they just had to name it because of course there was nothing they didn't have in stock at the Royalty. And your Grandfather Harnforth was sipping lemonade and looking rather glum. Mind you, he was *moody*. . . .' She taps out her ash into the large glass ashtray besides her. 'He'd sometimes hardly speak for days on end. For no reason at all. Your Grandmother Harnforth wasn't like that. More like us. . . .' She smiles.

'He was scarcely underground before she married again. Still, you can't help admiring her, nothing puts her down . . . Well, Thaddeus asked him what was the matter, and he said: *This lemonade's rather dull stuff, lad.*' She broadens her accent and deepens her voice. 'And Thaddeus says: *Can't I get you something stronger?* And that shocks your Grandfather Harnforth. *Nay, lad,* he says, *I'm strict temperance. I'd better have some tea.*' My mother draws out the last word the dialect way, pronouncing it *teeah.* 'And Thaddeus had had just a few, and he was ready for a bit of devilment. *There's a special temperance drink they stock here* he says. *Just for special customers. Leave it to me.* Of course, your Grandfather Harnforth was just a bit suspicious. *But it mustn't have even a drop of alcohol in it,* he says. *Give me your word.* Your Uncle Thaddeus knows how to keep his face straight. *Oh no,* he says. *I respect your convictions. I give you my sacred word.* And your Grandfather Harnforth believed him because he looked so dead serious. Well, to cut a long story short, Thaddeus has a word with Jim O'Hara and they go into the kitchen and get a big jug and put in white wine and sherry and a drop of champagne and a drop of cider and half a bottle of gin and cherry brandy and orange curaçao and whisky and brandy – and God knows what else – and top up with ginger beer and sarsaparilla and slice up an orange and a lemon. Then Thaddeus takes it to your Grandfather Harnforth and pours him a glass. *Are you sure there's nothing alcoholic in this?* your Grandfather Harnforth asks him. *May God strike me dead if there is,* Thaddeus says, still keeping a straight face. And he fills up his own glass and drinks it straight down. *As mild as mother's milk* he says, though he told me afterwards that he thought the top of his head would come off.'

She laughs, and keeps on laughing: she has a deep, almost contralto laugh which is genuinely infectious. 'And

Grandfather Harnforth sniffed the drink, then tasted it, then smiled for the first time, then drained his glass too. *By go*, he says, *that's summat like. Very fruity. What do they call it*? Which doesn't flummox your Uncle Thaddeus. *The Rechabite Special* he says. *I'll remember that*, your Grandfather Harnforth says. Well, they finish off the jug between them – '

'Was my Grandfather Harnforth drunk?' I ask.

'His feet scarcely touched the ground when he left the hotel,' she says. And he was singing *All Things Bright and Beautiful*.'

'Didn't he suspect anything?' I have a literal mind and a sceptical approach even then.

My mother looks rather impatient. I'm spoiling the story. 'Why should he? He believed your Uncle Thaddeus. But the next time he met him he said: *I've been trying to buy that Rechabite Special everywhere, lad, but no-one's ever heard of it. I've never tasted owt like it since. . . .*'

I used to like this story more once. Now I don't like the idea of my Grandfather Harnforth being made fun of. Now, as with the old women at St Bridget's, I'm on the side of the losers. Now, without being particularly chauvinistic, I'm on the side of the English. Not of course that the story would have happened as my Uncle Thaddeus told it: he was given to embroidery, as all my Irish relations were, as indeed was my mother. Though he was essentially sardonic, he couldn't help but dramatise, he put in highlights which weren't there. The truth of the story of the Rechabite Special, I suspect, would have been that he spiked my Grandfather Harnforth's lemonade with gin and naturally Grandfather Harnforth found it an improvement.

But I wish now the Irish side hadn't quite so much taken over, that I'd known the English side better. My father never talked quite as much about his family as my mother did about hers; come to that, my father simply never talked as much, no doubt considering that she could talk enough for both of them. But he did tell me about his brother Dick, a self-employed locksmith, whom I remember as having the larger blunter features of my grandfather rather than the neater, more planed-off features of my father. He was my father's height – taller than most men of his class and generation, but smaller than the men of my generation and more slimly built than his Irish in-laws. My father is smoking his pipe and drinking tea: I hear his voice again, light and carrying, with no trace of Yorkshire accent. He got rid of his accent when commissioned in the Devonshires, though in fact from time to time he quite deliberately relapsed into it on the proper occasions.

'Your Uncle Dick's a quiet one,' he's saying. 'Not one for throwing his weight around. But there was no better locksmith in Wetherford. Taught himself, really. Always messing about with locks when a kid.' He chuckles. 'Just as well he was always honest. He could have made a fortune as a burglar.'

'He has some peculiar friends,' my mother says. 'Like his cousin Leonard Walker.'

'Dick's a good-natured chap,' my father says. 'Leonard's a bit of a card.'

'Leonard's a thief,' my mother says. 'Too smart to be caught, though.'

'He's had one or two near misses,' my father says placidly. 'But he's innocent until proved guilty.'

My mother snorts and returns to her book, which is almost certain to be a thriller. My father relights his pipe. 'There's no lock your Uncle Dick can't open, he has a name for it. Well, there was this Sidney Gomershall on

Bradford Road – something went wrong with his safe on Friday afternoon when he was due to pay the wages out. And of course he thought of your Uncle Dick first and sent to his shop for him. And Uncle Dick looked at the safe and said to Sidney Gomershall: *Is it worth ten quid to you to open it?* And Sidney Gomershall says, *Yes, yes, but get on with it.* And your Uncle Dick took out a bit of wire, bent it, and fiddled about with the lock for just one minute. And then the safe door swung open. And Uncle Dick held out his hand. *Ten quid, Sidney*, he says. And Sidney Gomershall laughs at him. *You haven't been here for five minutes,* he says. *Here's a fiver; and think yourself lucky.* And your Uncle Dick just banged the safe door shut, and walked out. Sidney Gomershall had to get a blowlamp to open it. Yes, there's no-one like Dick.'

My sisters don't bother to listen: they're undressing their dolls by the fire. At five and six they're so near in age that most of the time they're quite self-sufficient: they're very happy in a cosy and safe little girls' world, safer by far than the vile world my daughters are growing up in. What I remember this bright summer morning in Hampstead is that feeling of being in a protective circle, that feeling of stone walls around us all; what I remember is the coal fire with the blue flames at the centre of each coal and the smell of my father's St Bruno and the sharper smell of my mother's Woodbine, and my sisters' voices like birds.

And now I'm climbing high, like the hero of *The Snows of Kilimanjaro*, but the things I've been saving to write about are not encounters with Armenian whores and nothing to do with sudden death or any kind of violence, but everything to do with gentleness, everything to do with loving kindness, everything to do with faithfulness and loyalty

86

and decency and unshakeable and absolute moral values. I don't remember any hatred in that world, or any real greed.

I had a shock, recently, reading Laurence Olivier in his autobiography and expecting theatrical anecdotes, the usual sort of ghosted job. And instead a real human being spoke – a Real Person is like the Real Place – and spoke about wine. The older wine is just as good as the young wine, in fact better. But open it and it must be drunk that very day. Otherwise it becomes vinegar. The young wine will keep its flavour until the second or even the third day. Olivier used the analogy because some time in his sixties he was rehearsing a TV play in the afternoon and appearing in a stage play in the evening. And on the day the TV rehearsal went well, only sheer strength of will and a lifelong expertise carried him through upon the stage in the evening without complete and utter disaster.

And that's how it is with me, dear reader. Even being able to talk to you now in this completely relaxed way is yet another proof of how much I've been healed since I came to Hampstead nearly two years ago. I couldn't have faced this truth about myself then, I couldn't face the fact that I hadn't the energy I had when I was younger. And I looked at my material in the wrong way. I rushed towards my memories as if they were inanimate, raw ore all to be excavated and processed. I relied upon my willpower, my sheer determination, I relied upon my professional skill, I thought of my memories as my property, as my material belongings. *Poems are not feelings,* Rilke said. *These we have soon enough. Poems are experiences.* And memories are living entities, like animals or little children. One must be quiet and calm and stay perfectly still.

The woman in the first-floor flat here, an amiable elderly widow, has a black cat who from time to time ranges in the front passage. When first I came here, as soon as I appeared in the passage he'd scurry upstairs and disappear from sight. Then after a few months he stopped at the first flight and sat looking at me unblinkingly. Then each time I appeared he seemed to stop further down the stairs. Now he sits on the second step up. He's still cautious, but he's not frightened. Always for a minute or so I speak to him in a low soothing voice and tell him how beautiful he is. Soon he'll leave the step and sit in the passage and one day he'll come to me. And that's how it is with memories: they have to be respected, they have to do the choosing, they must get to know you in their own good time.

Besides, I don't have the strength to run after them, nor can I play with them or hunt with them: I have to stay still. And now I remember my Grandmother Harnforth and her house in Marlside, a windy and bleak northern suburb of Wetherford, high above the city, with the main road approaching it named appropriately enough Arctic Parade. Grandmother Harnforth lived with her unmarried daughter, my Aunt Norma. Both were small and spare, straight-backed, fair-skinned, with lively blue eyes – speaking eyes – with brisk alert features. And what I recognise now is that they both had about them a curious innocence, the innocence of a generation which had grown up confidently expecting life to be better. Both of them, much to my mother's scorn, were die-hard Conservatives, but still there had been a time when they'd been sure that they'd live in a world of peace and prosperity and even of justice.

The house was a terrace-house of local stone, a little smaller than my home at Parker Terrace, the front door opening straight onto the street. It was a district of the respectable working class, the pavements scrubbed and the doorsteps yellow-stoned.

The furniture was all old and dark and heavy, really too

big for the house. I and my sisters always seemed to have to sit on the horsehair sofa, which was scratchy against our bare legs. I didn't like the furniture then – apart from the discomfort of the horsehair sofa, all of it had too many sharp corners, there wasn't any room to move. But now remembering it I like it very much: it was solid, it was strong, and as yet highly inflammable and toxic stuffing hadn't been invented.

'Norma's a caution, mind you,' my grandmother is saying. 'Do you know what she did the other day when the minister called in? She pulled out a *cigarette*! Yes, she did. . . .'

Norma smiles. 'Fair flummoxed him, that did.'

'He was more than flummoxed,' my grandmother says. 'He was shocked out of his mind. *Why, Norma*, he says, *I didn't know you smoked*.

'And Norma looks at him right cheeky, bold as brass . . .' My grandmother begins to laugh. 'And she strikes a match and says, *Why, I smoke all the time* – ' Now she's absolutely shaking with laughter. She pauses. 'But do you know what? It was a spice cigarette.' (Spice was Yorkshire for sweets.) My father smiles faintly, my mother manages an actual laugh, my sisters and I are puzzled because we're used to seeing women smoking. And I can see that my mother's rather scornful about this puritanism and lack of sophistication.

And now all those years after, living alone over two hundred miles away in a rented flat, I remember that moment with love. *Sancta simplicitas*, blessed be the innocent. And blessed be that solid stone house, which she owned, and blessed be the massive strong furniture, and blessed be the two lives centred upon the Methodist chapel, and blessed be the district in which, like Whitegate, everyone knew each other, and blessed be that vanished world, not a perfect world but, like Whitegate, a clean one.

My Grandmother Cloneen's house smelled of roast beef and tapers, both cosy and vaguely ecclesiastical. My Grandmother Harnforth's house smelled of baking bread and furniture polish. And there was a painting of the Cow and Calf rocks at Ilkley there, the work of my Aunt Ethel, who was married to a draper and lived in York. It was some three feet by four and had captured a sense of distance and space and height, and had come near to capturing the subtlety of the colours – the pale blue sky, the almost black rocks, the green of the moors, the purple of heather, the grey buildings of Ilkley down below.

And there was a tinted photo of my Uncle Dick in a corporal's uniform and my father in a subaltern's uniform. Their faces both seem now to me to have an expression of dawning bewilderment – not quite horror, certainly not fear, but the expression of someone who's just discovering that lies have been told to him. But at the same time there is endurance there, an endurance with no posturing or melodrama. And their faces are not brutalised: they went through the slow grinding hell of the Western Front and came home and put away their uniforms and became decent law-abiding citizens.

Another memory comes to me, quite without relevance, and since it has come to me of its own free will I must let it stay. It's the memory of the Wetherford Catholic Players production of *The Arcadians* in the Victoria Hall in the city centre. The Victoria Hall is a large building with a profusion of towers and a crenellated parapet which looks as if it couldn't make up its mind whether to be a cathedral or a fortress. It has long since been destroyed. But in 1947 it was still there, providing a hall at a reasonable rent –

granted that the acoustics were terrible, but that gave no-one appearing on its stage any alternative but to speak up.

It was in October 1947 that the Wetherford Catholic Players put on *The Arcadians*, a musical so rarely performed now that I can only remember one tune from it, 'The Pipes of Pan'. But I remember my Cousin Basil, Uncle Thaddeus' son and two years younger than me. Basil was small and sturdy, with dark hair and a singularly open expression, like his grandfather, someone whom everyone liked.

I can see him now in the racecourse scene, in a morning suit which is too big for him and a grey topper which threatens to extinguish him, speaking with great attack and preciseness his one and only line, *Here comes Peter Dinwoodie, the demon jockey*! And then he appears again in Arcady, in a short green tunic and baggy white tights, more like ill-fitting long johns, but this time only a voice in the chorus.

And now the memory goes away, scuttles up the stairs. Somehow or other I've frightened it, possibly because in 1947 I felt myself superior to the Wetherford Catholic Players and their choice of musical. Today I'd settle for *The Student Prince* or *The Red Shadow* or *Bittersweet*; today I want bright costumes and tuneful songs belted out by burly baritones and curvaceous contraltos, today I want escape.

Yes, I have digressed again: yes, I'm making judgements. But I am after all in the region of Mount Kilimanjaro and I have to make the right judgements. I don't want to be like the leopard whose frozen corpse was found at the summit. No-one knows what he was doing there or what he hoped to find, but I can hazard a guess – or will do so before this end of my story – because I, too, though not as beautiful as a leopard, feel the fascination of the heights and the snows; I, too, can sniff the clean air; I, too, am not frightened of the piercing cold. And perhaps what all these memories add up to is this: the smell of courage, the smell of the sea, the smell of the heights. God knows that with all my problems I've had a pleasant enough life. I was there on the beaches at D-Day in a state of great confusion, seeing men go down around me as if in a film. I was in two skirmishes in Normandy villages, I killed two Germans more through good luck than good management, then I broke two legs and an arm in a house-to-house winkling-out and by the time the complications had been cleared up in England it had been discovered that I could sort out Army bumf and type quickly – though only with one finger like a demented woodpecker – and for me the War was over. I've been lucky. But there is a price to pay and I will pay it.

But now this very moment, on a bright summer morning in Hampstead, it's as if I'd been given a fine meal by a pretty waitress and she'd asked me to pay in kisses. The memories at the forefront of my mind now all give me pleasure. And my immediate surroundings all give me pleasure. The breakfast things are all cleared away now and the partition concealing the sink and the cooker and the rubbish bin is closed. The other week Vivien gave me a bright flowered plastic tablespread: it gives a touch of colour to the room. I keep the milk jug and pepper and salt cruets and the table mats on it: the cruets and the jug are a set in cream porcelain with a pink flower motif, and there isn't much room on the shelves above the sink and I don't want to risk breaking them. For a year after I first came here I ate at the coffee table and used the milk straight from the bottle and didn't have any cruets. I lived like a slob.

I lived, when I come to think of it, as I never lived in my youth, or even in the Army. In my youth we ate at a table, unless we were ill and ate from a tray in bed. And in the Army in barracks we ate at a table, and didn't have our meals in the place where we lived. And even if the table was merely a bare trestle table, it had cruets. And at home I never saw a milk bottle on the table: that would have represented disorder and idleness and sloppiness; that would have been, to use one of my mother's strongest expressions of condemnation, *common*. *Common* had no snobbish undertones, and had nothing to do with money: to be common meant letting oneself go, having no style, having no pride in oneself. To keep salt and pepper in cruets, to put milk in a jug, was as much a part of not being common as polishing one's shoes and shaving every day and having a new outfit on Easter Sunday.

And now there's another memory: the girls of my youth, who washed their hair and set it, who put on freshly laundered dresses, who wore fully fashioned silk stockings, who wore just enough make-up, who smelled of face-powder and orange water and lavender and violets, who, above all, smelled clean. Clean but not deodorised, soap-and-water clean: close to, there was always that wonderful smell of feminity, as sharp as clean linen, as soft and sweet as grass, not quite musky, but on the road to it. That is Vivien's smell, that is the real cleanness, that is the enchantment.

And there are memories of walks on the moors and walks through woods and afternoons on the river at Casterley, and trips to the sea, and of plays and of films: I was Pepe Le Moko once, seeing the ship sail away with my beloved, pushing the heavy gates open, crying her name, walking forward to the sea and her and liberty and then falling to the gunshot, falling, falling. And still the sea is there, still the ship sails over the great waters, and still no love is ever quite wasted.

The memories are all coming up to me this fine morning, sniffing me, rubbing against my legs, purring, each one of them alive, fully itself and self-contained, asking for nothing and never being greedy, inhabitants of a world outside discontent and outside formulae and theories. And it's a privilege that they now so fearlessly come up to me and put their heads up to my hand to be stroked. And yet I see now that these are not just cats, they are lions and wolves and panthers and leopards and tigers, as real as the snows of Mount Kilimanjaro, as real as the frozen corpse of that leopard at the summit. And I am paying for my caviare and duck with orange and *Crêpes Suzette* and champagne with kisses, I am flying higher towards the snows, flying, flying.

Seven

And now it's eleven o'clock and I'm out in the High Street and turning just past the King William IV into the Community Centre Market. It's the best sort of English summer weather – which is to say, without being in the least chauvinistic, the best summer weather in the world: not humid, not brassy, not glaring – the weather for strawberries and peaches and watercress and cricket, the blue sky scattered with fluffy white clouds which have about them the suggestion of cherubim. And, this being Hampstead, high above the chalk bowl of the West End, there's a faint cool breeze from the Heath, the air isn't stagnant. I can breathe here, as I could breathe in Casterley in the West Riding; this is the clean world. And there are always the trees bordering the High Street, to give shade from the sun and to filter off the carbon monoxide.

And I'm dressed, as I seem to have been every day since May, in a sports shirt and slacks and canvas shoes, feeling light and free, casually dressed but not too damned casually. My grey slacks are pressed and my blue cotton shirt is freshly laundered and my white canvas shoes are immaculately white and, of course, my grey towelling socks and Y-Fronts are freshly laundered too. At sixty one never has to be less than immaculate, the daily bath and the daily shampoo and the cologne and talc must be used unsparingly: a dirty old man is offensive in more ways than one. There's a cobbled alleyway beside the Community Centre Hall where there's a greengrocer's, a delicatessen, a pet-food shop, and a real fishmonger's. I can smell the fruit and the vegetables and the cheeses and the clean sea-smell of the fresh fish. I've never been in the fishmonger's, but I look at it longingly. I can't cook fresh fish in a flat as small as mine, where cooking space is also living space, any more than I can cook cabbage or curry: but when my ship comes home and I have a house with a kitchen and a dining-room again, that's something to look forward to. There's a moment when I see this as a concrete possibility when, the cobblestones under my feet and the smell of fruit and vegetables and cheese and the sea, I'm in the normal world once again, almost in the Real Place; and then I work out what my debts still are, I remember the price of property in Hampstead, and I know that the ship will never come home. On the verge of self-pity, I buy a pound of veal-and-turkey pie for a pound sterling from the delicatessen, not being able to resist the bargain.

'Lovely, that, guv,' says the proprietor, a middle-aged man with a tough humorous Londoner's face. 'Smashing with lots of mustard – ' He smacks his lips.

'I'll report back to you,' I say. 'Enjoy your mustard whilst you can. Any day now, it'll be discovered it's bad for you – '

I move on. This is the small change of life, the trivial yet all-important human contact, all-important because the contact is more than a commercial transaction, all-important because no demand is made upon one's energies, no sort of conformity expected. And I move on to the greengrocer's and buy the red and green peppers and cucumber and tomatoes and radishes and spring onions and beetroot, which with the home-made vinaigrette –

olive oil, wine vinegar, shredded garlic – Vivien will bring to the flat this afternoon, will make up the salad, a salad of clean sharp tastes, raw and fresh (earth, water, sky, sun and rain) which we shall enjoy because of the taste, not because it is good for us.

For what is good for us any longer? I ask myself, passing the florist's at the entrance to the Community Centre Hall. This is another small pleasure: at this time of year there is so much in season, and there is an abundance of roses. *An abundance of roses:* I make my way straight to the Walden bookstall at the far end of the hall, mulling over the phrase.

It's a bare lofty hall, with steel bracers, a refreshment counter to the right, the market stalls round the walls, a trestle table down the centre, covered with a plastic cloth with pictures of children's board games. The stallholders come and go: I feel that they're one and all progressive *bourgeoisie* playing at being shopkeepers one day in the week. I also feel that the Community Centre Market is as much a social occasion for them as it is a serious attempt to make money.

And, I realise, making my way to the bookstall – which is the one stall always doing a roaring trade – I feel this with affection. Isn't it better then being at Brent Cross, buying, buying, buying, a light in their eyes on seeing a new piece of hi-fi equipment like Galahad seeing the Holy Grail? And aren't the notices on the notice-board – plays, ballet, concerts, political meetings, a plethora of good causes – better things to amuse oneself with than soft and hard porn and horror video, than amusement arcades and franchise joints and casinos and zonking oneself out with drugs and glue and alcohol? This, I am more and more beginning to realise, is the clean world. And a middle-aged woman is now distributing copies of an anti-apartheid newspaper. I have my own opinion of the anti-apartheid movement, as I have my own opinion of any sort of pacifist. But they are in there trying; no matter how clueless they may be, they have aspirations, they perceive that there is a larger world.

I choose my books – P. G. Wodehouse's *Laughing Gas*, Edmund Wilson's *To the Finland Station*, C. S. Lewis's *The Screwtape Letters* – and move to the refreshment counter and buy a cup of tea for fifteen pence. Not the least of the pleasures of the Community Centre Market is saving thirty-five pence on tea. This small economy gives me the feeling of being rich. The man beside me as I'm being served, tall and grey-haired in pale blue slacks and a red cotton shirt with a vivid green pattern which is rather too dashing for his age, is asking for a sardine sandwich with extra sardines and being, as he imagines, charming. Smiling wolfishly, pitching his voice lower, he says to the middle-aged woman behind the counter, 'Money is positively no object. I don't mind paying extra. . . .' If I didn't know English, I'd assume that he was inviting her to share his bed. I don't stop to hear the woman's answer. I move on, faintly smiling, and sit down with my cup of tea.

This is the best moment of my Saturday morning. I light a cigarette and sip my tea feeling completely at home. I've read all the books which I've bought this morning, but they are in my wife's house at Boxley, if she hasn't got rid of them. To have them again is for an instant as if I'd got back all that I'd lost. I was increasingly unhappy at that house, but it was a pleasant house, with a large garden and a study furnished and fitted exactly as I wanted it, with all of my books there. It was a real house with five bedrooms and a large kitchen and a dining-room and sitting-room and two bathrooms. A small flat, even in Hampstead, isn't the same.

But this is out of my mind before I take the next sip of tea because here I'm relaxed among the home-made muesli and chutney and jam, and the children's clothes and the rugs and the sweaters and the Navajo silver jewellery with the two young men on my left discussing Marxism and, more fully than at any other time, feeling that I live in a village. I don't have any feeling of being a stranger. There is nothing I want for, there is everything here that I need.

It's over two years since I last read – or rather re-read – *Laughing Gas* at Boxley, not long before I was driven from home. Wodehouse had become my chief drug then: it was either that or unremitting solitary boozing, for there were no pubs I wanted to go to, and no friends to go to either. And I'd lie on my sofa, sipping a drink very slowly rather than swilling it, always convulsed with laughter at the high points, always awestruck with admiration at his mastery of language.

Tonight I shall go to bed earlier with a mug of Ovaltine and *Laughing Gas*; this afternoon I'll go to bed with Vivien, we'll go out for a drink before supper, then we'll have the veal-and-turkey pie and the salad and Liebfraumilch and a nectarine each. And maybe with the coffee I'll have one very small brandy. The day will be quietly flawless, all the pleasures very simple. And all of the people here would understand it, particularly the pleasure of re-reading a book one loves.

'You seem happy, Tim,' a woman's voice says.

I look up and it's Pauline Carfax, my friend Joel Carfax's third wife, a small, rather plump blonde with a breathless little girl's voice. 'How nice to see you, Pauline,' I say, and kiss her as she sits down beside me. 'Can I get you anything?'

She shakes her head. 'I think I need something stronger than tea or coffee. Frank and I entertained a customer last night and I still feel a bit fragile. But what are you doing here? I thought you lived in the heart of the commuter belt.'

'I left there two years ago. My marriage broke up. I live in Hampstead now. Very happily.'

'You look better than when I last saw you. In fact, you look younger.'

I half-bow. 'And you always look younger every time I see you, dear Pauline. How is Frank?'

'Fighting for survival. All our bloody clients seem to be going bankrupt.'

'Don't worry, honey. Frank's tough – ' I stop. I don't know Frank very well. I've only met him two or three times: he's a small, dark, ebullient Montreal Canadian who runs a small advertising agency. How do I know he's tough? How do I know that he isn't, to use the word in the American way, *hurting*? *Tim's tough*: my mother's words come back to me and I remember how much the fall hurt. 'Ah hell, let's hope for better days. If it's any consolation to you, it's the same for all of us.'

'Except that sod Joel. You heard what happened to him? He hit the jackpot with this sex saga. A hundred thousand dollars for American paperback rights, Hollywood showing keen interest, the works – and what was it like when we were married? The bloody bailiffs were permanently camped out on our doorstep. . . . There's one consolation. Bloody Jill will really take him to the cleaners. Jill!' She lights a Gauloise with a gold Cartier lighter. 'What had she got that I hadn't got? She was ten years younger, that's all. . . . But how is it with you? Is Vivien still in your life?'

'Very much so. We see each other every day.'

'Is she getting a divorce?'

I know what's coming. 'It's too complicated to explain – ' Nevertheless I try to explain it: she listens with impatience.

'I don't understand. He's been going about with that Tracy creature for years, hasn't he? The children are growing up. Your divorce is on the way. What's the problem?'

I gesture helplessly. 'I couldn't explain it in under two hours. But we're very happy as we are. . . . Things will sort themselves out.'

'I suppose you know what you're doing.' Her tone plainly indicates that she believes the opposite. She glances at her stark black digital watch: she'll have a graceful gold analogue bracelet for evening wear. 'Time for a drinkie.'

I shake my head. 'I'd love to, Pauline. But I'm expecting a 'phone call from one of my kids. Let's get together soon – '

We exchange cards and kisses and promises, she stubs out her Gauloise and goes out, her hips swaying a little in the old-fashioned Lana Turner way, her jeans a little too tight. I go to the counter for another cup of tea. How do I explain why Vivien is still with Neil? I couldn't even in two hours. I don't have to, she doesn't have to. It has something to do with over thirty years of marriage, it has something to do with marriage for people of our generation – without bringing religion into it – being a living entity, bigger than the man and the woman who contracted it. It isn't even a question of a man and a woman making a marriage, but rather of the marriage being a sleeping monster which they both wake up. It may be a nice monster or a nasty monster, but it's still a monster – as the saying goes, it's bigger than both of them. It attaches itself to those who wake it up, and not even death will make it go away. 'Neil is lost,' Vivien said to me recently. 'He just doesn't know where he's going, he wants to be by himself, he doesn't want anybody except Tracy, and yet he doesn't want anybody. He came into my study the other day and brought me a cup of coffee and suddenly I looked at him and I realised that there wasn't anybody there. . . .'

And I reflect over my second cup of tea, my eyes fixed now upon the Snakes and Ladders part of the tablespread, that for Vivien and me there is no monster. I think that there was a monster for my father and mother, as there was for their fathers and mothers, but I think that it was a nice monster, a good monster like a huge P. C. Dixon, very kind and placid, but unshakeably sure of what was right and what was wrong. With Vivien and me there is only the two of us. We have come together of our own free will, we respect each other as individuals. I remember now how in the early days of both my first and second marriages, Shirley and Val wanted to devour me utterly. Or, rather, the monster ordered it so. They wouldn't have realised, as Vivien realised, how much I need time by myself, how much, for instance, I need this time by myself in the Community Centre Market on a Saturday morning. And Vivien needs time for herself, Vivien too needs solitude. We are never greedy.

And yet this is only the beginning of the explanation. The situation that Vivien and Neil are caught up in isn't like being in a production crisis at a factory, a crisis which can be overcome by repair or replacement of a machine, transfer or replacement of workers, doing one's sums again. It's an *organic* situation, like some wholly new and unprecedented natural catastrophe. It won't be altered by any conscious intellectual decision, there can be no master plan: it has its own laws and logic but fairness or common sense have nothing to do with it. Neil doesn't know where he's going, any more than his mistress knows where she's

102

going. But, however much they may protest, forces outside themselves will carry them away, like the gale of the world.

On the way out I buy a spray of pink orchids for Vivien. Orchids are flowers which I used not to like: lately they have become my favourite. It isn't only the delicacy of their colours, it's their absolutely unabashed sensuousness, that quality of fleshiness which makes them seem as much like a vegetable as like a flower, as if they should not only be visual luxuries but edible luxuries. I sit on the bench outside the King William IV with no thought of having a drink. On any other day of the week in weather like this I'd get myself a drink and sip it very slowly in the sunshine and enjoy the gentle glow which only comes when a drink is taken this way. But a drink, even only one drink, before making love is being greedy, is insulting Eros.

And, in any case, it's enough to sit in the sunshine. I don't even want to read, though I have in my large Sainsbury's shopping bag the books which I bought this morning and also the *Hampstead and Highgate Express*. It's enough to sit in the sunshine and look with pleasure at Hampstead High Street – predominately brick except for the white of Barclays Bank, a solid and dignified building with an imposing portico and a massive parapet which used, rather puzzlingly, to be a vicarage. I look around me and see nothing to offend the eye – even the new building, Millsdown House, across the road, doesn't quarrel too stridently with its surrounding, and in time its new brick will mellow. The High Street seems more full than ever of young people; I feel sustained by their collective vitality. I shall buy some bread, some wine and some fruit soon, but apart from that, there's nothing else I want. Books, orchids, bread, wine and fruit – that's my Saturday shopping in

Hampstead, that's real shopping and is untainted by the Brent Cross syndrome.

Two years ago at this time I would have been in the Boxley Shopping Centre, a huge redbrick block like a factory, and my supermarket trolley would have been heavily laden. I can see it now, and I can see Val frowning at her shopping list, and I can feel again the sickness which comes over me as I look at her. Her ash-blonde hair, her startlingly blue eyes, her dark eyebrows and eyelashes, her neat features and full mouth, her small but emphatic breasts, her long precise legs, all add up to physical desirability, and she is my wife and the mother of my children. And we haven't shared a bed for seven years and never will again. And I don't want her: I've schooled myself not to want her, I only want Vivien. But what is so wrong, what is a devastating grey horror, is that in the first instance only an act of will enabled me not to want her. And what, strangely enough, is still more terrible is that I know she hasn't a lover – she didn't only cut me off sex seven years ago, but also herself. If she had a lover, then there'd be a sort of balance preserved; and now, looking at her, I ask myself for the thousandth time what goes on in her mind. Fear of pregnancy and a fear of hospitals and even the most minor operation don't seem motive enough. There's a great emptiness somewhere in her psyche, a sort of black hole which swallows up all normal human emotions. And I look away from her; my strength has gone, I'm frightened of the black hole.

And then I'm back in Hampstead outside the King William, lighting a cigarette, with my hands actually shaking. Val is in my conscious mind less and less now, though often in my dreams. When I first came to Hampstead I was haunted night and day by her presence, by her implacable hatred. And now it's all over, the

104

monster which was our marriage is only a paper tiger. And I don't need a drink to soothe my nerves, as once I would have done. At last I've achieved tranquillity: here and now I'm at one with my surroundings, as once I was in Casterley, where I was born and where I lived until my first wife ran off to Harrogate with a Wetherford woolman. I left the year after this happened.

It's a small town where everyone knows everyone else's business and I could bear neither the gloating malice – the jeers at the cuckold's horns – nor the sympathy. I actually think now that there was rather more sympathy than gloating, but I was younger then and cared more about other people's opinions. Casterley is an old market town some seven miles from Wetherford; it isn't a tourist resort and has no buildings of any distinction, but most of the buildings are in local stone, and though it's been messed about with and there's a hideous redbrick Arts Centre and a hideous concrete multi-storey car park and a hideous redbrick supermarket and a hideous new redbrick public library, it hasn't been quite destroyed. And with the best will in the world they couldn't destroy the canal and the Three Rise Lock, they couldn't destroy the river which runs through Laurel Park, they couldn't destroy the hills and the woods and the moors. If my first wife hadn't left me, I think that I still would have been living in Casterley: it was only Shirley made it for a while hateful to me, poisoned it with bad memories.

But, looking back, the only bad memories are of the year that Shirley left me and the year after, finding myself alone in a small house which was suddenly large and empty and echoing. And that memory doesn't stay with me for very long: the memory which comes to me now is Gillian. Gillian was twenty years older than me, one of the bright lights of Casterley Little Theatre. I met her when I was twenty-three and had just got the job of Junior Master at Bilton Road Primary School.

The old Casterley Little Theatre isn't there any more. It was in a large high block of Victorian buildings on Webster Street, one of the narrow cobbled streets which ran off Main Street down to the river. It wasn't very large, but it had been the town's first cinema, and the floor was raked and there was a balcony. It was not quite a jewel-box of a theatre: the plasterwork was all too plain and the preparations both constricted and irregular. But the acoustics were surprisingly good and we had the use of the large hall above us, originally the meeting-place of the Oddfellows, a mysterious Yorkshire organisation whose purpose I've never quite understood, except that it's somehow connected with temperance, philanthropy, and insurance.

There are no bad memories of Gillian, no quarrels, no bitterness. And she now has gone; she died last year, quite peacefully. And now I'm in the Tram, the long narrow bar in the Duke of York's, the pub just opposite the Little Theatre. The Tram is the bar used by the Little Theatre crowd; if it's full they use the Saloon Bar, but never the taproom. The Duke of York is the only pub in Casterley into which a woman not a whore or an ancient biddy can go into unaccompanied by a man. The Duke of York has, of course, gone too: the multi-storey car park covers its site and indeed the whole of the area once bounded by Webster Street and Conray Street next to it.

And now I'm back there in the Tram and I'm twenty-three: the memory has come to me of its own accord, I didn't coax it. And though I'm happy now sitting in Hampstead High Street in the sunshine, the happiness of the memory is a different kind of happiness, the happiness of youth, the happiness of an infinite amount of possibilities, the happiness of aspirations without limits, the happiness of being boundlessly eager, the happiness of an overflow of energy. Now in the sunshine in Hampstead High Street I have settled for what I can get: I almost feel, in fact, that I've got more than I deserve, that I've had my full day's pay for coming in at the last hour. To mix my metaphors, I am not defeated, I am well satisfied with a negotiated peace.

But back in late September in the Tram in Casterley, at the age of twenty-three, I'm confident of total victory. And I'm in the Tram now at nine o'clock talking to my friend Chris Bandon. Chris has an almost comically Irish face with a long upper lip and snub nose and, at the age of twenty-three, black crisp hair with a red undertone. He's my height but more slimly built, with a cracklingly debonair vigour in all his movements and gestures: it's always as if he's about to break into song and dance. He's been my friend since primary school and we went to St Peter's Catholic Grammar School in Wetherford together and (I didn't know it then but, to do me credit, I was sure of it) we shall be friends for the rest of our lives. Chris works on the Wetherford *Sentinel* and, after a period there as editor, just to bring them into the twentieth century and also to make a name for himself, he's going to Fleet Street to become a national figure. He's not quite sure which of the nationals he's going to edit, but recently he's been favouring the *Daily Express* because of its typography: he says it's the only paper it'd be a pleasure to look at even if one didn't know English.

And now I see the Tram very clearly. It's a long narrow room off the saloon bar. Appropriately enough, it has much the same dimensions as a tram, though it is rather broader. The plasterwork was once white but now is the same shade of yellow as nicotine-stained fingers, the red carpet is worn nearly threadbare, the waist-high panelling is cracked, the framed photos of cricket notabilities of the

107

Twenties and Thirties dusty, their gilt frames peeling. There are benches round the sides of the room upholstered in black horsehair and three long tables each side. The tables are iron with fake marble tops; the ironwork is extremely elaborate and has a way of barking shins and laddering stockings. It isn't a very well-maintained room, nor is it in any way well proportioned. Looking at it dispassionately, it totally lacks charm, or even any sort of cosiness. It's rather chilly in the winter and suffocating in the summer: the old-fashioned central heating radiator at the far end gives out more noise than heat, and the two narrow sash windows have never been known to be opened. And yet at the age of twenty-three with the whole of life glittering ahead of us, having both of us had experience of the wider world (war well may be hell but it opens up new horizons) there is no other place where we would rather be.

For this is the one pub in Casterley where wonderful things can happen. This, for Casterley, is Bohemia. This is the place where we are in touch with the Theatre (it deserves a capital letter) and so with literature and so, for Chris, with Fleet Street. This is the place for poetry, this is the place for romance in the fullest sense of the word. And beyond it, which must never be forgotten, are the rivers and the canal and the trees and the uplands and the moors, beyond it is the wilderness. And beyond that, which then I was just beginning to understand, is the Real Place. I had not put it into words then. But speaking now only for myself, I know that I'm sensing in late September with the leaves falling, taking on newer and brighter colours, a proper change, a fruitfulness and maturity which is at the same time like spring. This is merely an approximation of what I'm feeling this evening in the Tram: the peculiar enchantment of the room is that at any moment someone may enter who will understand what I feel and who will help me to find exactly the right words. And, being healthy and strong and twenty-three and having no woman in my life at the moment, I hope for a mistress. To be accurate, I hope for a mistress who will also be the perfect friend.

At this moment, the only other people in the room are a middle-aged couple who are sitting side by side staring glumly at their half-pints. Chris and I have been here three-quarters of an hour and have each already begun our second pint of bitter: the middle-aged couple haven't yet spoken or moved or put their lips to their glasses.

'Bizarre,' Chris says. He doesn't look in the direction of the middle-aged couple, but I know that he's talking about them. 'I wonder if I'll ever be like them.'

'You're too fond of your ale for that. And the sound of your own voice.'

He takes a swig of beer and pulls a face. 'I'm not fond of *this* ale. I'll be glad when I've had enough of it.'

I lift up my tankard and stare at it for a moment, then sniff it. I broaden my accent. 'Aye. 'Orse fit for work.'

'Let's move on to the Wellington,' Chris says. 'This bloody place's like a morgue.'

'It'll liven up,' I say with confidence. And at that very moment two young men come in, both in dark grey suits and pale blue polo-neck sweaters, both with trench coats draped from their shoulders, both with brown casual suede shoes. Chris and I are wearing the young man's uniform of that era – brown Harris tweed jackets, dark grey slacks, highly polished dark brown brogues, check woollen shirts with plain woollen ties with large knots. And our raincoats are single-breasted fawn gabardine with detachable woollen lining, and we have check caps and woollen gloves and camel scarfs which were Christmas presents. We're neat and tidy enough, but we don't have the dash of these two young men, and our raincoats aren't the type which can be draped from the shoulders.

'Ray! Martin! Come and join us,' Chris says, his face lighting up.

They come over, and I know that my face is lighting up too. Ray Holbeach and Martin Hillmore are curiously alike in this: they are both the life and soul of the party, they have the actor's gift of creating a sort of festivity around them, bringing to the most ordinary occasion a touch of glamour. Ray is the taller and slimmer, some two inches above six foot, with a long thin face, a hair's breadth away from being hatchet, with sleek brown hair rather longer than is worn at that time, but razor-cut and never untidy. Without seeming to try very hard, he's always perfectly groomed, never dapper, never dressed up, but always in tune with whatever event he's throwing himself into. Martin is some five inches shorter, more sturdily built, with a round cheerful face and black curly hair. Martin is more the valued straight man, the Allen to Ray's Flanagan, a person in his own right but his function being to accentuate Ray's brightness. For Ray's gift is to give light, to turn the stage lights on and start up the band. He carries everyone along with him, he's a born leader.

'How's things going, Ray?' I ask him as Chris goes off to fetch the drinks.

He takes out a silver case and offers Churchman No. 1 all round. Churchmans are the usual length of cigarettes but fatter, a penny more for twenty, and of course non-tipped. And that's another thing I remember in Hampstead – the way everyone smoked back in the late Forties and early Fifties. It wasn't a world where people worried so much about their health, it wasn't a world in which there were so many things to be frightened of. And it was a world which was full of solid, durable objects like Ray's silver cigarette-case, a world of solid durable objects designed to be kept for a lifetime and handed down to one's children.

'I don't think amateurs should be allowed to do Coward,' he says. He has a light clipped voice, a true tenor. 'It's a question of exact timing and professional instinct. I did warn them. Mind you, the dear old Casterley public will love it – as always.'

'Gillian will carry us through,' Martin says.

'Oh yes, dear Gillian. She's a real tower of strength. But then she's one of the few who really could have been a professional. . . .' He turns to me. 'Loved your piece in the *Argus*, Tim. Mind you, I didn't recognise the dear old Duke of York's. Or any of us poor old rogues and vagabonds. My God, what a romantic you are!'

Chris brings in the drinks. 'Too true, Tim's a romantic,' he says. 'That's why he's such a bloody good writer. Me, I'm just a reporter, no damn nonsense about me. But Tim sees things his own way.'

Ray looks at me speculatively. 'You'll have to do something for our revue,' he says. 'We're always short of original material.'

'Nothing Tim can't do,' says Chris loyally. 'He can be damned funny too.' And, looking back, I realise that Chris has never changed in this: he has a generous spirit, he doesn't know what envy is.

'Here's Gillian,' Martin says, and she sweeps in, bearing along six others with her, all chattering loudly. She's tall for a woman, with dark brown eyes – 'Bournville chocolate eyes' I am to call them – and fair skin and brown hair worn longer than was the fashion then; her breasts are full but I can't see her legs because she's wearing fawn slacks. But it's her face I look at – it's so vivid and expressive, like all real stage faces, a shade larger than life, not coarse-featured but bold-featured: like Ray, she belongs behind the footlights, like Ray, for her the band strikes up. And this is the moment in my life when my life takes off, when St Brendon's Primary School, Casterley and St Peter's Grammar School, Wetherford, and the Army and Casterley Teachers' Training College are all behind me, all the exams and all the training are over, I have at last found my vocation.

She is forty-three now, twenty years older than me: she doesn't try to look younger than she is, but she does look younger, there's always a youthfulness of spirit about her, she always moves gracefully, as if each step, each gesture were part of a ritual. Her face, above all, has been lived in, the dark brown eyes are speaking eyes. And the strange thing now is how sure I am that our meeting is crucially important, that we never have been strangers from the start. Of course, there is sexual attraction, of course I imagine her naked, of course I feel a stirring in my loins. For at that time most unmarried people are sexually repressed – and quite a few married people into the bargain. I'm not a virgin but there have been no more than half a dozen casual couplings, all during the War, none of them very satisfactory. With the sort of girl that I would marry, there can be no more than heavy petting – which actually when now I remember it in Hampstead was extremely pleasurable.

What else do I remember? She has an off-white wool coat with a red silk lining, worn draped from her shoulders like Ray's and Martin's, and a dark brown silk shirt, low-cut, and a red-and-blue silk scarf. Introductions are exchanged but hers is the only name I catch and there's confusion and more buying of drinks and to-ing and fro-ing, and then she's sitting down opposite me asking searching questions, instantly communicating, holding nothing back. She smokes, of course, – Passing Clouds, an expensive oval cigarette – but I notice that she wastes more than she smokes, inhaling only infrequently and stubbing them out half-smoked.

'Let me guess how old you are,' is the first thing she says. 'No, don't tell me – twenty-four.'

'You're only a year out.'

'I'm very good about ages if I go by my first instincts. That's a good rule, Tim. Don't rationalise, don't do party tricks. Go by your instincts.'

'I loved you in *A Doll's House*.'

'That's kind of you, Tim. I think you are a very kind person. Not that that article about the Duke of York's is always kind – '

'I'm sorry – it was just as I saw it, it's not to be taken seriously – ' I find myself beginning to stammer.

'You've got to write about things as you see them, darling.'

I notice how precise her enunciation is, each syllable distinct. I also notice that it's with her gin-and-tonic as it is with her cigarette – it's only a kind of stage property, she scarcely touches it.

'I try to,' I say. 'But what I see isn't what other people see.'

'What do you do for a living?'

'I teach at Walton Road Secondary.'

'Teach?' She lifts her eyebrows. 'I should have thought journalism would be better.'

I shake my head. 'It's not what I want. I want writing to be about what I want. I don't want to be ordered what to write – '

'It would be good discipline.' The brown eyes never leave my face. The room is crowded now, and everyone seems to be talking at the top of their voices, being relentlessly theatrical, *darlings* and *loves* flying thick and fast, regardless of sex. And there are three young men sitting together in the far corner who are, as we'd say now, camping it up. I take all this in automatically but only really see Gillian.

'Discipline has to come from inside. I write something every day whether I feel like it or not. If I were a journalist I absolutely wouldn't feel like it.'

Chris, who's been talking to Ray Holbeach's group, chips in. He has the facility of being able to take in more than one conversation. 'I never feel like writing,' he says. 'I just like meeting people, that's all. Then I just slam everything down quickly. Tim's a perfectionist. He'd go mad.'

'No. He's very tough. He has a very strong face.' She takes my hand. 'Very strong hands too.' Her hand is thin, with long fingers; the nails are beautifully shaped and glistening from what must be a recent manicure. It's not hot, but it's warm, with a life of its own; and now I feel my erection growing embarrassingly and have the feeling that she knows it and is pleased about it.

'Talking about hands,' Chris says, 'I met a chap today who knows the hangman. Do you know where he lives? In Bradford. Necropolis Road, by the cemetery. I had to go there once on a story. Funny thing, it was a cold day, but bright. About eleven o'clock. And there was this lovely smell of roasting meat. Made me quite peckish.' He pauses for effect. 'Of course the smell was from the crematorium.'

Gillian gives a mock shudder. 'I think you're embroidering,' she says. But Chris has his audience.

'Old Tom, the hangman – he's a very quiet chap. But Annie, his wife, she's a fat jolly woman. They keep hens. And, according to this chap from Clayton, Tom won't

114

wring their necks. Annie has to do it.' He assumes a woman's voice: 'ee, Tom's a queer 'un. Can't bear to wring his birds' necks. You'd never think it, would you? But me – ' he mimics a screech – 'why, it's nothing to me. But Tom can't bear to look at it. Ee, he's a funny one, isn't he?'

There's general laughter: somehow or other Chris seems to have taken over the conversation, somehow or other everyone is listening to him. Gillian lets my hand go, giving it a little pat, giving me a half-smile. I'm content to lean back and let the third pint of the evening get through to me: I'm not drunk or in any way near it, but I've left the ordinary world, I am escaping, and I'm on the verge of something big, I've sighted the white whale. It isn't merely that I'm on the verge of an affair with Gillian, though even when we're not talking to each other we still are communicating with each other, we still are together. It's more than sexual excitement I feel: I recognise it as creative excitement, I sense a theme emerging and I sense a change coming, a change from merely being a camera, a change from merely recording. For what I see and hear now is without shape, and until it has shape there's a danger it may escape me. I'm happy to be there and to be with Gillian; but with another side of me I long to be home in my attic bedroom, making notes in my diary, searching for the shape which is there in this evening in the Tram, just as a sculpture is within the block of stone it is carved from.

And outside are the hills and fields and the woods and the moors and darkness and cold, outside there are narrow roads twisting and turning upward, and high on the hills looking down the lights of Casterley will be golden, and I have a picture in my mind of Gillian beside me on a hilltop, her hair blowing across my face. As I look at her

115

now I see how soft and smooth and shining it is, smell a faint floral smell, and I want to stroke it, but stroke it very gently.

And now in Hampstead nearly forty years later I'm full of triumph in the sunshine. I have no property of my own left or even many possessions. But I have Vivien in my life and the capacity to enjoy merely sitting in the sunshine, and I have that memory of Gillian and that autumn evening in the Tram when I knew that I had found a theme, though exactly what it would grow into I couldn't yet tell. But the joy I felt was the joy of foreknowledge, of knowing that I wouldn't always be a primary school teacher, that I wouldn't live my life through and then die and have it as if I had never existed. Now in Hampstead at the age of sixty, mess though my life may be in many ways, I know that I'll be remembered, that after I'm dead my books will speak for me, that, like everyone else, I'll go away into the darkness, but part of me will stay and be there, part of the sunlight.

And now Gillian and I are leaving the pub, going out into the small car park and Gillian's car, a black Mark V Jaguar, huge compared with the other cars beside it. By then Jaguars are no longer the Bentley of Wardour Street, the name is a synonym for solid luxury, yet still has overtones of roadhouse raffishness.

'It isn't my car,' Gillian explains as she opens the door for me. 'It's too damned big. Mine's in dry dock at the moment. This is my husband's passion waggon. He's at home for once.'

'Is he away a lot?'

'He runs a firm which mounts exhibitions. And does PR work generally.'

It's revealing of how things were at that time that I nearly find myself asking what the initials PR stand for, and then work it out from the context. In these innocent days in this country there was no PR, only advertising, and few two-car families either. I'm rather overwhelmed, overwhelmed too by the smell of leather and the violet glow of the instrument panel, more like a bomber's than a car's, and the deep leather upholstery and the lingering smell of cigars and some musky perfume, a perfume not Gillian's, but heavier, somehow younger. I've only been in small cars before, not counting riding in the back of large hire cars at weddings and funerals, and have always thought of these hire cars as superior buses, no more than a kind of public transport. But this car is privilege, with its smooth-running engine, this car is more than transport, this car is meant for a background of *de luxe* hotels, racecourses, big deals, evening dress, boxes at the theatre, obsequious servants, holidays in the South of France. And if I had asked how much it cost to maintain, I couldn't have afforded it.

We're going up Alexandre Road now, the long steep road off Main Street. Casterley is in the centre of a heavily wooded bowl with the moors beyond it. I know all this without looking out of the car and the darkness won't let me see much anyway, but I'm always happy to know that it's there, and happy to be climbing towards the freshness and the coldness and even then towards the cleanness, somewhere in the wildness the Real Place.

'I live in Parker Terrace,' I say. 'It's off the third right.'

Her hand pats mine quickly, so quickly I almost feel I imagined it. 'Let's have a drink first – the night is still young.' I'm now more aware than ever of her physical presence, and her light floral scent with undertones of jasmine is driving out the other scent, and the big car is climbing effortlessly and I desire only for it to keep on climbing, going faster and faster, an enclosed world, a world of power and privilege, a world insulated from poverty and suffering and defeat, a world where all are winners and the winners have taken. I don't think then, as I am to do some forty years later, about the old women at St Bridget's laying their burdens down, I don't think about the men at the Somme, I don't think about Thermopylae. I am young and I rejoice in my youth and I too one day will have a Jaguar. I too will invite people to my home for a drink. For at Parker Terrace there's only a bottle of sherry for special occasions and one half-bottle of brandy for emergencies. When alcohol is wanted it's bought strictly in the quantities needed, and tea is drunk with all meals.

'A drink would be nice.' I say.

'Toby's a real wine aficionado. Goes on about it rather boringly. Can't have a glass of sherry without composing a prose poem about it. Goes on rather about cocktails too – I think he likes talking about the stuff more than he actually likes drinking it.'

We're turning left now along a broad road, a road of big houses with names instead of numbers, a road of Jaguars and Rolls and Bentleys and Humbers and Rovers, a world of cigar smokers and wine aficionados, a world within easy walking distance of Parker Terrace, a world light years away, and turning into a long drive through a gateway with stone pineapples on top of it, and drawing up in front of a big stone house with steps leading up to the front door. I can't name the period: the windows are large and square with all the lights downstairs blazing, there's a classical portico and a rather spindly parapet but projecting bay windows upstairs and dormer windows on the roof. There's a light on in one of the dormer windows, and

118

I wonder if whoever is there at this moment is looking towards the Real Place.

'My God!' I say, 'there's a lot of it.'

'Absolutely ridiculous really. Most of the time there's just two of us. And, as you see, my husband likes plenty of light. It's like Blackpool Illuminations, isn't it? And four fucking acres of land.'

Four *fucking* acres: the *fucking* adds to the enchantment of the evening. It's important for me now to remember how important the word was then: used in the proper context with the proper person, it was a password, a sign that neither of you were peasants. It was, I came to know later, along with *cunt* and *shit* and *piss*, a word rather extensively used at the Casterley Little Theatre. It wasn't a word which one ever used towards one's inferiors. I valued it highly, it added to the mounting enchantment of the evening.

And now we're in a large hall with two large sofas and a long oak table with a litter of letters on top of it and an illuminated recessed china cabinet and red velvet curtains and cream thick fitted carpet and the same smell of cigars as in the Jaguar and two large vases full of chrysanthemums and the sound of music from the room on our right – *Roses are Blooming in Picardy* – and I stop and shrug off my raincoat and put it on the big oak chest next to the door. And I don't think about Gillian, and I don't think about the Jaguar, and I don't think about the significance of these fucking four acres. *Roses are Blooming in Picardy, But there's never a Rose like you* – and I can't move for the moment, my eyes are beginning to moisten, it's the unfeigned sweetness of the music, from a world of lost innocence, it's all the suffering, all the heartbreak – and then I see Gillian looking at me, her hand on my arm.

119

'You funny boy, you're crying.' Her tone is amused and tender.

'Those World War One songs always get me. It's one of the things I want to write about – '

'I bet you do.' She pats my hand. 'Darling, it's all ahead of you, you'll do it.'

We go into a book-lined room where a man is stretched out in an armchair, his jacket carelessly flung across the back of another armchair. There's cream fitted carpet here too, and not only a three-piece suite but a sofa at the far corner which is a full four-seater. The man gets up in one quick movement and kisses Gillian very quickly and deftly on both cheeks. 'Darling, how lovely to see you!' He looks inquiringly at me.

'Tim Harnforth,' Gillian says. 'Met him at the Tram. Tim's a writer.'

He shakes my hand. I notice something which I've never seen before – that he too has had a recent manicure. His hands are small and with long fingers, unexpectedly strong: they ought to be effete, but aren't; the manicure and their gracefulness are somehow like the elaborate decoration on a heavy rifle.

'Tried to write myself once. Too much like hard work.' He's a few years older than me with fair hair, worn rather long, and what I recognize as a typical upper-class face, not far from being cherubic, with a smooth skin and regular features and white teeth all his own and long dark lashes and dark blue eyes. The eyes are very sure of themselves and he knows how good-looking he is: there are no doubts there and, I feel, little pity either.

'It's not really hard work,' I say. 'It's always a pleasure. Like acting for Gillian.'

'Ah, that's where I went wrong.' He moves to the drinks cabinet. 'Drink, old chap? Gillian?'

'I'll have a Horse's Neck. You know the way I like it.'

'No sooner said than done. And – yes, by God, there's some ice. What about you, Tim? My name's Toby, by the way.' I notice that his accent is different from the clipped Noel Coward Standard English of the Casterley Little Theatre: it's a shade fruity, again absolutely sure of itself, with more than a touch of narcissism, enrapt with its own perfection.

I'll have a Horse's Neck too, Toby.' It's important that I prove to him that I too know what a Horse's Neck is. There's no reason why I shouldn't feel well disposed to him, but I'm comparing my accent to his, comparing my Harris tweed jacket and shirt and heavy brogue and steel Services watch with his silk shirt and silk tie and grey-blue suit in what must be mohair, and heavy gold Rolex bracelet watch and his black unwrinkled casuals fitting so neatly round the ankles. The shirt is loosened at the neck – its collar attached, but he's wearing heavy gold cufflinks.

Most of us then wore collar-attached shirts only with sports jackets: the reason for separate collars, I suspected, was the necessity to save on laundry, washing machines having only just come on to the market. At this moment, I don't work all this out: I only know that there's a difference between us, and now it's all to my disadvantage, but one day I will change it.

He pours me a stiff brandy, adds ice, and hands me the glass and a bottle of dry ginger, mixes Gillian a drink and hands it to her, and goes back to his armchair and pours himself a glass of red wine.

'A shade metallic, this,' he says, puckering his mouth. 'Still, good enough to get gently pissed on.'

Gillian shrugs. 'You got it for free, darling.'

'No bloody wonder,' he says. 'I'm doing a little PR work for these wine importers,' he explains to me. 'They have the ambition of making the British into wine-drinkers. A noble ambition, but I feel they're fighting a losing battle.'

The music has stopped. There's a lot of silence in this house, just as there's a lot of furniture and ornaments and, to be fair, a lot of books.

'I think people are changing,' I say. 'It's not going to be the same as before the war.'

He smiles. 'Forward into the golden future with Mr Bloody Attlee!' he says. 'You may be right, old man. We must have a chat some time.' He yawns and then empties his glass. 'I must, in my old Nannie's words, go up the wooden hill to Bedfordshire. Got to work like the clappers tomorrow. Nice to have met you, Tim. Goodnight. Goodnight, Gillian *darling.*' There's some significance in this last word which I can't quite understand, but I sense tension. We say our goodnights and he's gone, leaving the room very quickly and quietly. All his actions are like that – *deft* is the only word which fits.

When he's gone, Gillian and I look at each other for a moment in silence. I'm very aware of how big and rich, how insolently big and rich, the house is. . . . My erection is beginning again. And yet this moment is more than merely sexual. It's a moment when I'm taken up into a high place and shown all the kingdoms of the world and even tempted to throw myself down for the angels will bear me up. For there are angels there, there are the hills and the trees and the moors and the wind and the cold high places and the consciousness that one day I shall use all this, that one day I shall fix it for ever.

And remembering it in Hampstead now in the sunlight, I know that I didn't use what happened exactly as it happened, that when I did use it, Gillian and Toby became different people, because, as they were, they satisfied me – but I thought they wouldn't have satisfied you, dear reader, they were never believable enough, Gillian would have been too much the middle-aged female predator, the rich bitch, Toby too much the young upper-class ne'er-do-well, the scapegrace with a good war record.

But at this moment at the age of twenty-three this is something to be treasured, tasting the brandy and the dry ginger, the flame of the brandy not diminished but rather diffused by effervescence. And there is the half-smile on Gillian's face and I join her on the sofa and kiss her. Her arms tighten round my neck and she opens her mouth to kiss, and I taste brandy and ginger ale and tobacco and her lipstick, and her hand touches my groin very delicately and then I'm unbuttoning her shirt and my hand feels a miraculous softness and a large nipple and then she is holding my hand to her nipple with her own hand and then suddenly she's pushing me away and buttoning up her shirt again.

'No, no, darling. It would be wonderful, but not now. I'm sorry – I was being greedy.'

Yes, that's what she said, dear reader. *I was being greedy.* I got my first real lesson in love when I was young and then it was repeated later. That's what Vivien would have said, that's what real women say. But at that time, being only twenty-three, I don't quite understand her. My voice may even be a little sulky.

'I don't understand – you've messed me up – '

'No, no, darling. I'm not a prick teaser. And you're not stupid. You're not just here for a quick fuck, are you?' She takes out two Passing Clouds from a silver box on the table, lights them both, and gives me one. 'You're not like the rest of them. You'll wait for the proper moment. This isn't it. Not that you'll hear again from Toby. Or the housekeeper. Toby doesn't give a damn. Haven't you seen how it is?'

'Goodnight, *darling*.' I mimic Toby's enunciation as best I can.

She squeezes my hand. 'Yes, you've put your finger upon it.' She takes my glass and goes over to the drink cabinet. 'One more drink and we'll go, my darling. You're not a bit pissed. I do like that.' She looks at me searchingly. 'Yes, you've a strong face. But you can be hurt. You can be hurt very much. What was it like during the War for you?'

'Not so very terrible. I was there at D-Day and broke both my legs in a silly skirmish in Normandy. Ended up a corporal in West Berlin. Nothing to boast about.'

'Toby had what they call a good war. Volunteered in September 1939, ended up in the Western Desert and Italy. Christ, he has a chestful of decorations. Doesn't talk about them, but somehow or other everyone gets to know about them. Major, mentioned twice in dispatches, an M.C., a great favourite of Monty's. Still sees the old bugger. Every now and again his old military chums come to see him. They have a great time killing Germans.'

'I only killed two, more through good luck than good management.' The second Horse's Neck is even better than the first and I'm really enjoying the Passing Cloud. Those who've been brought up in an age of filtertips never know what the taste of strong pure tobacco is, they only taste plastic.

She sighs. 'You didn't enjoy it, did you? Tell me the truth.'

'I was scared stiff and that's the truth.'

'Toby enjoyed the War. He and his chums enjoy killing. And being stiff upper lip and slightly frivolous and very very deadpan – *By God, sir, I've lost my arm! By God, sir, so*

you have! The mimicry is perfect and I take up the Wellington and Waterloo reference.

'I'm not a gentleman,' I say. 'Just a survivor.'

'A survivor? That's all I want to be too.' She strokes my
hand. 'No. You're not a gentleman, love. I've married two
gentlemen. Left the first one – a R.N. captain, no less –
when I came home one day and found him on the sofa
with one of his sailors. Toby's not that way, but he's a
thoroughgoing shit just the same. I'm not a lady either.
Just the only child of an appalling old sod of a woolman.
This is the old sod's house. God knows why I don't leave
it. But I feel at home here, God knows why.'

'I think I know why,' I hear myself saying.

'Why, love? Just you tell me.' Her voice is appealing,
almost childish.

'I can't tell you now. But it has all to do with the way
Casterley is. And the country round it. Not really anything
to do with money.'

'Not really anything to do with money?' She hugs me –
there's no sex in it but there is warm and spontaneous
affection. 'That's it, love. You understand. You are a funny
boy – there's so much of the masculine in you, and yet
you're so feminine. No, no – ' she holds up her hand.
'Don't misunderstand me. Nothing queer about you, my
darling.' She glances at her watch. 'Time to go very soon.'

'I can walk.'

'No need. We'll see each other again very soon.' She
laughs. 'It's funny. You're so young, you're so eager,
you've so much talent – ' She squeezes my hand again. 'I
was feeling a bit despondent until I met you – '

And there I end, dear reader, at the moment when it all
began. I end only for an intermission, there is more to tell.
But it isn't as it was in my first novel, it isn't so neat and

so romantic. The only correspondence between fiction and reality is simply this: to use a cliché, we were twin souls. I have no memories of Gillian which are not happy, beginning with that very first meeting and the taste of brandy and dry ginger.

Eight

I feel a hand on my shoulder and come back to Hampstead. I look up and it's Neil Canvey, Vivien's husband, a tall, gaunt-faced, grey-haired man about my age. I haven't seen him for something like seven years, and then our meeting was brief and casual, but of course his face is familiar to me from family photos which Vivien has shown me from time to time.

'A long time since we've met,' he says, and sits down beside me. 'Settled down in Hampstead?'

'Very much so. I feel it's my village.' I'm aware of feeling nothing at all beyond a mild curiosity. Something has changed about him: his whole bearing is placatory, aggressive no longer, and there's a stoop to his shoulders which wasn't there when last we met.

'It's a wonder we haven't run into each other before. Not that I go out these days very much.'

'So Vivien tells me.' What she tells me is that when he's not away directing films he's always around the house, drifting round every room except her bedroom, apparently ubiquitous. *He's like Withers in that novel of C. S. Lewis', he appears where he can't possibly be.* . . .

He takes out a packet of cheroots from the left-hand pocket of his shirt, which is coarse khaki twill with the sleeves rolled up and looks like Army surplus. His jeans

127

are patched and he has white scuffed track shoes, and he has a large watch with a profusion of dials and panels and buttons.

'I suppose Vivien presents me to you as the villain, doesn't she?' he asks me.

'People are as they are. It's not for me to sit in judgement.'

'I should have thought that that was your *métier*.' There is no aggression in his tone.

'It used to be. I used to go on rather about Hampstead – it was full of lefties, decadent intellectually and decadent morally, a mutual admiration society . . . I don't give a damn any more.'

'Maybe you're becoming decadent yourself.' He smiles. His teeth are very good and he has an even suntan, but the smile belongs to a younger man, his face is too gaunt for it to belong there.

'My agent says that I'm not as abrasive as I used to be.'

'I'm a bit tired of being abrasive myself.' He sighs. 'I'm all for a quiet life. As for being left-wing and all that shit – Christ, I don't know! I've met all the politicians, I've even let the buggers use me – ' He grimaces. 'What a shower!'

'"A politician is an arse a man has never sat on,"' I quote.

He smiles, this time without showing his teeth; this time, the smile is more in fitting with the gaunt face. 'Bloody good. And likewise: "Don't tell my mother I'm in politics, she thinks I play the piano in a brothel."'

I glance at my watch. 'Have to be going – expecting a 'phone call.' The conversation is becoming all to easy and civilised; too much so, I feel, between a husband and his wife's lover. I also have a feeling that Neil derives an almost voyeuristic pleasure from it precisely because it's so cosy and civilised.

'Why not have a quickie at the King of Bohemia?'

'No, no, I really am running a bit late.'

'I don't really know what to do,' he says suddenly. 'It's a very confused situation I'm in. I can't do without someone, yet I can't do with her. It's really impossible. I'm damned if I know ... Things are getting on top of me.' He's not really speaking to me; I think he's really speaking to someone who isn't there. I realise that he has about him a strange blankness: it isn't the blankness of insanity, but simply that the gaunt face is not now tenanted.

'You'd better take action,' I say briskly. 'The wrong action is better than no action at all.'

'Vivien wants us to sell the house and split up,' he says. 'I'm not sure. I've been there a long time ... You are sure of yourself, aren't you? Of course, that's the attraction. She's a very decisive person. ...' His voice becomes pleading. 'Why not have a drink, old chap?'

'Some other time.' Another day I would have had a drink with him: though I feel nothing towards him personally. I'm beginning to be interested in him as raw material: even compared with someone like me, he's so exceptionally and unselfconsciously selfish and selfcentred. But this is Saturday and on Saturday his wife and I make love. I get up. 'Nice to have met you.'

'We'll meet again.'

'The Village is a small place.' I nod to him and walk away down Perrins Lane. I feel suddenly tired: I've been robbed somehow of part of my vitality and it's like having had my pocket picked. *He's what someone once called a parasite person*, Vivien once said to me. *He never gives, he takes. Even when he's going to some trouble to be charming, he's taking, he literally leaves me tired. ... You give, my darling, you're always giving. ...*

That sums it up: he's a parasite person. I remember now all those nights going back to Boxley and the way my spirits would sink as the train approached the station, going through the pinewoods which bordered the town, and the bleakness of spirit which always came over it as I got out at the bleak little redbrick station where there always seemed to be the same ticket-collector, a middle-aged man with a pale face and incongruous David Niven moustache, who always looked at everyone with unconcealed hatred. And I remember that walk through the deserted town, a town which had had its own seedy individuality once and a working-class quarter in the town itself, but which now seemed all concrete and glass and fluorescent lights. And I remember taking the road off by the Town Hall – a straggle of old redbrick houses and concrete one-storey extensions – and walking down Woking Road, a long winding road, which eventually led to Woking if one really wanted to go to Woking and off Millerton Road down a narrow side road to the cul-de-sac of large detached houses, not one alike, and my house standing at the top of it.

My house has bay windows on the ground floor and a grey slate roof and a dormer window in the loft and, being built in 1924, it's not displeasing to look at and isn't jerry-built. It's set well back from the road and the garden's about one-third of an acre, and it's always in tolerably good order. The road wasn't made up when we first came, but there's an active Residents Association and we had the road made up ourselves at half the cost the Council would have done it for, and had a better job done into the bargain. And it's lined with trees with a little tree-planted roundabout at the entrance. It's a very quiet area – all too damned quiet, with few lights on as I approach it, and around it one road of more detached houses and more trees and in the distance lush and rolling pasture-land.

But one can't see the Real Place from here; if anyone has the vision of the Real Place in Boxley it's a mixture between Harrods and Brent Cross. And even if I'm rather pissed, I sober up momentarily as I go up the drive to the front door with its rather too ornate porch.

And Val will be there up to one in the morning, sitting in the drawing-room looking at TV or listening to Radio Two. She won't be waiting up for me, she rarely even looks up when I come into the room, but goes on smoking, puffing noisily, and very slowly sipping red Spanish wine or tea. When it's tea she has a habit of giving a little grunt of satisfaction after each mouthful, a habit I've never noticed in any other person. She doesn't speak until I've spoken, unless something exceptional has happened. But nothing much happens in Val's life except looking after the house and the children and shopping.

And I know that if I say anything about the play or the film I've seen, particularly if she detects real enjoyment in my voice, her eyes will slide away from mine, as if I were telling her something both distasteful and tedious. She can only with an effort bring out bromides like *Sounds interesting* or *You seem to have enjoyed it*. It isn't that she's a fool: but, after getting a passable School Certificate, she has closed her books for ever, has got on with the serious business of life which, after the house and the children, is simply buying new things. Or, rather, spending money – there are many other ways of spending money than buying things and she knows them all.

But I am a big earner still and none of this would matter if there were love. If there were love, she'd be waiting up for me, she'd get up to kiss me, she'd be glad to see me, she'd pretend interest in what I'd been doing if

131

she didn't feel it; and we'd go up to bed together after a nightcap, go up to bed together and snuggle down happily, in the words of the Gracie Fields song, as snug as a bug in a rug or a pea in a pod.

And that is it, that is the trouble, and that has been the trouble for a long time: that large cosy room with the oversize Heal's suite in the blue floral loose covers and the blue fitted Axminster carpet and the blue Sanderson's curtains is my Gethsemene. I do not want her, especially do not want her if I've been with Vivien: I don't think that after all these years of separate bedrooms I'd be able to make it with her. But she's still an attractive woman with a good figure, ash blonde with blue eyes and dark eyebrows and eyelashes and a full mouth, and she's had three children by me. It's an obscenity that we never sleep together simply because of her fear of pregnancy and her equal fear of the side-effects of birth control and of even the most minor operation. Every day of my life with her I'm hurt and I'm tired of being hurt, I'm tired of there being no love there. One doesn't grow toughened to it, but every day more sensitive, every day more tired of not being regarded as a human being, but a cheque book on two legs.

And now back in Hampstead going home, a good morning behind me and a good afternoon and evening before me, I can't believe it. Because now for something like two years I've not had anyone in my life who hurts me, I've not had anyone in my life who wants anything from me but myself. Every day of my life I've been loved, every day of my life my strength has been built up, every day of my life I've been respected at my proper worth, every day of my life my knowledge of myself has increased. My knowledge, not my interest — true self-knowledge doesn't mean self-preoccupation but rather a greater degree of detachment, a greater interest in other people. *You'll really get to know yourself when you come to Hampstead*, Vivien once told me; and in that, as in everything, she's been dead right.

And that is why I can think of Gillian now and see what she meant to me and how much she taught me and how much I used her. And I even see now what for years I never faced, which is how she saw me, how everyone else saw me, how much I blundered, how greedy and uncaring I once was, how much, in my own way, was perhaps even a parasite person, how much even I hurt people. No-one has pushed me this way, no-one has lectured me, no-one has brainwashed me, least of all Vivien: but now, on this sunny morning, I'm beginning to see myself in perspective, just as it's nearly too late; at an age where it's said no-one can change, I'm beginning to change. I'm learning what love is.

Gillian died last year, peacefully, from natural causes. She'd been living in Spain for twenty years, very happily from all accounts, with a Frenchman some fifteen years her junior. From all accounts means from Chris Bandon's account: he ran across them in Seville on a touring holiday some ten years ago.

'She doesn't look her age,' he told me at the time. 'Hair with not a tinge of grey, though I fancy she helps it on a bit. Still a good figure too — those lecherous dagoes were eyeing her. Her husband's quite nice for a Frog. She asked after you.'

She asked after you: but I've hardly thought of her until now, until the age of sixty: I have used them and moved on. And now I am remembering her, remembering every detail, remembering that for the next five times we met there was friendship, there were quick kisses on meeting

133

and quick kisses saying goodbye, there was the occasional squeeze of the hand; but we met only at the Tram, she was part of a group, she was almost entirely taken up by the Little Theatre. It was as if I'd dreamed that first meeting and that first embrace.

And now it's an October evening and I'm twenty-three again; and it's just past ten o'clock and unusually mild for that time of the year and that part of the country, and unusually clear, too, for the era before the Clean Air Act, with a new moon into the bargain. And Gillian and I are in her Jowett Javelin, a nice little car rather like a scaled-down Lincoln Zephyr with a genuine top speed of eighty and immaculate road-holding, but too highly stressed for reliability and not in keeping with the long-established image of the Jowett as a reliable workhorse.

Something like this is in fact passing through my mind very briefly: in those days, before I was a car-owner, cars meant more to me than they do now and the different marques were genuine marques, not merely badges, each with its own identity, its own quirks and its own virtues. And the mere possession of a car meant more than it does now; merely to ride in one was still something of an adventure. I can drive, having learned in my father's Hillman Minx, but the Minx hasn't the glamour of the Javelin, and doesn't have Gillian in it. So I'm quite content this evening as it speeds up the hill, quite content with being in a new Javelin, quite content with Gillian's scent and proximity.

I've made up my mind to expect nothing, I've settled for what I can get, and what I can get is not only what I have now, but what I had when she took me for a drink to her home in September; and when I get home and am in my room I can relive that moment, I can carry on from the moment she pushed me away gently but firmly. That is what I have this mild moonlit evening, that is what cannot be taken away from me.

And she's slowing down before turning for Parker Terrace now and I'm prepared for the goodbye and the quick light kiss.

And now she suddenly says: 'Fuck it!' she speeds up again and passes Parker Terrace.

'You've passed Parker Terrace,' I say.

'I know I have.' She squeezes my knee.

'Where are we going?' I feel a choking excitement.

'It's a mystery trip.' She laughs.

'Will it be somewhere I haven't been before?'

'I think it will, darling.' She puts her hand briefly on my groin. 'Yes, I'm sure it will. You won't have been to a place quite like it.' She slows down to take the narrow steep road winding north of the town.

'Has something happened, Gillian?' It's the cold part of me which asks this, the camera part, the writer; the real Tim Harnforth only cares about what his instincts tell him is going to come, and doesn't care what price he pays for it.

'Toby has been playing silly buggers. . . . Godammit, you see how it is. We go our own way, we keep our mouths shut, I finance his bloody business, I buy his bloody Jaguar. . . . But there are rules. Jesus, we've got to live by the rules. God knows they give us plenty of latitude. . . . *I* keep them, Toby doesn't.'

'I won't inquire any further.'

'No, you won't.' Her voice is surprisingly tender. 'You're a very odd person for Casterley, Tim. Part of it, but you don't belong here. You won't stay here, any more than you'll always be a teacher.'

'I like it here. I want to write about it.'

135

'You'll move on. Remember I told you. *You'll move on.*'

And I am to remember it nearly forty years later in Hampstead, physically in Hampstead, but physically only. And this is the real truth about me, dear reader: only with Vivien have I ever experienced complete reality, only with Vivien has there not been the feeling of displacement, the feeling of not being where I ought to be.

For this October evening I don't want to be anywhere else, am aware that what I'm approaching is the sort of incandescence I've always hoped for, am being taken out of ordinary life, the water changed to wine; and yet what matters is the moment when I shall be alone in my room afterwards, I am taking notes, the camera is clicking.

And now we're high above the town, its lights glittering below us, the Javelin taking the bends on its torsion springing as if on rails, and now there's another scent beside her floral scent, now there's the scent of her excitement, and we're bumping down the narrow road to Wharton Woods, bordered by silver birches, ghostlike in the moonlight, and she's parked the car well back from the road in a grove where she seems to have been before, a sort of alfresco car park, where there is already a Morris-8; and we're going over the stile and branching off the main path up a narrow steep rocky path, half-running, and we've reached the Wharton Woods Spring and the little stream fed by the water from the large rock above it and we're in a clearing by the spring among the dead leaves hearing the sound of the stream, hearing the sound of the running water, hearing the faint rustling of the trees, hearing the hoot of an owl, hearing a dog distantly barking, almost hearing the sound of the earth breathing, but hearing no traffic; hearing our own breathing, smelling the woods and the earth and the night air, smelling even, I give you my word, dear reader, the water of the spring, that cold clear water, so live, almost effervescent.

Some say water has no taste and no smell: they're wrong. Water which rises high in the limestone country and makes its way downwards through the rock has a smell and a taste all of its own: it can't be explained until you've tasted it and smelled it – it's clean but not sterile, it's clean but not disinfected, and once you've tasted it you'll want no other water.

And I throw my trench coat down and she kisses me open-mouthed, taking the initiative, her hands efficiently busy at my loins and then her mouth doing things which to me then are highly surprising and there's nakedness and the wonderful sensation of the fresh air, the fresh moving air on my whole body, and there's the plunging and my mouth on large nipples and my mouth on her mouth and then us both crying out and an orgasm for me which seems to be through my whole body, through my skin as much as through any single part of me.

Afterwards we lie quite still, our arms around each other. I don't seem to have any weight, I feel as a spirit must feel, and at the same time I am conscious of the minutest detail, I can feel the texture of the grass and the texture of my trench coat. I can hear the faintest of the sounds of the night, hear the rustle of each separate leaf and the scurryings of the smallest insect. I feel very warm.

'You're wonderful,' I say to her. 'I love you.'

She kisses me. 'That's nice. That's what you should say. But it won't last, you know.'

'I was wondering what you felt about me.'

'I think you know, darling.' She stands up and begins to sort her clothes out. As she bends, her breasts drooping, as she stands, her knickers and her slacks in her hand, I see something which I have never seen before except in paintings and photos and on the stage. I am seeing a naked woman after love, a naked woman utterly unselfconscious, I am seeing her all the more clearly because of the background, the night, the grass, the trees, the silver of the moonlight, the sound of the stream. And I can see her body all the more clearly because for the moment I feel no desire; can see her body as a spontaneous work of art, a song, a poem.

I put on my own clothes. Dressing together, even more than undressing, seems to bring her very near, moves me to tenderness, a tenderness which astonishes me. I don't feel that I could ever hurt her because I have seen her body and entered it; I see her not as a body but a person.

'I don't know if you don't tell me,' I say. It's suddenly colder; I dress very quickly.

'Actions speak louder than words, darling. I don't do this with everyone.'

'I really do love you.' I don't really know whether I mean this, but my instinct tells me that it's the right thing to say.

'Don't say that, darling, it's unlucky. Let's just say we're friends.'

'I've never felt like this before. You've changed my whole life.'

She kisses me very gently. 'You'll feel like this again. Many times. Do you know what you are? I knew as soon as I saw you in the Tram. You're one of the men who likes women.'

'Don't most men like women?' I pick up my trench coat and put it on my shoulders in the Little Theatre fashion. It's a recent purchase, not a Burberry, but a good make, with all the trimmings, even the rings for hand grenades.

138

I'm very pleased with it, it even seems to give me a sort of glamour.

'Not in this country, darling.' We go hand-in-hand to the car; I feel very warm now, almost as after a cold bath, my skin glowing.

In the car she switches on the interior light and we're in a small world of our own. I comb my hair.

'Your husband likes women, doesn't he?'

She's combing her hair too and taking out her lipstick: the car is full of the smell of make-up, sweet and oddly innocent, and it is full, too, of the scent of love. 'Toby's not queer,' she says. 'Sex for him means women. Any amount of them.' Her tone is bitter. 'But he doesn't *like* women, he doesn't like their company. Yes, yes, he has nice manners, he's a real English gentleman. But what he prefers is a night out with the boys. Particularly his old Army chums. And of course he loves golf and fishing and shooting. Mind, he understands women well enough. He has all the makings of a high-class gigolo. But he doesn't like them. You really do. You can't help it. It's how you were born.'

'Actually, I only like you. I've never met any woman quite like you.'

She laughs. 'Ah, darling, I'm nothing very special. Just a poor little rich girl amusing herself as best she can.'

'It's something more than amusement to me.' I'm aware that my voice is sulky: for the first time in my life I seem to be treated as a thing.

She squeezes my hand. 'Tim, Tim, don't be so touchy. It was more than just a quick fuck to me. I told you, I don't do it with everybody. I was interested in you from the first moment I saw you.' She lights two cigarettes and hands me one. 'You're not bad-looking, but there's something more. You've a *live* face. You want a lot of things very badly, don't you?'

'Doesn't everyone?'

'No, darling. Most people are content just to get by. Most people are scared of what's outside their experience. You're not scared, are you?'

'I couldn't live like that. It wouldn't be living, it'd be so damned grey, so boring – '

'You'll have to leave Casterley, of course. It's too small for you.'

'I expect I'll stay here a bit longer. There's something I want here. I won't find it anywhere else.'

'You'll find it only when you go away from here. You'll go away from here. You'll go a long way.'

'How do you know?'

It's a very good moment in the small self-contained world of the Javelin: I can smell her make-up, I can smell her scent, I can taste the tobacco, the window is open a little and I can smell the cool night air and the grass and the trees and even, I'll swear, I can smell the cool running water and smell the windswept distance of the moors.

'How do I know? I go by my instincts. I'm never wrong. If I'm guided by my instincts, my very first instincts, that's fine. You can do that, Tim. But don't rationalise, don't try to be clever. When I first met Wilfred, when I first met Toby, I knew they were shits. But then I rationalised it – they were so beautiful, they had so much style, I had to have them. I gave them trial runs too, and there wasn't a damned thing wrong with them. . . . Well, I've paid dearly. The only thing I've done right is to hang on to the house. Bloody ridiculous really, the only time when I really use it to capacity is when the boys come home. And when they do, they're not in it very much.'

'Don't you ever think of the professional theatre?'

140

'Too late now, darling. I went to a not bad little stage school in Wetherford and had one or two jobs in rep., but it wasn't for me. No-one liked me for having so much money. I stayed in grotty boarding-houses to muck in, be one of the gang, but they didn't really like it. They wouldn't have liked it if I'd stayed in a decent hotel either. No, my face didn't fit. And someone was always trying to put the bite on – if not for a quid until pay-day, then they were trying to get me to finance some loony venture. Yes, there are problems if one's rich.'

I laugh. 'I think I'd manage to get over them. I wouldn't let them depress me unduly.'

'Oh, love, don't kid yourself. It's nice having pots of money. It doesn't buy happiness, but it enables you to be miserable in comfort. I can't imagine how ordinary people live, it seems so odd to me. Of course, I'm very nice to ordinary people, I treat them just like human beings. But they're another species to me.'

'You'll find we're uncommonly like you,' I say drily. I'm not taking offence, because I don't really see myself as an ordinary person.

She puts her hand on mine. 'Darling, you're not ordinary. You'll have plenty of money one day, I can smell it on you. Besides, you're not exactly a horny-handed prole, are you?'

I have never had a conversation like this with a woman before, nor have I ever met anyone so utterly frank. This was the first of many conversations: we were never short of something to talk about. I often wish I'd kept in touch with her after I left Casterley, I often wish I'd had the experience of having her as a genuinely platonic friend, having her guidance and counsel. As it was, she was a good teacher. It wasn't just sex she taught me: she ironed

141

out the remains of my Yorkshire accent, she forbade me hair oil, she told me where to go for a haircut, she told me how to dress, she told me about wine and about food and about tipping, she told me about acting and public speaking and painting and music, she was my Pygmalion. No doubt I should have learned all this anyway, but with her as my loving teacher I learned painlessly, and I was a quick learner.

I wouldn't like you, dear reader, to think that on that October night I was anything other than a warm responsive person, that I was anything other than grateful, that I wasn't fully committed to the experience. To look at it in any other way would make me a monster, simply an intellect, simply a cold intelligence. What I always have had, and what appealed to Gillian in the first place, was my emotional vitality, my capacity for feeling. And that night it was entirely engaged, I valued every second. And that was Gillian's great gift. All the time spent with her was out of the ordinary: boredom and depression were abolished; I could feel myself becoming the person I was meant to be.

And now I'm coming home to Parker Terrace; Gillian has left me at the bottom of the road to save comment and awkward explanations. My mother is reading by the fire as I enter.

'You're late,' she says.

'I've been to the Little Theatre.'

She looks at me and sniffs. Despite all the Woodbines she smokes, she has a keen sense of smell. 'You've been with a woman.'

I shrug. 'You know how these theatrical types are. Always kissing each other. Doesn't mean anything.'

'Doesn't it? I think you're making a cheap wife out of some poor girl.'

'Come off it, Mother. I've just had a quiet social evening.'

'Is that what they call it?' She's rather enjoying herself, I note with affection. 'It was different when I was young. I met your father on the Monkey Parade in the Park in June, 1914 that was, a lovely summer. Mind, he was good-looking. He can be an awkward sod at times, but he was good-looking. . . . Of course we didn't have cars then, coming home at all hours. . . .'

I sit down and light a cigarette; suddenly I'm rather tired. 'Mother, I'm grown-up and I've been a soldier. Anyway, you've nothing to worry about. There were four of us given a lift home.'

'Want a cup of tea? Or anything to eat?'

'Just tea,' I say. I'm glad now to be home. I was glad when I came to the front door to see the lights of home.

She goes into the kitchen, a small kitchen just adjacent to the living-room, and keeps on talking. 'There's a bit of cold beef left from tea-time. Or I could fry you some bacon.'

'Just tea, Mother.' And this is a thing I remember in Hampstead. We didn't have a fridge, only a tiny scullery off the kitchen, but there were always the makings of a meal at any time, there was always milk enough not only for tea, but for a hot milky drink; there was always somehow a fresh loaf; there was always somehow more than enough; there was always somehow the materials of comfort.

And I remember now in Hampstead that in Boxley, despite all that I paid out, despite all Val's shopping expeditions, despite the large fridge-freezer, despite all the money I paid out, one couldn't count upon there even being enough tea or coffee or milk or bread or butter or marmalade or cheese. We were always running out of everything except cigarettes and booze. But my mother in Parker Terrace never ran out, and that's why that house in Parker Terrace was a home, that's why nearly forty years later I look back to it with love.

And now we're drinking tea by the fire and we're very close together. My mother is close to my sisters and loves them; but I am her favourite. They are good girls: Josephine at Wetherford University reading English, Christine a nurse at Wetherford Royal Infirmary, both of them living in Wetherford but both of them frequent visitors, and she's close to them, she's their friend, she talks the same language; but I am her favourite because I have the streak of wildness they haven't, the Irish side of me has always got the upper hand in me, I'm more like the sort of men she grew up with.

And now in Hampstead nearly forty years later I realise what I had in Parker Terrace and how short a time there was remaining for me to have it in. Perhaps that night I was even a little annoyed at the way she still tended to treat me – just as if I were still a teenager – perhaps I wanted my independence, a place of my own. But that now, remembering coming home that October evening when I was twenty-three, is not how it was. I was glad to be back in Parker Terrace, near to the Real Place, I was glad to be drinking tea with her, I was glad to be home.

'Your father still thinks you should go to the University.' she says. 'If Josephine got a place, why not you?'

'I just want to be a writer, Mother. I don't mind being a teacher. I quite like kids.'

'You're a rotten devil sometimes, but you do like children, I'll give that to you. Time you were married and had some of your own. . . .'

And here I am again, dear reader. It always comes down to you. Vivien loves me, and she's the best thing that has happened to me in the whole of my life, but I can't even talk to Vivien about Gillian. Though it's so long ago, though she's now dead, Gillian in a sense took something from Vivien. That's the way the sexes are. More and more these last two years in Hampstead I've become more keenly aware of what men and women have to give to each other; more and more I've become aware of the fundamental differences between us.

My mother, when I was twenty-three, lived in an ordered world. I was home from the War all in one piece and, though I didn't go to University as my father would have wanted, was still a son to be proud of: not an ordinary person but a teacher. I think that all she really wanted was for me to get married and give her grandchildren. And she would have given me and my wife love, she would have given the grandchildren love. I remember that now about her, remember that along with her harsh realism, her outspokenness, her black-and-white standards, her fierce and rigorous Catholicism, she would have been on my side. And if she were alive now, which isn't entirely impossible, she would have got along like a house on fire with Vivien.

The oldest cliché of all: men marry their mothers, girls marry their fathers. All I know is that the sort of emotional comfort that my mother provided for my father, Vivien provides for me.

And now I'm in my room at Parker Terrace, and before I undress I look out through the dormer window and I know the Real Place is there, and I know, too, that before I go to sleep I must put down all that has happened to me in what I call my Notebook which is always kept under lock and key in the battered old mahogany desk which dominates my room. There's a big frayed square of carpet beside the bed, there are darkstained floorboards, there's a divan bed with a large red woollen rug over it, there's a big wing chair with a shabby green loose cover, there's a built-in cupboard and built-in wardrobe, there's a large deal kitchen table, there's two rather dilapidated fireside chairs in dirty green and orange, there's two large oak bookcases crammed full, mostly with Penguins, and there's an old spluttering gas fire. And I've wrapped my pyjamas round the stone hot water bottle, and I'm smoking a last cigarette and I'm remembering.

I don't know now how significant this moment is, what use I shall make of it. It was all different in my first book, it was much neater. The older woman wasn't all that much older, and not all that rich. Her husband was richer than the hero; but he had the money, not her. And the Little Theatre was entirely different, much less sophisticated. When I settled down at the desk I wrote it all down as far as I could remember, not in diary form but as the synopsis of a story. And I didn't put in any real names. I wrote in buff exercise books which I pinched from school, and I kept them under lock and key.

My other manuscripts were kept in the cupboard along with my Olympia typewriter: I'd taught myself how to type by the hunt-and-peek system in West Berlin, but I always wrote notes and synopses and rough drafts in longhand. I didn't care who saw these or, in particular, who saw the finished work and in fact hoped that a lot of people would see them: but what was written in the notebooks was private. I wouldn't be able to use it yet.

I look back at that room with genuine nostalgia. When I come to think of it, there was everything I needed there, and considerably more space than one would have in any

Earl's Court bedsitter. And, above all, always there was the view from the dormer window of the path which led to the Real Place: I always look out of it each time I come to the room and tonight the silver of the new moon seems to bring the Real Place nearer; with a little effort it almost seems that I'll be able to see its buildings.

In my notes I'm reasonably explicit but don't use four-letter words. I indicate them plainly enough, but at that period it was a waste of time for writers to depend for their effects upon something which was strictly forbidden. The curious thing about writing it all down is that, since I'm a healthy twenty-three, the capacity to feel desire has returned, but though I can remember every detail of making love to Gillian, I feel no desire, nor will I when I read over it tomorrow. I write very easily now, with no corrections: the only time I slow down is when I try to analyse my moment of triumph afterwards, the feeling that the Jaguar and the Javelin don't matter, that I've conquered Toby, that I've conquered that big house, that I've conquered the silver box full of Passing Clouds, that I've conquered the Little Theatre, that I've conquered the rich world, that I too am one of the lords of creation.

I don't like writing this because it doesn't show me in a good light, because whatever her faults may be Gillian gave me herself, whatever her faults may be she doesn't think of sex in terms of status. But that is what I felt, whoever *I* may be, and to tell the whole truth about myself, in this context, is my only claim to any real integrity. But my father in my shoes, assuming an impossibility, would have conceived of the sexual act as something totally and utterly private between two people.

This thought passes through my head, but I discard it. I love my father, but I have never been as close to him as to my mother. It isn't that her personal standards are any less unremitting than his, it isn't that she has any doubt about her moral values. But she's more outgoing, more extrovert, more given to dramatising herself and, indeed, all the life around her; she's a great gossip and scandal-monger, she has a devouring curiosity about other human beings. My father is more reserved, my father measures his words, my father keeps his thoughts to himself, my father's always calm. His face gives nothing away; my mother's face reveals every thought. My father would never dream of opening other people's letters, of prying where he had no business to pry; I wouldn't put it past my mother.

My father is closest to my sister Josephine, who's one year younger than me, and now taking an English degree at Wetherford. Both my sisters are like my mother in colouring with clear fair skin and blue eyes and black hair, but Josephine is the most like my father in temperament. She and my father together have a way of sharing a companionable silence; and when they talk together use less words than other people, but get more satisfaction from these words. And Josephine is an academic high-flier, a scholarship winner, who has fulfilled vicariously my father's own dreams of going to university. I scraped through School Certificate and had a one year's teachers' crash course at Casterley Training College and, although I am at least a teacher, I'm a sad disappointment to him, though he never reproaches me.

Christine is three years younger than me, a nurse at Wetherford Infirmary. I don't mean that my mother didn't love her daughters, or that they didn't give her something I couldn't give; I'm now trying to understand, nearly forty years later, just how it was in Parker Terrace. And, looking back there, late that night after I've made love to Gillian, I can understand this, having now myself had daughters.

And I know now in Hampstead why my father was never depressed, had never thought of depression as being an illness, something one had to see a doctor about, but nevertheless missed my sisters. Though their marriage wasn't perfect – both of them being so different – my mother was his wife, the only woman in his life, the only woman with whom he'd ever had sexual intercourse. And he made the best of it; he put up with his Mick relations; he did his job at Inkerman Road Primary School as headmaster, climbing up slowly. And Inkerman Road, Wetherford, is where my Irish grandparents lived, where St Bridgets was: he often remarked upon the coincidence. To me at the age of twenty-three and definitely Left Wing, the name meant exploitation, the nineteenth-century ruling classes commemorating battlefields, another insult to the working classes. But to my father – and, God knows, he'd seen his share of battlefields – it was simply coincidence.

Sancta simplicitas, I think now, going along Perrins Walk. Blessed be the innocent – and then, as I go into my flat, I have the rebellious feeling about the innocent, all the people like my father who don't stir up trouble, who don't make waves – I have the feeling that I'm on the side of the rebels, the awkward buggers, those who do make waves. Do you know, dear reader, the origin of that phrase? A very wicked man is condemned to Hell, and gets the choice of two doors. He hears at one door loud agonised screams and howls for mercy. He hears at the other door a soft, sibilant sound, almost a whisper. And this is the door he chooses. And when he goes in through the door he sees a great pool with a thousand people neck-deep in shit. And the message they're all whispering is this: *Don't make waves. Don't make waves.* I'm sure that my father never heard the story. But when I come to think of it, he ran his whole life as if it were true.

And now after another large orange and a large Red Leicester cheese sandwich and a large mug of strong tea I'm lying on the sofa waiting for Vivien, listening to pop music on Radio Two, perfectly happy. I haven't ever known such happiness since my mother died; I'm recovering from what has happened to me two years ago. I'm happy because I'm living in a world of love and friendship. And, all on tea, I'm as if mellow with drink, reflecting that always now I'm going to love as the pagans love, I'm going to love only those who love me. And how right the pagans were! Christ got it right from time to time, Christ could be extraordinarily wise, but for most of the time He was a lunatic. Yes, dear reader, I know. I can't help using the capital. He is still the Son of God to me. And what I realise, lying on the sofa waiting for Vivien, is that there is no reason why a superhuman being can't be wrong, why the whole universe can't be a gigantic balls-up. And none of it invalidates what those broken-down women at St Bridget's believed, none of it invalidates what I saw once at the Cathedral of the Sacred Blood in Leningrad, none of it must ever take anything away from the poor, the old, the broken-down, the defeated – and not just the old.

And now the doorbell's ringing and she's there in a dark green print frock and sandals and the pleasure on meeting her is always as if for the first time, and I'm taking her parcels and carrier bags from her and not having quite enough hands and wondering – though wondering with affection, not annoyance – how one human being can accumulate so much impedimenta – and we're drinking tea and we are resuming our conversation.

Resuming our conversation, dear reader: this conversation has never stopped. This is why I love her, because this conversation, this long dialogue, began a long time ago at Brotton Manor, when I met Vivien for the first time, when I was dead drunk and despairing, when we instantly communicated, when all the despair was over, when I knew I'd found the right person. There's even more to it than that, I know, lying on the sofa: for one thing there is absolute commitment, absolute faithfulness. I think of all this and time passes by.

I don't mean this to be dismissive, dear reader. We don't have long upon this earth, and every moment is to be cherished. But it's always with Vivien as it was once with Gillian – no aspect of life is ordinary, the most commonplace details have splendour. And when the door-bell rings, hours have passed, I'm in a happy trance. She's a little late, because she always takes too much on, she's always at least a quarter of an hour behindhand. And she's always doing something for someone else, she's always giving, particularly to me. And I don't care about the time, because what she has to give me is well worth waiting for, because once again I'm going to be in the Real Place.

And that's it, that sums it up. With Vivien I'm living in the Real Place. With Vivien, there's no unhappiness. She would never hurt me. And, waiting for her now, I ask myself who else would do? Who else but my mother and Gillian ever cared about me? Who else ever loved me? And so now I'm waiting for Vivien, waiting to tell her about Pauline, waiting to tell her about running across Neil, waiting to bring her another item to add to our long conversation.

I tell her about Pauline first. Oddly enough, though when I actually met Pauline I felt no irritation, I feel myself growing angry. Vivien is angry too.

'What does she mean, "Why doesn't she divorce him?" What the hell does she know about it?'

151

'I know. But that's how some people are. It never occurs to them that they're in no position to give anyone good advice, having made such a mess of their own lives. I might well have asked her why she married a disaster area like Joel in the first place, knowing his track record. . . . Goddamn it, I don't give other people advice – not unless they ask for it.'

'It's thrown you a bit, hasn't it?'

'It didn't at the time, but it does now. Just a bit. What the hell, she doesn't matter. All that matters is that we're happy. The rest of our lives is for us. . . . Like the September Song – *September, October, November – these precious days I'll spend with you.* . . . No, these golden days. These are the golden days, darling, these are the best days of our lives. . . .'

She comes across and kisses me. Her eyes are moist. 'Oh God, you do say lovely things. . . .' She pours out more tea. 'But you were going to tell me something else, weren't you? You said you ran across two people you hadn't expected to see.'

'Neil was the second person I ran across. Actually, he ran across me. I was in a trance, sitting in the sunshine.'

'*Neil?* Of all the people – still, it was bound to happen sooner or later. The Village is a small place. What did he say? Was the atmosphere fraught?'

'Very matey. He invited me to have a drink with him.'

'I bet he did. I bet there's nothing else he'd like as much. He often talks about you. What he'd really like would be a nice cosy foursome with him and Tracy. *Design for Living* stuff. All very, very enlightened. There's a lot of the voyeur in Neil – I'm sure he'd love a blow-by-blow description of how you and I get on in bed. . . . He often tells me about him and Tracy. Complains she's rather tiring. Not that I want to listen. . . . It's indecent somehow. . . .'

'Don't worry, darling. I didn't tell him anything. I was quite polite, but kept my distance. He was rather gloomy, in fact. Says he's tired of being abrasive. Sounded off a bit about politicians. Then went on alarmingly about what a quandary he was in, how he couldn't do without Tracy or do with her. . . . At least, I take it he meant Tracy.'

'I'm not so sure. I think it's me he means sometimes. . . . He doesn't really like change, he's a very frightened person. That house means a great deal to him, and so does that damned operating theatre of a study. . . . When he's not actually at the studios or on location, he sometimes hardly goes out for days on end. . . . It isn't a house, to him, it's a womb. . . .'

'He seemed rather resentful that you want to sell the house and split up.'

'He changes as the wind changes. Sometimes he's all for it. I wish to God he'd make up his mind! I suppose I should chuck him out and divorce him – but after all these years, it's easier said than done. He's not like you, he's no earthly good at looking after himself.'

'Why can't Tracy look after him?'

'I've told you before – she's too damned selfish. Most of the time she's working anyway. Not that I think she could look after him – Neil says she hardly knows even how to boil an egg. . . . The wonder is how the affair's lasted so long. It certainly isn't making him very happy.'

'I found him damned depressing.'

'You can say that again! He never was exactly a laugh a minute, but these days he's permanently glum. Never opens his mouth except to grumble. Every time I talk about selling the house, he puts me off, or says, "Yes maybe next month" or, "Yes maybe when I've licked the cast into shape. . . ." Then if I do pin him down he argues about price. . . . It's like trying to fight a giant jellyfish.'

'Don't think about him, honey. This place is just for us. . . . Today when I came back from the Community Centre Market it suddenly occurred to me – here is a place where never a harsh word has been spoken. No-one's hurt me here – no-one in the whole of the Village has ever hurt me. And here's our fortress. We're absolutely safe here. It's the first home I've had since my mother died. My stepmother wasn't a bad sort, but she didn't give me a home. She really just wanted my father. And Shirley and Val didn't give me a home. How could they? They didn't love me. But you do, and that makes all the difference. It's so marvellous loving and being loved, it really does change the water into wine. . . .'

She looks at me and smiles. 'I think we should taste some of the wine,' she says, and gets up.

I follow her into the bedroom, the excitement always mounting, it being – as always – as if it were the first time. As I undress, my own words come back to me: *the first home I've had since my mother died.*

That night after Vivien has left I go to bed at ten o'clock with a glass of cold milk, a bar of Toblerone, and *Laughing Gas*. This is the moment of the day which I most enjoy, this is the final couplet in the sonnet. I escape into the happy, enchanted innocence of Wodehouse's world, into a fantasy which never puts a foot wrong. It's all the more enjoyable for being so familiar to me: I gain more pleasure from it, find fresher felicities in it, each time I reread it. I nibble two pieces of Toblerone, very slowly, tasting the honey, and again half the pleasure is in its familiarity, in the fact that it hasn't changed since my childhood. And I sip the milk very slowly, soothed by its cold blandness.

And when I've finished it I have a last cigarette, but stub it out halfway because wave after wave of sleep is coming over me, my eyes are closing. There is no better soporific than sunshine and good food and good wine and true love; it's better than any sleeping pill, which bludgeons one into sleep rather than coaxes one, which leaves one the morning after with the beginnings of a headache and a feeling of open-eyed desolation.

And on the borders of sleep, almost in a dream, the realisation comes to me – *This is the first home I've had since my mother died*. And still almost in a dream, I'm back at Parker Terrace at the age of twenty-four, almost to a day a year after the time of my first meeting Gillian. And it's the day after my mother's death and we're in the living-room in the evening, and Christine and Josephine are there and my Uncle Thaddeus and Auntie Norah and Grandmother Harnforth and Auntie Norma. I note that Josephine's eyes never leave my father's, that it is her upon whom he leans, and I note in my grief who she is. She's Daddy's girl, as I am Mummy's boy. We have had our rôles fixed very early in life, our sexual identities established. God knows, my mother didn't spoil me, God knows she had fixed ideas about men and women, God knows that I still don't forget that I'm tough, that everything which goes wrong with me is my own fault, that Tim mustn't cry. God knows that my father took it for granted that Josephine would one day get married and have children and centre her life upon her husband and children. But I think he learned in Flanders in World War One to live in the present, and just now she is his best friend, his comrade. And what I'm conscious of now is of being part of a family. We don't have to explain anything to each other, we understand without words. And I am noting now, amidst my grief, that the men are sipping whisky and the women are sipping sherry. Even

155

my Grandmother Harnforth and my Auntie Norma are sipping sherry: this is a special occasion, the beat of the Black Angel's wings can be heard.

'I told her about turning right into a main road,' my father is saying. 'I told her, I told her, I told her – ' I've never heard so much emotion in his voice before. 'Stop. Look left, look right, look right again – but that's what I used to tell her about crossing the bloody road. She just used to *dive* across, there was always something on her mind.'

'She was excited about Tim's broadcast,' Christine says in a hard voice. 'Couldn't think about anything else.'

I can't cope with it, I can't answer her, but Uncle Thaddeus breaks in. 'What's wrong with the lad broadcasting? Of course she was pleased. Wasn't his fault she was such a bloody awful driver.'

I'm beaten down, there's this terrible void in my life, everything has changed, I'm no longer in charge of my life, but when Uncle Thaddeus speaks, the ranks are closing, the Regiment is looking after its own, I hear the voice of love. And, come to think of it, and remembering how my father has spoken about his colonel, the motivating force behind a good regiment is this sort of sustaining love, the willingness to close ranks in the face of adversity.

And then suddenly I'm awake and I'm hurting. I thought that I would sleep easy; but I made too thorough a job of remembering. And I get up and I put on the maroon lightweight dressing-gown that Vivien gave me, and I go back into the living-room and I open a bottle of brandy. It's only eleven o'clock. But I have the radio on Radio Two and I'm going to get an unending stream of pop music and I'm going to finish the bottle of brandy very slowly and I'm going to top it up with dry ginger and I'm going to taste Horse's Neck again. At sixty, aren't I an old man? Why should not an old man sit up late, listening to pop music, weeping gently into his brandy and ginger? I'm hurting. What more do you want of me?

And I'm sitting now in an armchair with a bottle of Martell and two large bottles of Schweppes Dry Ginger beside me, a man of sixty, a mother's boy. And after two stiff drinks I'm going to cry. And what could be more pathetic, dear reader? But I made my mind up when I started this book: because you've given me such a good life, I've always got to be completely honest with you. And that's how it is now in high summer in Hampstead – an old man remembers, an old man weeps.

Nine

It's September and I'm at Bertorelli's in Charlotte Street
and totally happy, sitting in one of the booths in the
ground floor with Kevin and Vivien sipping strega. The
strega is yellow in tiny tulip-shaped glasses. It is to be
sipped – really sipped, on the tip of the tongue – very
slowly after a good meal. It is not to be hurried. It is sweet
and potent, a little sticky, and I'm smoking a Dunhill
Luxury Length with it and Kevin is smoking a Panatella.
And that is an extra pleasure. A good cigar is like incense,
designed for others' pleasure.

Kevin is my son by my first wife: taller than me, lean
and quick-moving, with fair hair like his mother's and
eyes a deeper blue than mine, his mother's again. He's
very well dressed, in a maroon silk jacket and blinding
white shirt and blinding white silk display handkerchief
and pale-pink slacks and brown Bally casuals and a blue-
and-white floral tie which looks to me like Liberty's Tana
Lawn. His hair is worn short, with no fuzz on the nape,
and he has a heavy silver identity bracelet and an octagonal
Seiko watch, and I'm very proud of him; he is indeed the
fruit of my loins.

I used to think of Kevin as an instrument of the
revolution: clean, bright and slightly oiled, the way the
Army likes its guns to be. But today at lunch it's been

different: politics haven't been mentioned. Instead he's talked about his new girlfriend Samantha, a lecturer in English at the university where he's teaching. And now he's showing us photos of a young dark-haired girl. She has a happy face, an open face, and now Kevin's face is happy and open.

'She's actually going to have a baby,' Kevin says, almost offhandedly. 'So we shall get married. The funny thing is it's much more cheerful – one's in the mainstream.'

It is Vivien who has brought him out: before he met her there was always a sense of remoteness; we were friendly but cool. And he never volunteered conversation, I always had to take the initiative. I don't think that he's ever forgiven me for not keeping in touch with him after his mother left me. He told me once in a rare moment of intimacy that when he was small he used to cry himself to sleep at night, wondering what he'd done wrong that I shouldn't want to see him.

'I'm so happy to hear it,' I say. 'Now there's three of you, now you're in the human race. And I shall have more people to love.'

'She'd like very much to meet you,' he says. 'She's a great fan of yours. And she'd like to meet Vivien.'

'We'll all get together.' I smile. 'Life's opening out for you now – I can't tell you what difference it makes to centre your life upon one other person.'

'I was tired of playing the field,' he says. 'It all ends in tears.'

I have a vision of the future, of a small house and a bright indefatigable baby; I have a memory of little children, of trips to the country and the seaside, and small hands in mine and small warm soft bodies on my knee.

'You'll be a grandfather at last,' Vivien says to me. 'You've got away with it for long enough.'

'I think she made up her mind to marry me as soon as we met,' Kevin says. 'I always thought I was going to keep myself free for the Revolution, but somehow I've gone off it.' He holds up his hand. 'No, don't say I'm growing up. I'm not about to join the Tory party. Or even the SDP. But I want to go in another direction. Where I don't know.'

'There's time to find out,' Vivien says. 'As long as it's the direction you personally choose.'

'It's *we* now,' he says. 'We work things out together. God, it's marvellous! I was getting to be lonely before. I was tired of never loving people And never being loved.'

'I know the feeling.' I pause. I'm coming closer and closer to him and it's because of Vivien, who draws him out without apparently trying, always warm and concerned, always unfeignedly friendly. And this is the way I should always have been with him, this is the way a father should talk to his son.

'There can be a kind of desolation,' he says, 'if you sleep with people and don't love them. It took me a long time to realise it.'

'You won't feel that any more,' Vivien says gently. 'With Tim and me it gets better all the time.'

And this, dear reader, is exactly what was said. And it's more difficult to put it down than to put down the most realistic blow-by-blow details of sex and violence. What we say we believe in: happiness is just as real as unhappiness, just as nice people are just as real as nasty people. And the clean world is just as real as the dirty world, and a great deal more pleasant to live in. There will be other things to talk about with Kevin and with my other children, and if I live long enough there'll be other grandchildren and children-in-law, more people to love. I've been out of the normal world for too long; too many nights I've not wanted to wake up, I've had this appalling feeling of displacement, of true happiness evading me. I've had the feeling of only being regarded as a source of money and not as a human being. And now, in the words of the Maurice Chevalier song, I'm living in the sunlight. These our revels are not ended, these our revels are just beginning. And Kevin and Samantha and the bright indefatigable baby are among those revels, and in the fullness of time my other children will join them.

And we go out into Charlotte Street into a bright afternoon and a taxi comes by at exactly the right moment and we lean back happily. I wonder sometimes, a little sadly for once, whether I'll have enough strength left to do the work I need to do. And then I reflect that I have Vivien and I have my children and will have a grandchild, that now after all these years I'll be part of a proper family.

I look through the window and don't like what I see – all that traffic, all those people, all those shops, and the sensation of being in a huge bowl full of carbon monoxide, and the sensation of being surrounded by strangers. And every now and again I see young people with blank faces and in a shop doorway there's a young man zonked out. And I see older faces, faces sagging with loneliness, and I see men and women in ragged clothes muttering to themselves. Camden High Street is more human, Camden is a place where people live all their lives and are more than brief sojourners, but it's tatty, it isn't clean, there are too many shabby little shops, there is the smell of greasy food cooking.

'Kevin's changed,' I say to Vivien. 'I used not to be able to get near to him. But I did what was best at the time. I'll swear I did.'

'There are no good divorces for children,' Vivien says.

'Oh God, what can you do? That's why I didn't leave Val a long time ago. I'd left one child, I couldn't leave three.'

'At least you've seen them grow up. So have I seen mine grow up.'

'But at what cost? What have I got now? A small rented flat and an overdraft?'

'You'll get through, darling.' She takes my hand. 'You're a strong brave man.'

I feel tears pricking my eyes. I weep less frequently since I've come to London but weeping still overcomes me. 'I'm tired of being strong and brave. I want to rest, I want to take things easy, I want to stop worrying about money, I want not always to be writing another bloody book, I want time to think things through.'

Swiss Cottage, Archway, Belsize Park, and we're passing the Post House Hotel; I feel my spirits rising, I am going home. And we're out of the chalk bowl.

'You've done wonderfully, darling. Remember how it was when you first came to Hampstead and stayed in the Post House?'

'Oh God, will I not!'

'You just about had the clothes you stood up in, and your book was half-finished. Don't you remember, you could hardly walk a hundred yards without stopping to rest! You've done wonderfully in two years, darling. I really am proud of you. And so is Kevin.'

'The worst of it was missing the children. They let me go with hardly a word.'

I see them now – Penelope with blue eyes and fair hair, Vanessa with blue eyes and black hair – the gentlest of all of them, always Daddy's girl like my sister Josephine – and Simon with fair hair and a curiously unguarded face.

162

When I think of Simon even now, I feel unaccountably guilty. He was the only one who sent a Christmas card to me that first Christmas in Hampstead two years ago, he was the one who sent my clothes and books on. He was twenty then, Penelope fifteen and Vanessa fourteen. And again I feel unaccountably guilty when I think of how young they were, how terribly vulnerable. I miss them all still, but when I came to the Post House, their faces came between me and my sleep and again and again I saw them at the moment of my leaving, again and again I saw Val's face contorted with anger: 'We all hate you, we wish you'd go, then we'll be happy!'

And even Simon didn't say anything; they heard her impassively. And now, nearly all that I worked for has gone, and now I'm growing increasingly tired, now when I should be working I have to lie on my bed, not sleeping, just resting, licking my wounds.

'They're always on their mother's side,' Vivien says. 'It's a fact of life. It's most unfair, but that's how it is.'

'She could have had so much, she could have had a marvellous life. I gave her so much, I really did. She only had to ask and she got what she wanted. They all got what they wanted.'

'She's got her comeuppance.'

We're approaching Rosslyn Hill now and this is the real Hampstead. This is the proper place for me to be in, this is tree-lined, the air is fresh here and there are no strangers: here I have had nothing but love and friendship and my eyes moisten again.

When we get inside the flat Vivien puts the kettle on, and then looks at me searchingly. 'You're looking green all of a sudden. You should lie down. Put your pyjamas on and lie down. I'll bring you some tea.'

'You're sure you don't mind?' It's been a happy day so far, but now I can't go on. I'm defeated, I lay down my arms.

'Of course I don't mind. You've got to have a *rest* rest. You're worrying too much. I'll look after you.'

I find myself trembling all of a sudden. 'God! I don't know what's wrong with me.'

'It's nervous fatigue, you've been through too much. You won't get over all that's happened to you that easily. You're a sensitive man, you have deep feelings, and you've been shamefully treated. Put on your pyjamas and lie down and let go, my darling. I'll look after you.'

'You are good to me. No-one else has been so good to me.' The tears start flowing, I'm appalled by my weakness.

She sits down beside me and puts her arm around me. It's a strong arm, but it's a woman's arm, it's enormously comforting. 'Let go, darling, you don't have to be macho. You've had too much of being tough, of not crying. Cry all you want to. And if ever you fall ill, don't worry. I'll bring a camp-bed, I'll be there all the time. . . .'

And I'm going back to childhood, remembering the time when in Wharton Woods a big rock fell on my toe and smashed the big toe nail, and I limped home in agony, frightened of only one thing, that my father would see my foot and look sorrowful and make me feel worse. I was seven at the time, already training to be truly macho: *Tim is tough.* My mother took my shoe and sock off and washed my feet and then applied iodine. Iodine was the first thing to be applied on wounds in those days, and it stung ferociously and I couldn't help crying, the pain was too much to bear. And I remember now that her face became vulnerable, no longer efficient and matter-of-fact, and she hugged me to her bosom, and I remember the softness and the warmth and the clean laundered smell of her cotton apron.

And I go into the bedroom and throw off my clothes, letting them lie where they fall, and put on clean pyjamas from the chest-of-drawers and collapse onto the bed and let go. And in a moment she comes in with a cup of tea, and puts it on the bedside table and sits on the bed. 'Stay here as long as you like, you don't have to go anywhere. There's two of us now, my darling.'

'Yes, there's two of us, we're not ever going to be lonely and unwanted again.' I drink the hot tea. 'God, I remember how bloody awful it was at Boxley. The week-ends were the worst. And they always seemed to be giggling, and they'd fall silent when I came into the room. . . .'

'It's all over now, sweetheart. Finish your tea and rest. Just ask if there's anything you want.' I kiss her hand and she goes out and I finish my tea and close my eyes and absolute fatigue takes over, but I'm happy knowing that she's in the room next door, and again I've not known such security since I was a child.

And, half-asleep, I remember my first house in Casterley, a two-bedroomed terrace-house with a tiny bathroom and a tinier kitchen. There was, of course, no garage; I kept my second-hand Austin A40 – a sort of bastard estate car – outside. And I have let myself in and the house seems curiously empty, somehow large and echoing and dusty. This is two years after our marriage, in September, and Kevin is a year old. There's a teapot and two cups on the small gateleg table and cigarette ends in the ashtray, State Express 555, not my brand. And Shirley doesn't smoke. And then I see the envelope on the mantelpiece with my name on in Shirley's large dashing hand. I take it to the armchair and light a cigarette before opening it.

> *Tim: This will be a shock to you – or maybe not such a shock as that – but I've gone off with Jack. You and I were never right together. I'm sorry about this, but we're just not the same kind of person. Jack will bring Kevin up as if he were his own, and I want nothing from you – Shirley.*
>
> *P. S. In case you wondered. Kevin is yours, no doubt about it. I would never have done that to you. . . .*

No, it isn't such a shock as that. I see her and Jack Cessnock together, I see her blonde hair and generous mouth and startlingly blue eyes, I see his bony cowboy's face and his grey eyes, I see the way they look at each other; and I remember them before she and I were engaged, and I wonder how I failed to notice how they were together and how frequent a visitor he was, always with a friend as a chaperone, always on some plausible pretext, generally on Little Theatre business. And I remember quite soon after Kevin was born her saying that she'd go crazy if she spent another evening indoors, and I remember all the excuses and her coming home, her cheeks glowing after what she'd describe as a little hen party, and I wonder how many lies were told to me.

And I go to the kitchen and take in the teapot and the two cups and throw them in the litter bin and then hunt up another teapot and make myself tea and take it into the living-room. I'm twenty-eight and I haven't all that much of a job and nothing much published except a few articles and broadcasts and stories and poems and two stage plays which never got off the ground, but I had a house and a wife and a son and was happy in the place I lived in. And now there is nothing, nothing but a sense of failure. This is the worst moment in my life, worse even than the death of my mother. My mother's death was a visitation from outside, I couldn't blame myself.

But now I know what people will be saying – nudge, nudge, he couldn't keep up with her, he wasn't man enough for her, Shirley's a lively girl, a real goer, and he's one of those dreamy kind. May not have found out what it's for; and there'll be masculine laughter and tobacco smoke and re-ordering of pints all round.

And even if I find them at it I can't fight them all; I can't in fact even fight Jack Cessnock, who's bigger than me and was a Commando, much decorated, as every member of my generation seems to be except me. And, though hatred will come later, I don't feel it now, I'm too sick, indeed on the verge of vomiting: I don't finish the tea but have to rush into the kitchen to spew into the sink. And, indeed, that's the worst of this memory, it's so ugly, it's so humiliating.

And I go to the bathroom and brush my teeth and wash out my mouth with Listerine, but feel no better. For the bathroom cupboard is crammed with her talcum and cologne and bath oil and hair spray and there's a rubber duck in the bath.

And I go downstairs and make myself fresh tea and keep it down this time and tell myself that the reason for Shirley bolting the coop are obvious. He has the latest Jaguar, he has a partnership in a Wetherford wool firm, he, like her, is all for tennis and golf and racing and bridge. Money is the answer, all the more the answer because her parents have never had any, have in fact had much less than mine.

You may think dear reader, that my consolation here is the knowlege that I would use the experience. You would be wrong. It hurt too much. I couldn't face it. Like poetry, fiction is emotion remembered in tranquillity, and the knowledge that one would use it would make the emotion sterile. I did write what happened in my diary, but it was no more than a brief agonised note. I didn't want to write about it, I wanted to expunge it from my mind.

I look at my watch: it's just past five o'clock, the time the children have all come home from school. I've never known the house seem so big or silent or shabby or dusty before, and never before felt that there wasn't any hope for me. And then I look out into an ordinary stone street with, as always in Casterley, the trees and the moors in the distance. And I no longer look at it with enjoyment, it's as if it were against me, as if it were in league with Jack and Shirley, as if it somehow should have told me what was going on. And on the uplands there isn't any Real Place, but quiet corners where Jack can make love to Shirley in the Jaguar. Jack and Shirley have dirtied the whole place for me, Jack and Shirley have quite casually killed the love I feel for my birthplace.

I was hungry when I first went into the house but all of a sudden the idea of food is nauseating. I don't feel as if I will ever eat again. And the images of Jack and Shirley naked are crowding in on me, intolerably sharp and clear, and I can see her full breasts with the big nipples and hear her peculiar whining childish cry during orgasm. And now for the first time I wonder if she didn't fake orgasm, whether the way she cries out for Jack is quite different, a sound I'll never hear.

There isn't much to drink in the house: a bottle of cream sherry, half a dozen bottles of Tetley's bitter. I'm tempted to open a bottle of bitter, but 'phone my father's home. There's no reply: he often stays on late at school doing small administrative chores, and he and Lucy attend all sorts of meetings. I feel unreasonably resentful about him not being there when I need him. 'Fuck you!' I mutter childishly and slam the 'phone down and open a bottle of bitter and take it very slowly. And I'm drinking it on an empty stomach and it has an immediate effect, and by the time the second bottle is finished a sort of sleazy cheerfulness has taken over; I even, oddly enough, feel myself free, remind myself of the increasing gap between me and Shirley, remind myself that the main reason we got married was that Kevin was on the way. We told everyone he was two months premature, but since he weighed ten pounds, no-one believed us.

And I become realistic when the third bottle is finished, and realize that, her pregnancy apart, I didn't really want to marry her for her own sake. I wanted a home of my own. Living with my father and his second wife Lucy in their new house off Alexandre Road didn't suit me. My stepmother was an agreeable person and made me welcome for my father's sake, but they were a self-contained couple and only really needed each other. And I realise now on the third bottle that my mother and father were too different, that though they got along well enough, my mother's life also took in the Church and her brothers and sisters. Lucy suited my father in a way my mother never did, and although I could understand it and didn't begrudge him his new happiness, I could never quite forgive him.

And at the fourth bottle I know that I don't want to see him and Lucy, I don't want to tell them. And I reflect in my stupidity, because I was younger then, because I didn't know enough about parenthood, that Kevin is too young really to have known me, that it's best for him to think of Jack as his father, that Jack will give him a better start in life than ever I could have. (But this isn't the story that Kevin told me years later; and that night under the unfluence of alcohol I hurt my own son.)

And then the sixth bottle is finished and already I'm drunk. But the house isn't so large and empty now, it's more comfortable, it's become a sort of spacious bivouac. If there were more beer I'd stay here, but drunk as I am I can't mix sherry with beer.

It's strange now, looking back upon my youth, how offhand we were about drinking and driving, how we would go for pub crawls in cars and no nonsense about the driver staying sober, either. But I do remember now that as I start up the A40 I'm aware of a certain apprehension, I can scent death in waiting; and I drive more cautiously than usual, in fact a little too cautiously, because a passing policeman looks at me suspiciously. And now I'm in the Tram and there's only half a dozen there and again a sort of contentment comes over me. I've stopped trying, I've stopped aspiring, I've stopped even observing because I don't care about my surroundings: the wounded beast has crawled into its lair and is licking its wounds.

And I'm thinking of Gillian now, but have made my mind up not to expect to see her. I'm thinking of all our conversations (the kind of conversations which I'm only to have again many years later) and the way we talked about everything under the sun, but chiefly the arts. And I'm thinking of the stupid conversations I had with Shirley, conversations in which nothing of importance was really ever said, conversations which were all about personal matters or material objects. All my conversations with Gillian have been about things outside ourselves, so there's never any running out of things to talk about, and I'm always learning something new.

170

And now on my fourth pint I'm turning gently melancholy and I'm not seeing double yet but everything is hazy, the room is filling up with the people from the Little Theatre and when I greet them I know that my words are slurred. And what's rather bizarre about it is that I don't acknowledge I'm drunk, that in fact when I've finished my drink I'm going to prove it by going home an hour before closing time and I'm not going to buy any booze on the way.

And then Gillian comes in and I look at her blearily. 'Gillian! How lovely to see you.' I get up to kiss her, then have to sit down suddenly.

She sits down beside me. 'Tim, you're absolutely pissed. You look *awful*! Why aren't you with your wife and baby?'

'They're not with me any more.' I enunciate the words with great difficulty. 'She's run off with Jack Cessnock and taken the baby with her.'

Drunk as I am, I know that once I've spoken these words tomorrow morning they'll be all round Casterley and round Wetherford too.

'She never was the right woman for you. Still, no point in going into that now. Did you drive here?'

I nod. 'Yes. The car found its own way here. . . .'

'You idiot, you might have killed yourself. I bet you were pissed before you came into here. Give me your keys.' She holds her hand out.

'I shall be – all right. All right.' I try to get up again and subside again.

'You can hardly walk, let alone drive.' She holds her hand out and I give her the keys, and a moment later she's helping me out into the car park and into the Javelin: she's surprisingly strong. And I'm conscious, as I wasn't until many years later with Vivien, of letting go, of being looked after, of having a true friend.

And then she's helping me into the house and I'm slumped in an armchair and she's looking at me rather amusedly.

'You loony, when you get sloshed you really do make a job of it. I never realised the full meaning of *legless* before.'

'Don't be unkind to me, Gillian. Not you.'

'I'll make you some coffee.' She goes into the kitchen and for the first time since reading Shirley's letter I'm back in the normal world, even back in the world I lived in when my mother was alive. Because this is how my mother would have treated me in similar circumstances: there'd have been no shock and anger, only help.

'I couldn't help it,' I say to her over the coffee.

She lights two cigarettes and passes me one. 'You mustn't do it again, darling. Once is enough. It sounds an easy thing to say, but you've got your whole life before you.'

'I've got nothing before me.' The coffee is working with extraordinary rapidity.

'You're just feeling sorry for yourself. And who shall blame you, poor darling? But you've got enormous talent. You've got to believe in yourself, Tim. Or no-one else will.'

'People must have suspected. Why did no-one tell me?'

'Would you have been pleased if they had? Wouldn't she have denied it, and wouldn't you have believed her?'

'I don't know.' I feel overcome by absolute helplessness. 'I don't know what to do.'

'Divorce the bitch and make a new life for yourself.'

'Chance would be a fine thing. But – oh, Christ! I can't stay here; everybody will be talking about me.'

'They talk about me. They talk about me and you, for that matter. It's always the same in small places.'

'You see, Casterley suits me, too. There's everything I want here. . . .'

'You'll have to go away, Tim. A long way away.' She pauses. 'Not just to escape gossip. But because that's the only way in which you're ever going to be able to see it properly. There won't ever be any other place for you. But you can't stay. Do you know something? The worst thing that could ever have happened to you would have been if Shirley had been a good wife. You'd have been happy here, you'd have had other children, and then one day you'd find yourself forty-five and nothing done. These are the crossroads, Tim. *You've got to leave Casterley.* I want you to leave for your sake, not mine. I shall miss you. Yes, I shall miss you, I'll miss you very much.'

'I shall miss you. I'll miss a lot of people.'

'You have to go,' she says firmly. 'Believe it or not, there'll be other people.'

And, over thirty years later, there have been other people, many other people and there has been the one person. And now in Hampstead I drift off to sleep, I let go, knowing that that one person is in the next room and she loves me and will look after me always.

Ten

In the autumn the year after Shirley left me I came to Boxley. I came for no other reason than that I was able to get a job there. I often reflect with some bitterness that if I'd stayed on in teaching I now should nearly be due for a huge tax-free handout and an index-linked pension.

The first year in Boxley was the worst year in my life. The town still had some individuality, the two main shopping streets in uniform Pont Street Dutch and a solid Victorian Gothic Conservative Club and a small cramped market place. And off the High Street was a warren of little houses with little shops and there were local stores with a large range of old-fashioned goods and the draper's still had an overhead change-carrier. And at Sainsbury's there were two long counters and at Woolworth's they still sold biscuits and cake by weight, and the off-licences delivered. Boxley wasn't very friendly, and didn't give the impression of ever having been loved. Having tried three pubs in the centre I mostly drank at home. They were too rough, too unfriendly. Home was a small flat on the top floor of an old house in the suburb where I taught at the comprehensive. I had about the same amount of living space as I had in my bedroom at Parker Terrace and a dormer window too; but there was no view of the hills and the moors beyond them, no chance of seeing the Real Place.

Boxley has changed now with a new shopping centre and multi-storey car parks, and virtually all the old buildings gone and the working-class streets off the High Street are now an ill-planned maze of dual carriageway and huge concrete buildings, more oppressive even than Victorian prisons, calculated insults to the human spirit. Even then Boxley had no social life, but at least that warren of working-class streets off the High Street ensured that some sort of life continued after half-past five. Now the centre is quite dead in the evenings – dead and also menacing.

And so, by myself, more lonely than I'd ever been in my life, there was nothing to do but write. That flat, though green, landscape in the suburb where I lived gave me no nourishment. I turned back to Casterley, knowing I could never live there again, but feeling at the time that there was no other place where I could be happy.

And so five years after it all came together and my first novel was published and the money and the invitations poured in and the film rights were sold at a sum far below their market value but enough to buy my first Jaguar and a five-bedroom detached house. I had married again a year before this to Val, whom I met at a party. Val was ten years younger than me, which always irritated her parents, who kept a small newsagents. They thought that she could have done better for herself. She was extraordinarily like Shirley at certain moments with the same ash-blonde hair. (I reflect now that to marry her was rather as if having had nothing but trouble with a car I were to change it for a newer model of the same make.)

I had, in fact, made the same mistake again: and it's mystifying to me why for so long I couldn't face it. I hadn't married Val for her own sake, though I found her physically attractive: I had married her for a home, I had married her for children, I had married her to get back into the human race, I had married her so that never again I need be lonely. I'd even married her to have in-laws, to once again be part of an extended family. Her parents weren't bad when I got to know them, and her father had at least been a bomber pilot.

And now it's all coming out, dear reader. And I shan't speak to you again like this. There isn't time. I have now to do what I've never done before; I have now to extend myself, I have now to forget myself. I've begun to know myself in Hampstead, to find out what sort of person I really am, after over twenty years of increasing pain have come into calm waters. I've used this story to get to know myself, because at my age I can afford no more illusions either about myself or others.

I don't often think about my first book now: I'm always interested more in the next book. But the first book wasn't autobiography. The hero of my first novel was a pushing working-class boy come to a small town like Casterley from an appalling mining and chemical town in South Yorkshire. That was for contrast, that was for dramatis-ation, that was to give him a special vision of the town like Casterley. Not many people die for love. And, although I got Shirley in the family way, she didn't have a rich father like the girl in my first novel. Rich young girls marry rich young men: that's a rule of life.

And having said all this, dear reader, what I always return to, one of the few things I feel guilty about, is that what I felt about my mother's death I used in my first novel. I couldn't have used it directly, that would have been merely journalism. But somewhere in my mind there must be a coldness, what Graham Greene called the splinter of ice in the heart. And I think that my father and my two sisters knew about this without ever consciously working it out, and I think that is why that first book put a distance between us.

Yes, we send each other Christmas cards, we write, we occasionally visit each other; but that first book hurt them and hurt them all the more because I covered my tracks so well. And I have a shrewd suspicion that my father has never been keen on my hero being so emphatically working class in origin; though a lifelong Socialist, he remained proud of having held a commission, of being a headmaster, of being very emphatically middle-class – and all by his own efforts, his father having been a millhand. And it wasn't until I came to live in Hampstead, this middle-class enclave, that I came to realise this, that I came to realise that for him that first book somehow devalued his achievement, that my book was a sorrow to him.

Not that any of this occurred to me when my first book was published, when all the reviews were glowing, when I was suddenly a Name. And, of course, there was money, more money than I had ever had before, and I acquired an agent and an accountant and a part-time secretary and gave up my job.

And I'm back now to that September when I gave a farewell dinner to the headmaster and staff of Hexley Road Comprehensive School at the Manor Hotel in Boxley, virtually the only place in Boxley then where dinner was available, and I'm driving home afterwards with Val, not drunk, but relaxed and expansive.

'It wasn't a bad dinner,' I say. 'My God! Now I'm free!'

'You mean you haven't got a salary coming in any more,' Val says. 'Of course I couldn't stop you, could I?'

'For God's sake, there's enough in the kitty for a year, even if we don't sell the film rights.'

'And what if you don't? Have you thought of that?'

'I'll have written another book.'

'And what if it's a flop? What if you're a flash in the pan? That's what some of these people who are making such a fuss of you now are thinking. You should be thinking of your wife, you should be thinking how much I want children. . . . Not that I'm successful there, am I?'

'Oh, for Christ's sake, whose side are you on?'

And the dreary complaints continue long after I've put the Austin A35 away (the Jaguar came when the film rights were sold). I can hear them now in Hampstead: I'm back again in the small living-room of our first house in Boxley, crammed now with a Heal's three-piece suite and all kinds of bric-à-brac, redecorated and recarpeted, with a full drinks cabinet, I'm absorbing Glenlivet single malt Scotch rather too rapidly, I'm hearing that shrill voice, seeing her face distorted with anger: *It's all you, you, you. I don't seem to exist, there's no thought of what I've gone through with my miscarriage. . . . When these bloody people talk to you, it's as if I'm just your reflection, just the admiring little woman. . . . You've got what you want, you're the big man, people keep stopping me to talk about you. They don't even ask me how I am . . . .*

And then there are the tears and suddenly she's more reasonable and saying that she's giving up her job now and talking about new dresses and coats she's got her eyes on: actually saying that she hates me is to come much later, when there are the children, when she has power over me. And of course in the new brass-railed bed afterwards there is the usual reconciliation, and as usual she wakes up in the small hours and says she can't breathe and says she has a pain and asks me to rub her back. (Shirley with all her faults didn't grumble and after sex slept as if stunned.)

'I ask myself now why I ever put up with it,' I say to

Vivien twenty-two years after. 'Why did I put up with such a lunatic?'

'Darling, you'd only been married some eighteen months. Your first marriage only lasted two years. You'd have looked bloody ridiculous.'

Vivien isn't here physically, but this is what she would say, has in fact said. She is never cold, but whenever I'm disturbed by what cannot be altered, whenever I reproach myself to no avail, she is cool, she is sensible, she takes the heat out of the situation. Takes the heat out of? Takes the hurt out of, makes me see in perspective what made me hang on to the marriage.

However after that night Val then made a perceptible effort to support me socially, having by then, I suppose, begun to count her blessings. The Jaguar and the new house clinched it: she wasn't going to kill the goose which laid the golden eggs. Even if it were I and not she who was made a fuss of, she had a better house and a better car and was better dressed and altogether lived in better style than most of her former schoolmates.

Nothing could persuade her to take any interest in my work or indeed in anything outside her constricted and timid personal world. And when Simon was born – I see it now – more and more she ceased to regard me as anything else than a good provider, to be fed and have shirts ironed for him, and to be given sex from time to time, or rather to be used as a sex-object. For she wasn't cold sexually, and was, more than any other woman I've ever known, the aggressor.

And now all the poison is out, dear reader. Now it is September in Hampstead – mild and bright but with a faint and refreshing hint of coldness – and I've left that

179

world of hatred and malevolence. I don't wake up in the small hours with a sense of waste and loss and ruin –

> When in the hollow night the tower
> Jussle the bells amid,
> Then on my tongue the taste is sour
> Of all I ever did.

On my tongue there is no sour taste, only a taste like the taste of the water from the spring at Wharton Woods, the taste of fresh air, the taste of the air on the hills. For nothing that has ever happened to me has been wasted, I've turned even the ugliest of it into stories, as civet is turned into perfume. I am not the civet cat, I am not the person who produces the civet (there is an uglier name for it) from the civet cat. I am the perfume maker. Out of what happened to me in Casterley some thirty years ago I made a romance. It was a romance and not a documentary, but it was based on real life and was a living entity and not a fabrication from the front of the mind. The front part of my brain – or the left side – is lively and inventive and a show-off, so that at times in journalism I've enjoyed myself enormously. I've danced on the right rope, I've swung on the trapeze, I've jumped through all the hoops. But that has all been mere cleverness, that has all been evanescent. What lasts is the story, the romance, from deep down; what lasts is the story which I sometimes feel is already finished and perfect before one begins it.

And perhaps my first book was finished and perfect that day I came home to find that Shirley had left me and taken my son with her, and perhaps what kept me from drinking myself to death or suffering a nervous breakdown was that knowledge, though I didn't have that knowledge consciously. And that is the privilege all story tellers have.

180

But, being human, this doesn't console us. And perhaps the true story of what happened to me in my youth was what happened in my first book. That, of course, is mere speculation.

What is not speculation, and what gives my life some justification, is that no matter what happens to me, that story of the poor boy and the rich girl and the older woman who kills herself for love continues unchanged. Long after I'm dead, dear reader, I'll continue to speak to you. And at my worst moments that's always been the one great consolation: when I die, it won't be as if I've never existed. I couldn't bear that. I would never have gone so far as to commit a crime or gigantic folly to get my name in the paper, but I can't bear the thought of not being noticed. Perhaps this is ignoble. But if I don't freely admit to being ignoble, neither will you take me seriously when I tell you of my higher aspirations, neither will you listen when I tell you of my increasing desire to live only in the clean world.

I think of that world more and more these days, just as I think more of the Real Place. What concerns me more and more, talking to Vivien, is that for all that I've had, a high price must be paid. If I have given more, I must give more. It isn't enough to give money, it isn't enough to take part in demos, it isn't enough to write letters. I have to give myself. And why have I left this part of myself out of all my books? It's just as authentically part of myself as my weakness and wildness, my laziness and cowardice.

And so I'm moving nearer and nearer towards being the person I was meant to be, so at last everything's beginning to make some sort of sense. There is a shape to my story, it was already finished before I began it. And part of its conclusion has to do with the sea, our great grey mother, the sea which Vivien and I love. She is a Medway Town girl, she loves that part of England just as Dickens loved it. We love the sea at all seasons; but particularly out of season we love, rather than the larger tourist resorts, the small places like Deal where the sea is a way of earning a living, where the sea is treated with great respect, where it's part of life.

And now later in September we're at a rented bungalow in Deal at dinner – garlic sausage, tongue, roast beef, roast port, salad, a bottle of Chablis. There will be Brie to come and, since this is our last night, single malt whisky to be sipped very slowly. We take our time, savouring each kind of meat, each kind of raw vegetable in the salad, taking the wine very slowly. It's sharp, but not in any way acid and, if taken slowly, a gentle euphoria, a rational and sensible warmth comes over us.

The bungalow stands at the end of a row overlooking the seashore. It's a solid redbrick Thirties building, and because of its position there's a view of the sea from two sides. We eat at the table by the front window, looking out onto the sea. There are the lights of the lightships now – Cape Gris Nez, South Goodwin, East Goodwin, North Goodwin, North Foreland – and there's a large ship, all lights blazing, sailing by, which looks like a private yacht. There is a row of boat-houses on the beach – the sea at Deal is a playground too, though, as always, a tough and rough playground. There is enough light to distinguish land and sky and sea and yet there is the feeling that they all are one, they all add up to voyages and discoveries.

The lounge – if that's the word – is a large comfortable room which, unlike some rented property, feels like a home, gives the sense that a family has lived here. Best of all, there's an open fire, by the light of which we're eating

182

now. And the absolute contentment which Vivien and I now share isn't entirely due to the sea and the lights and the large comfortable room and our sense of leisure, but due to the fact that we're sharing a meal. Each meal that she and I share is a sacrament. We want nothing else but what we have at this moment, we don't even need to speak very much. We are not bored, we always have plenty to say to each other, but we also know how to share silence, we know how to listen to the sea.

But what matters even more than this is that I awake at six next morning and can't sleep any longer. Both Vivien and I have gone to sleep immediately the night before in the double bed in the front bedroom with bird-medallioned wallpaper and white furniture and, above all, a view of the sea. We don't make love at night; for us the afternoon has always been the time for that, because seeing each other's bodies is part of the pleasure. And we don't often have the opportunity to really sleep together; when we do have that opportunity we experience utter security in each other's presence, we drift into sleep as in the nursery with the night-light burning. But when I wake at six I wake immediately, I wake rested, I wake crackling with energy, I have had no bad dreams.

I go through into the kitchen to make myself a mug of tea. The kitchen is a large, cheerful, orange-tiled room, sparklingly clean but not inhumanly hygienic, with a bay window with window seats and a view of the beach and a large table by the side window. It's, above all, a well-lit and cheerful kitchen, with a battery of brand new electrical gadgets, and now the sun is rising and the sky is a very pale pink and all is very quiet. And I see that the table is set for two places, with two plates and knives and a large plate and two breakfast cups and two paper napkins and a pot of black cherry jam and strawberry and thick-cut marmalade and a butter dish and two glasses. Our breakfast is orange juice and croissants and *café-au-lait* with chicory. This is a habit we've built up together.

The strange thing is that Vivien must have set this table for breakfast many times. It's simply that I never noticed it before. And now I make myself a mug of tea and sit by the window and light a cigarette and look out at the dawn and look at the table. This is the way I always ought to have lived. Yesterday we did our shopping at Tesco's in Deal and had a pub lunch and walked on the pier and had a cup of coffee in the cafeteria at the end of it and explored Deal yet again and came home to make love and then have dinner – dinner with love, a sacrament – and now we're beginning the day, we're having breakfast with love. This is what those plates and glasses and knives and breakfast cups and butter dish and two kinds of jam and the marmalade mean.

We're living now as we always should have lived, and neither of us is ever again going to live in a world without love. God knows, we have problems to solve. God knows what disasters lie ahead of us, but there's nothing we can't do together and the sun is rising above the sea, and we'll never again be lonely or rejected, we'll always have each other.

And now four days later in Hampstead on a September evening the story ends, as far as it will end while we're alive. I'm sitting in my flat waiting for Vivien at six-thirty, sipping a whisky-and-soda. This isn't my usual habit but I've written a two-thousand word article, today in one sustained burst, having left the work until the last possible moment (as is my invariable practice with journalism), and I need to let myself down immediately with something stronger than tea; I need to slow down.

And now Vivien's here, shedding her parcels as always, and as always glowing, and as always seeming to me as she was the first time I ever met her, the bright one, the eager one, going forward unafraid.

'Darling, give me one of those. Not too weak. I need something.'

I mix the drink. 'My God, what's happened?'

'Oh, no disaster. Neil's gone. He's giving me a divorce. Everything's down in writing, all duly signed and delivered – permission for me to sell the house, division of property, the lot – ' She drinks her whisky-and-soda. 'He's in charge! The big macho male! As usual, doing exactly what he wants to, making everyone dance to his bidding – '

I freshen my drink. 'I presume he's going off with Tracy.'

'Wrong. That's all over. She's too demanding and capricious. And terribly promiscuous. He looked very stern and puritanical when he said that. My God, I've been married to that man for thirty years and he never ceases to surprise me!'

'When did all this happen?'

'Not so long ago. He came in, delivered his bombshell, left me the documents and disappeared again. He'll return tomorrow to dot the 'i's and cross the 't's. God, I've never seen him so brisk and efficient and determined.'

I smile. 'But this is exactly what we've both been wanting. He's been hovering for months, he's nearly driven you out of your mind – '

'Don't you see, he's got the better of me? He's taken the initiative, he somehow has come out on top. When it suited him he was a human jellyfish and I was the one who suffered for it, I was the one who wasted time seeing bloody buyers, only to have him cry off at the last moment. And now that it suits him, he's off to bloody Australia, to carve himself a new career, no doubt. As always, he wins.'

'You'll be better off, darling. It's what we've been wanting. You'll soon get a smaller place of your own.'

'A smaller place? You can say that again. He has a load of debts. Pleasing himself again. . . .' She is silent for a moment. 'He always pleases himself. He always does exactly what he wants to. . . .'

'But *we'll* please ourselves now, darling. We'll really be together – '

'We'll need space for ourselves,' she says. 'It's funny – I wanted to take freedom myself, not have him give it me as a favour.'

I sit next to her on the sofa. 'He's given you no favours. No matter what happens, we'll always love each other. We'll manage somehow.'

'Oh yes, we always will.' She kisses me. 'But he's won somehow, he's flushed with triumph, the bastard! He's done just what he wanted to do. We were managing already, you and me.'

'Yes, indeed we were.' I smile. 'But now you'll have to get used to the idea of being a wife and not a mistress.'

'I like being your mistress. After all Neil had done to me, I liked the idea. I was superior to him. . . .' She sighs. 'It's interesting, isn't it, Tim? You couldn't really invent it, could you?'

'I couldn't invent Neil for a start.' I tighten my arms around her shoulders. 'I'm always with you, darling. Look, we'll go out for dinner. What the hell. We'll push the boat out – Bentley's, Langan's, the Café Royal, you name it. And no bloody going Dutch. You can treat me when you sell the house.'

'That'll be lovely, darling. It's just what I need.' She

takes another drink. 'It'll be strange leaving that house – the end of an old song.'

'The beginning of a new one. Just you and me. The rest of our time is just for you and me.'

'Just for you and me.'

I kiss her and then we cling together in silence. And all of a sudden we have our happy ending and our happy ending has come from outside ourselves and taken us by surprise. But we shall go on together to the end of our lives and every morning I'll wake up to a table already laid for breakfast and we both shall be the people we were meant to be and lead the lives we were meant to live. Yes, this is a happy ending.

And I shan't talk to you again like this, dear reader. I shan't ever talk to you again about myself. I shall talk to you about yourself.

*Also available by John Braine
in Methuen Paperbacks*

One and Last Love

'And when he thinks he's past love, then he meets his
one and last love . . .'

It's a chance meeting that brings Tim Harnforth and
Vivien Canvey together. Both are successful writers.
Both are married with teenage children.

Suddenly Tim and Vivien fall in love . . .

But theirs is a mature love and they share true friendship as well as a passionate affair. It is the complete
merging of two opposites: she a sophisticated and
urbane Londoner, he a brash and individualistic
Yorkshireman. Together they develop a love and
happiness that comes to fill their lives . . .

Life at the Top

At the end of *Room at the Top*, Joe Lampton's ambition seemed to have found its reward. Married to a rich man's daughter and with a good position in his father-in-law's company, the future looked rosy. *Life at the Top* takes up the story ten years later. Joe is well off, with two children and two cars, but his life is heading for a crisis. Once again his restlessness drives him towards other women. Joe is ready to break out . . .

Stay With Me Till Morning

Clive and Robin seem to have a perfect marriage. A nice house in a fashionable Yorkshire village, three reasonably pleasant children, a successful career and the settled contentment of middle age – what more could any couple want?

But the calm surface of their married life begins to crack when Robin meets up with a former boyfriend and Clive drifts into an affair. Both seem to be seeking excitement and escape from the humdrum of everyday life . . .

Top Fiction from Methuen Paperbacks

While every effort is made to keep prices low, it is sometimes necessary to increase prices at short notice. Methuen Paperbacks reserves the right to show new retail prices on covers which may differ from those previously advertised in the text or elsewhere.

The prices shown below were correct at the time of going to press.

All these books are available at your bookshop or newsagent, or can be ordered direct from the publisher. Just tick the titles you want and fill in the form below.

Methuen Paperbacks, Cash Sales Department,
PO Box 11, Falmouth,
Cornwall TR10 109EN.

Please send cheque or postal order, no currency, for purchase price quoted and allow the following for postage and packing:

UK   60p for the first book, 25p for the second book and 15p for each additional book ordered to a maximum charge of £1.90.

BFPO and Eire   60p for the first book, 25p for the second book and 15p for each next seven books, thereafter 9p per book.

Overseas Customers   £1.25 for the first book, 75p for the second book and 28p for each subsequent title ordered.

NAME (Block Letters) ....

ADDRESS..

....

 W9-CFW-531

Death Wind

Death Wind

William Bell

EMMAUS HIGH SCHOOL LIBRARY
EMMAUS, PA 18049

orca soundings

ORCA BOOK PUBLISHERS

FIC
BEL

Copyright © 2002 William Bell

All rights reserved. No part of this publication may be reproduced
or transmitted in any form or by any means, electronic or mechanical,
including photocopying, recording or by any information storage
and retrieval system now known or to be invented, without
permission in writing from the publisher.

Library and Archives Canada Cataloguing in Publication

Bell, William, 1945-
Death wind

ISBN 978-1-55143-543-5 (bound) / ISBN 978-1-55143-215-1 (pbk.)

I.Title. ps8553.e4568D42 2002   jc813'.54   c2002-910138-7
pz7.b41187de 2002

First published in the United States, 2002
Library of Congress Control Number: 2002101408

Summary: When Allie fears she is pregnant, she leaves home with Razz, a
skateboard champion. Returning home she is caught up in
a tornado that threatens to destroy everything. She learns to
believe in herself and face her future.

MIX
Paper from
responsible sources
FSC® C016245

*Orca Book Publishers is dedicated to preserving the environment and has
printed this book on Forest Stewardship Council® certified paper.*

Orca Book Publishers gratefully acknowledges the support for its publishing
programs provided by the following agencies: the Government of Canada
through the Canada Book Fund and the Canada Council for the Arts, and the
Province of British Columbia through the BC Arts Council and
the Book Publishing Tax Credit.

Cover photography by Eyewire

ORCA BOOK PUBLISHERS
PO BOX 5626, Stn. B
Victoria, BC Canada
v8R 6s4

ORCA BOOK PUBLISHERS
PO BOX 468
Custer, WA USA
98240-0468

www.orcabook.com
Printed and bound in Canada.

17 16 15 14 • 11 10 9 8

Dedicated to those who suffered through the Barrie Tornado, and to those who helped.
—W.B.

Chapter One

Allie's parents were arguing again.

Allie slammed her bedroom door, rolled onto her bed and stared at the ceiling. *Eight o'clock in the morning and they're at it already*, she thought. She tried to block out the noise, but the harsh words made their way upstairs and through her door. Her mother was a shrieker. The madder she got, the higher her voice went. Her father was a rumbler. When he got mad, his voice got deeper—and he would have the Hurt Look on his face.

They were arguing about Allie again. It was the old story. Her mother said her father was "too soft" and let Allie get away with too much. After she shrieked for awhile, Allie's father would say her mother was "too stiff" and she should give a little. *Right on*, thought Allie as she lay on her bed. *I wonder what you guys would think if you knew the mess that I'm in now.*

Allie climbed out of her bed and plunked herself down in the chair at her little desk, leaning on her elbows and cupping her hands over her ears. *Stop!* She cried, inside her head. *Stop arguing!*

The report card lying on the messy desktop caught her eye. She groaned, flipping the stiff yellow booklet open. There were three bright red circles on it.

She had failed three out of four subjects. Last year she had stood near the top of her class, but this year, since she started going out with Jack, her marks had dropped. Her nickname used to be "Brainy"—Razz had given it to her in grade seven—but no one was using it lately.

Allie looked across the room to the calendar. There was a big photo of a pink kitten batting a ball of blue yarn with its tiny paw. The yarn was all tangled around the kitten's legs and head. Below the photo the days of the month were arranged in neat rows. May 1 had a red circle around it, drawn in crayon. Today was May 6.

Allie was five days overdue. She was afraid she was pregnant. *Wouldn't that be just my luck*, she thought. Jack had dumped her three weeks ago. He had told her in the cafeteria at lunchtime, while stuffing fries and gravy into his mouth. He told her he didn't want to be pinned down anymore. But they could still be friends, he had said. *Yeah, sure,* thought Allie, *you'll be my buddy if I'm knocked up, won't you, Jack?*

Allie wondered now what she had ever seen in Jack. He was cute, sure, and a lot of fun. And it had made Allie feel good when she stole Jack from that snob, Angela Burrows. But for the last couple of months he hadn't paid much attention to her. Except for sex. Allie knew she could never tell him about the red circle on her calendar.

The shrieking and rumbling downstairs got louder. Her parents were arguing about money now. Allie looked down at the three red circles on the report card, then back at the red circle on the calendar. She could imagine what would happen when her parents found out. Her father would put on the Hurt Look and make her feel super guilty. Her mother would put on the I Told You So Look and start to wind up the shriek machine.

Worst of all, Allie admitted to herself, they would be right.

Allie wished she could disappear. She wanted to be like that soft white fluff on a dandelion and float away on the wind. Somewhere, anywhere but here.

Then Allie made up her mind. Maybe she *could* disappear—get away from her parents' arguing and from the four red circles.

She went to the dresser and got a scrap of paper out of her purse. She stepped outside her room to the upstairs phone and punched in the numbers on the piece of paper. Allie cupped her hand around the mouthpiece of the phone.

"Hello."

"Hello," said Allie. "Is that you, Razz?"

"You're talkin' to him."

"This is Allie," she said. *Will he remember?* she thought. *I hope so, or I'll look like a total goof.*

"Hey, Brainy! How are ya?"

"Okay, I guess."

Allie took a breath. *Say it,* she said to herself. "Umm, I was wondering if your offer still stands."

"Well, sure, Brainy, but I thought—"

"Things have changed," she cut in. "I'd like to go with you now. When are you leaving?"

"In about two hours. Can you be ready?"

"No probs," she answered.

"Okay, where?"

"Umm, park around the corner. Ten o'clock, right?"

"See you then, Brainy." He hung up.

Razz and Allie had been friends since forever. He lived on a farm outside of town now, but he went to the same school as Allie. Last week, she had been complaining to him about how her life was falling apart. Razz had been really concerned about her. He had even offered to take her on tour with him. The skateboarding season was starting, and Razz was leaving today.

From downstairs, Allie heard some more shrieking and rumbling. Then the kitchen door slammed. As she went back into her room and closed the door, she heard the Chevy roar to life in the driveway. She knew her mother was taking off in a fit again. She always raced the engine like that when she was throwing a fit.

Allie got her little suitcase out of the closet. It was pretty banged up—the result of a few summers at camp. Soon, the bag was packed. She sat on it so she could close the snaps. Then she got her backpack and threw in her hair dryer, brushes, combs, can of mousse, toothbrush, and makeup. Next came the Walkman and a dozen tapes, along with a couple of movie mags. Finally, she stuffed in a new box of maxi-pads.

Here's hoping, she said to herself. When she was packed, Allie went to her desk and ripped the report card into shreds. She dropped the pieces into the waste can. *Only one red circle left*, she thought.

Then she put a tape in the deck, turned it up high and settled down at her window to wait.

Just before ten o'clock, Allie yanked at the window. It creaked and groaned as it slid up. She dropped the suitcase and the pack out first. Then she climbed out and dropped to the flat garage roof. Allie looked around. She tossed her stuff into the backyard and slid down the drainpipe, scraping her hands.

Allie slipped between the garage and the hedge and was soon headed down the street. Before she turned the corner, she looked back at the house. The bright morning sun blazed in the windows. Her dad would be in the kitchen, working. He'd be going over the accounts, shaking his head and worrying. Behind the house, the big maple swayed in the wind. That tree was the only thing she liked about the house.

When her mom got home, Allie wouldn't be there. They would find only the note she had pinned to her pillow:

Dear Mom and Dad,
I'm going away. You'll be better off without me.
Love, Allie.

Chapter Two

The first thing Allie noticed when she climbed into the van was the mattress in the back.

"Hey, wait a minute," she said.

Razz was dressed wildly, as usual. Green running shoes, unlaced. Yellow pants and a cherry red shirt. A green painter's hat.

All of her friends thought Razz was cute. He was seventeen, tall and dark.

Allie thought so too, but she had known
him too long to be interested in him that
way. *Besides*, she thought, *I have enough
of that kind of trouble as it is.*

"Relax, Brainy," he laughed. "I'm
not putting the move on ya. Take it
easy."

He started the van and pulled away
from the curb. Looking around, Allie's
eye was caught by the skateboards.
There was a rack along each side of the
van and at least eight boards hung from
them. They were all different colors,
with wild graphics on them. The decks
were different shapes, but each one
had the name *RAZZ* in big letters on
it. Behind her seat was a big wooden
box with dozens of stickers showing
company logos plastered on the lid.
Behind the driver's seat was a blue
SkyGrabber BMX cycle. Razz had been
a BMX racer in grade nine, but now he
spent all his time on a skateboard.

"Better buckle up, Brainy," Razz told her.

Allie turned around and snapped the seat belt on. "New van?" she asked. "Just picked it up last week," he answered. "Like it?"

Allie checked the interior. The red carpet felt soft under her feet. The seats were covered with real sheepskin throws. There seemed to be a thousand dials and gauges on the dash. Music thumped from a tape deck that was covered with buttons.

"What kind of music is *that*?" she asked, wrinkling her nose.

"Skunk music."

"Huh?"

"Skunk—you know, skateboard punk. Like it? No? Well, there's some other stuff in the rack."

She flipped open the box on the console between the seats and got a Killjoy tape. She put it into the deck.

"Hungry?" asked Razz. He pointed to a giant jar of peanut butter and a bag of red twisters on the dashboard. "They taste great together."

"No, thanks," said Allie, trying not to screw up her face at the thought of the taste. She settled back in the soft bucket seat.

They were turning onto Highway 400. The van picked up speed. Allie kicked off her shoes and put her feet up on the dash. She watched the scenery flash past, wondering how long it would be before her parents noticed she was gone. Would they phone the cops?

Hours later they were on the outskirts of Ottawa. They stopped at a restaurant to eat. Razz had a big plate of fries with hot dog relish and ketchup on them. The green and red mess on his plate looked like one of those dumb modern paintings

Allie's art teacher raved about. Allie ordered a hamburger but couldn't eat it. When they were finished, Razz pulled a wad of money from his pocket—all twenties. He peeled a bill from the wad and handed it to Allie.

"How about you pay and I'll bring the van out front?"

"Okay, but I can pay for my own," she said.

"You can pay next time, Brainy, okay?"

When they got to the fairground, it was packed with cars, vans and people. Razz showed a pass to the cop at the gate and they drove under a huge white banner that read "Ontario Skateboard Championships." They parked on the grassy infield and got out.

"I gotta spend the afternoon practicing," said Razz. "You can do what you want. But do me a favor and keep an eye on the van, okay? Last year, Slammer— he's my biggest opposition—sent a few of his goons to wreck my boards."

"Okay," said Allie. "I'll just look around. I'll watch the van."

Allie didn't know much about skateboarding, but she knew Razz was last year's national champion. He made a lot of money from sponsors. That's why you could buy boards all over North America with his name on them. This meet was the first one for the season. He was touring the whole country, and if he held onto his championship, the sponsors would keep paying. They paid enough to make Razz the richest seventeen-year-old she'd ever heard of.

Razz unlocked the back doors of the van and hopped inside to change into his gear. Allie looked at the painting on the bright silver panels of the van. It showed Razz doing a hand plant and grabbing a lot of air. He had a big smile on his face. She knew the same picture was painted on the other side of the van.

When Razz hopped out, he was wearing red tights, yellow jammers and pink shoes. He had a white helmet on and pads protected his knees and elbows. On his sky-blue T-shirt it said *Skate Tough or Go Home*. In his hand was a green board with *RAZZ* written in blue stars.

Three guys came up to them. They were all decked out in skateboarding gear. And they were all holding *RAZZ* boards.

"Hey, Razz. Just get here?" the tallest one said.

"Yup."

"Slammer's lookin' for ya," said another of the guys, smiling.

"Yeah, well, tell him I'm not home."

Razz walked away, saying over his shoulder, "Lock up for me, will ya Brainy?"

An hour or so later, Allie was sitting on the grass beside the van, soaking up the spring sunshine. She had her eyes closed.

"Well, well, well. Looks like Razz has a new chick."

Allie opened her eyes. Standing in front of her was a tall, well-built guy with pure white hair with a black streak up the middle. He was wearing skateboarding gear, but everything was black. On his T-shirt was a picture of a white skull with an ugly buzzard on top. The buzzard had an eyeball in its beak. On the shirt it said *Cheer Up and Die*.

Allie said nothing.

The guy in black grinned at her, showing his yellow, mossy teeth. "You guarding the new van?" he sneered.

Allie looked away.

The guy took a knife from his pocket and slowly opened it. He looked around. Allie's heart started to pound. He walked to the front of the van and pressed the point against the new silver paint.

"Wanna come and stay with *me* tonight, Sweetie? I can show you a better time than that loser."

"Why don't you fade away, man?" she answered, trying to keep her voice even.

The guy's grin disappeared. He began to walk along the side of the van, dragging the knife. It screeched on the metal as he went.

"Hey, you creep!" Allie shouted, getting to her feet.

The guy in black kept at it. She grabbed his shoulder as he passed her. He turned and brought his knee up into her stomach. Allie felt a sharp pain as she dropped to her knees, gasping.

He kept walking slowly, dragging the squealing knife along the side of the van. As he walked away, she saw in big letters across the back of his shirt, *Slammer*.

Chapter Three

The next morning Allie woke to a pounding on the van doors.

She groaned and rolled over. The mattress in Razz's van was too comfortable. She closed her eyes again.

The pounding came again. "Hey, Brainy! Wake up!"

Allie pulled on her baggy jeans and unlocked the door. She checked her watch. Eight o'clock. Razz hopped into the van, dragging his sleeping bag in after him. He had slept outside on the ground.

"There are showers at the edge of the infield," he said. He searched inside a leather bag and pulled out his skateboarding gear. "I've gotta warm up. The Street competition starts in half an hour."

Allie found her backpack under the sleeping bag Razz had loaned her. "OK, thanks," she said.

"By the way, Brainy, did you see anyone hanging around the van yesterday? Some scumbag did a job on the paint."

She told him about Slammer, leaving out the part where he kneed her in the gut. Razz looked angry for only a second. Then, to Allie's surprise, he smiled.

"No sweat, Brainy," he said. "That scum is trying to get me hot, so I'll lose my edge today. But I won't let him.

I'll take care of him after the meet. Catch you later."

After Razz left, Allie hopped down from the van and locked it. She looked at the dull gray sky as the wind snatched at her long hair. *Wonder what Mom and Dad are doing now*, she thought. *Probably arguing about whose fault it is that I left. What would they think if they knew* why *I left*?

Allie headed toward the showers. She was looking forward to the competitions, to seeing Razz at his best. She hoped that it wouldn't rain.

By the time the Street competition was over, Allie knew that Razz was in a class by himself. There was only one skateboarder close to him and that was Slammer.

All the boarders wore wild clothes. Some, like Razz, wore classy rags in crazy colors. Some went the other way, trying to look poor as beggars. One guy came out in a wet suit! But all of them wore pads and helmets. They swerved, jumped off the low ramp and did all kinds of unbelievable tricks with goofy names like the Ollie, the Truck Grind and the Acid Drop.

Razz and Allie took a break and had a couple of sodas back at the van.

Razz was surrounded by kids who asked him a million questions and wanted him to sign their boards. He finally had to shoo them away.

Taking a smaller board from the rack in the van, he walked over to the big cement square. The Freestyle part of the meet was about to start. Allie followed him after carefully locking the van.

She couldn't believe what Razz could do. He swerved, danced, spun in circles, did handstands—all on that little board. There were no ramps in this competition—just the flat cement square. Razz made the Pogo and the Finger Flip look easy. The crowd yelled and cheered through his act so loudly that she could hardly hear the music. Allie caught sight of Slammer on the sidelines, waiting for his turn. He was scowling.

Razz won the Freestyle and Slammer came second.

After lunch, Allie got a good seat in the stands for the Half-Pipe competition. This was the most exciting part, and the most dangerous. Razz was winning the meet, but he and Slammer were close in points, so if Slammer made a really good showing on the half-pipe and if Razz messed up, Slammer could win overall.

Allie's seat was right above the rail, in the center of the half-pipe. When the skateboarders came up the side of the half-pipe and grabbed air, they'd be right in front of her.

The first few guys weren't very good. They didn't grab much air and she could see the fear in their eyes as they flew into the air in front of her. Not that she blamed them. This was scary stuff! One poor guy, dressed in a clown suit, missed the coping trying to do a hand-plant. He flipped into the air, then dropped back to the half-pipe, tumbling down the sides like a broken doll. The guy lay at the bottom, without moving. They took him away on a stretcher. Allie could see a little pool of blood where the kid had been lying.

Next came Razz. He was directly across from her on the other side of the half-pipe. The crowd was dead quiet, waiting for him. He took his time, strapping on the helmet, adjusting his pads. Then he did something amazing. He leaped into the air! At the highest point of his jump, he slapped his board under his feet and dropped like a stone onto the half-pipe. The wheels on the board began to sing. Razz crossed the bottom of the half-pipe, rolled up the wall in front of Allie and flew high into the air.

"Ooooooooooo!" was the sound the crowd made. Allie looked at Razz's face as he flew past her. She could tell he saw nothing except the picture in his mind of what he was going to do next. He spun in the air and dropped past her again.

Razz did his 360 Hand-Plants, Rocket Airs and McTwists like no one else. He was smooth. But he was also daring. The crowd never stopped oooo-ing and ahhhh-ing until he was finished. He rose up the half-pipe across from Allie, flew into the air. He landed on his feet with his board in his hand. Then he smiled and bowed, holding his board across his chest so everyone could see *RAZZ* written across the graphics.

Everybody in the stands knew that Razz had the meet in the bag now.

Slammer was next. He started safely, like the other skateboarders had. He swept up the half-pipe in front of Allie, grabbed some air, turned and dropped back down. He came back. This time he looked straight at her and, as he passed, sent a big gob of spit sailing at her. It splattered onto the bench beside her.

Then Slammer turned and dropped back. The next time he came past, he was sneering again. Allie gave him the finger. A look of surprise twisted his face into hatred.

When Slammer turned in the air, his timing was off. He dropped onto the coping. With a crack like a whip, his board snapped clean in half. The crowd gasped as he fell down the half-pipe and tumbled to a heap at the bottom. The two halves of his board clattered down beside him.

After a few seconds, he struggled to his feet. He looked back up at Allie, his face dark with hate.

Chapter Four

That night there was a dance to wind up the skateboarding meet. It was held in a community center nearby. Razz asked Allie to go with him and she said yes. *I've got nothing better to do except worry,* she thought.

The center was packed with kids when Allie and Razz arrived. There were banners and posters all over the walls, advertising skateboards and gear. At one end of the room a few kids were doing a Freestyle demonstration on a wooden platform. The music was so loud Allie thought the roof would fall in.

Allie danced with Razz a few times. He was good. She danced with a few other guys, too. But she was nervous and kept looking around for Slammer. *Maybe he'll turn up and give me a hard time*, she thought.

At about nine o'clock Razz said to her, "Brainy, I've gotta go phone my sponsor. They wanted me to tell them how I did today. I'll be right back."

Allie sat down on one of the metal chairs, sipping a Diet Pepsi, thinking about her parents. Maybe she had made up her mind too fast. Maybe she shouldn't have left home after all. What was she going to do when Razz's tour was over? She had to admit to herself that she hadn't thought things out too well.

"Did the big shot leave you all alone?" a voice asked.

She knew the voice without looking up. It was Slammer.

He was dressed in black—black leather pants and cycle jacket. The light shining on his white hair made him look like a ghost. Standing with him were two other guys.

Slammer leaned over and hissed, "I'd have won today if it wasn't for you, bitch."

Allie could smell the beer on his breath. She didn't answer, knowing that what he said was a lie. She decided to get up and walk away. Slammer roughly shoved her back into the chair.

"Get lost," she said, wishing she felt as brave as she sounded.

"For a good-lookin' chick she's got an ugly mouth on her," said Slammer. One of the guys behind him, a tall blond kid, laughed.

Allie crossed her arms over her chest and looked away.

"Come on with us," Slammer sneered, "and we'll show you how to party."

Allie was scared. She looked around, but there was no one near her. All the kids on the dance floor had their minds on other things.

Slammer reached down and grabbed her arm, squeezing hard. He pulled her to her feet. The two goons moved in and the three of them surrounded her. Someone grabbed her other arm and yanked it behind her back. She twisted and struggled. She heard her shirt rip as a jab of pain shot into her shoulder.

"Let me go, you losers!" she yelled. But the music was so loud her voice was lost. Slammer and the two goons hustled her out the back doors of the community center. Allie shot a frantic look back over her shoulder. Just as the door slammed behind her, it flew open again. It was Razz, and he looked mad.

Slammer and the other goon let go of Allie and she stepped to the side. Slammer had his knife out—the one he had used to do the job on the van. He and the other goons separated so they could come at Razz from two sides. They paid no more attention to Allie.

"Come on, scum," hissed Slammer. "Let's get it on."

"Drop the knife, hot dog," Razz said. "Let's see if you can fight without a blade in your hand."

Slammer looked around, then folded the knife and put it into his jacket pocket. He grinned.

It was dark behind the community center and there was no one around. The cold wind whipped Allie's hair in her face. All she could do was watch as Razz and Slammer took off their jackets.

They began to circle, each fighter bent over a little, looking for an opening. Slammer struck first, aiming a kick at Razz's stomach. Razz stepped back and caught Slammer's foot. He twisted it and Slammer fell to the dirt. Razz waited for him to get up again.

Allie could see the hate in Slammer's eyes. Razz looked calm, but he had the same look of concentration he showed when he was up on the half-pipe. Slammer threw a punch. Razz ducked and the punch whacked his shoulder. He stepped forward and shoved Slammer away from him.

Again, Razz stood and waited for him. Slammer looked really mean now. *He isn't looking too good in front of his friends*, Allie thought.

Fast as a snake, Slammer bent down, grabbed a handful of dirt and flung it into Razz's face. Razz threw his hands up. Slammer lunged forward, driving his head into Razz's chest. The two of them went down, grunting, and rolled in the dirt. Fists flew. Legs jerked and kicked. Finally Razz broke loose and got to his feet, blood trickling from his nose. He wiped it away and waited for Slammer to get up.

When Slammer was on his feet, panting, Razz stepped into him and punched him just below the ribs. Allie could hear the air *whoosh* out of Slammer's lungs. With a loud grunt, Slammer dropped to his knees.

"Want some help, Slammer?" said the blond goon. *He doesn't sound too hot on the idea*, thought Allie.

"No, man. Stay out of it," Slammer wheezed.

Razz said, very calmly, "Had enough?"

"Yeah."

"Then you and your friends leave Brainy alone, all right."

Slammer looked up at her and pasted on a weak smile. "Yeah, all right."

"Okay, suppose you guys split."

The goons left, two of them helping Slammer. He wasn't walking too straight.

Later, Allie and Razz were in the van, sipping sodas and listening to the radio.

"How come Slammer hates you so much?" she asked him.

"Because I'm champion and I beat him all the time. And because of the sponsors. They pay me a lot more. That's why he wants to win so much. He'll earn twice as much money."

"Razz, you didn't really fight him hard. I mean, you just kept pushing him away and ducking his punches. A couple of times you really could have finished him."

Razz tipped up his drink, slurping down the last drops. Then he tucked it into the little bag hanging from the dash.

"I don't like fighting, Allie. It doesn't solve anything."

"Anyway, thanks," she said to him.

"No probs, Brainy. Now, let's check the gear. We gotta roll tonight."

"Where to?" she asked.

"Back home. My sponsor wants to set up a TV interview on the cable station in Barrie. And get this—they want me and Slammer on the same program! What a drag. Now we gotta backtrack."

Backtrack? Allie didn't like this news one bit. She didn't know what she wanted anymore. But she wasn't ready to face her parents yet—she knew that much. The last thing she wanted was to go back home.

"No, Razz, I can't go back!" she said.

"Relax, Brainy. We'll go back. You can wait in the van while I do the taping, and we'll be out of there in a couple of hours. We'll leave now, stop along the

way and get some sleep, and be there in
lots of time for me to clean up."

"But—"

"We gotta go," Razz cut in.

"Okay, okay," she said angrily. *What
choice do I have?* she thought.

Chapter Five

Razz drove for a couple of hours, dipping red twisters into the peanut butter jar before he chomped on them. The night was dark and rainy, with high winds that shook the van.

Allie sat with her feet up on the dash and tried to listen to the music. Her mind was a mess. She was mad at Razz for heading back home, and she was thinking about her parents a lot. And she was worried about the four red circles—especially the one on her calendar. She was still overdue.

Every once in awhile Razz would tell an elephant joke. "Hey, Brainy! How many elephants can you get into a compact car?"

"Who *cares,* Razz?"

"I thought you were Alison the A student. Come on, how many?"

"I don't know."

"Four—two in the front and two in the back!" Razz would laugh like a crazy man.

Allie would groan, but laugh anyway. Sometimes Razz could act pretty strange, but he had always been able to kid her out of a bad mood.

Finally, Razz pulled off the highway onto a gravel side road and parked the van. "Time to catch a few winks, Brainy. I'm whacked. This has been one long day."

Razz pushed a button and his window rolled down. Rain blew into the van.

"Guess I'll have to sleep in here tonight, okay?" The window rolled up, shutting out the rain.

"No probs, Razz. I'll curl up in this seat."

"No, you take the mattress."

"I don't *want* the mattress!" she snapped. *What's wrong with me?* she thought. *I'm starting to sound like my mother.*

"Okay, Brainy. Whatever."

Allie knew that some of her friends wouldn't have stayed up front while Razz slept alone on the mattress. But no way was she moving. She'd had enough of that stuff to last a long time.

Razz set the alarm on the dash clock and climbed in back. He tossed Allie's sleeping bag up to her and turned out the lights. Allie adjusted the bucket seat and tried to get comfortable.

For a long time she couldn't sleep. She stared at the soft blue clock light and listened to the rain beat against the windows and drum on the roof. She had the strangest feeling that something was wrong at home. She was worried about her parents. *They must be sick with worry too*, she thought. *They must be wondering where I am.*

Should I go back? What would that solve if I did? Nothing, that's what. And what happens if I really am pregnant? I couldn't *go home then.*

Allie had been pushing that thought away all day. With the excitement of the skateboard competition and the problem with Slammer it had been easy not to think of—that. But now the thought pushed into her mind, and it made her afraid.

It took her a long time to get to sleep.

In the morning the storm was worse. Thunderclaps slammed the dark sky above them as Razz struggled to hold the van steady in the high wind. The lightning was wicked. The wipers flapped like crazy and still it seemed like the van was driving underwater.

After an hour, Allie's thoughts were interrupted by Razz.

"What the—?" he exclaimed.

Allie stared ahead into the rain. Off to the right, she saw red lights flashing. Razz slowed the van and crept toward the lights.

"It's a pickup, with its nose in the ditch," he said. Then he pulled the van onto the shoulder of the highway. They could see a white truck, with a black stripe along the side from headlights to tailgate.

"Hey, that's Slammer's rig," Razz said.

He rammed the shift into Park and opened the door. Rain blew in as he climbed down, slamming the door behind him.

A few minutes later, two shapes floated out of the rain and came toward the van. They disappeared and the back doors opened. A suitcase was tossed in. Razz and Slammer climbed in and Razz crawled forward into the driver's seat. His clothes were soaked. Slammer looked awful. He was drenched, and his white hair was plastered to his head.

A drowned rat, thought Allie. *That's what he looks like.*

Slammer looked up at her and grinned. Then he blew her a kiss. She remembered what Razz had said about fighting, so instead of giving him the finger, she smiled as hard as she could. Then she turned around just as Razz pulled the van onto the highway.

"What did you pick *him* up for?" she demanded.

"What could I do, Brainy? He went off the road in the dark and smashed his rad."

"You could have left him there," she answered.

"But we gotta do that stupid TV show."

"Come on back here, Sweet Marie," Slammer sneered. "This mattress is real soft."

Allie stared straight ahead. "Take a hike, loser," she mumbled.

"Hey, gimme a break, you two," Razz snapped. "It's hard enough driving without a fight in the van!"

Finally they were on the 400 again, heading north. The traffic was moving slowly because of the heavy rain. Allie tried to get a weather report on the radio, but all she heard was static. The lightning was too close.

When they got near Barrie, the rain stopped but the wind was worse. Razz was having a hard time holding the van on the road. Allie could see the muscles of his arms bulging as he fought the wheel.

"Hey, Brainy. How many elephants does it take to drive a van through a hurricane?"

By the time they reached the ramp to Essa Road, Razz was creeping along, far below the speed limit. He turned off the highway onto the exit ramp.

Allie peered through the windshield. Past the Holiday Inn, over the hill, was her house. *Wonder if they found my note yet*, she thought.

Razz stopped the van on the gravel shoulder. Then the engine died.

"Hey, look!" he exclaimed.

Slammer scrambled forward and knelt behind the engine cover. "Looks *bad,*" he said, his voice shaky.

Ahead of them, to the northwest, the sky was weird. It was a dark purple-gray with a sickening yellow streak across it. The sky was quickly getting darker as the yellow faded. Soon, it was like dusk—but it was only ten o'clock in the morning.

"Look!" Razz said, and pointed to a black cloud up the highway. It seemed to be moving. It wobbled and shifted. Then Allie could see what looked like a crooked black finger coming out of the cloud and reaching down toward the ground.

The cloud *was* moving! It grew larger and larger. The roaring wind was punching the van like giant fists. Dirt from the shoulder of the exit ramp swirled into the air.

"Look," Allie said. "Are those birds flying around in that black cloud?"

"I don't—oh, no, no!"

"Razz! What's the matter?"

"Those aren't birds, they're—they're *boards* or something!"

The black finger was moving through the fields beside the highway, coming right towards them. Allie squinted, trying to figure out what she was seeing.

Then she knew.

In the black cloud, just above the finger, she saw boards and trees and huge, twisted sheets of metal spinning! The finger moved along the edge of the highway, sucking up dirt and gravel and spewing it into the air. It came to a car stopped on the shoulder. Dirt and stones swirled around the car as the whirlwind touched it. The car almost disappeared from sight.

Allie didn't believe what she saw next. The car flipped into the air and landed on its roof, like a toy.

"Razz!" she screamed. "It's coming toward us! Get going! Drive!"

Razz frantically twisted the key. The engine wheezed and groaned and died again.

"Come *on,* man!" Slammer yelled.

"Too late, Allie! Get down!" Razz cried.

But she couldn't. She stared, bug-eyed, out the windshield as the whirlwind came on. It swallowed the main building of the racetrack across the highway from them. The building just seemed to explode. The roof popped up and flew to bits, spinning up into the black cloud. The walls blew outward as if a bomb had gone off inside, and bricks scattered across the track.

The whirlwind came across the highway, flipping two more cars over and sending a tractor-trailer rolling down the bank. Chunks of wood and shingles and pieces of branches began to slam against the van. Something whacked the windshield, cracking it. The fierce wind roared around them.

"We gotta get out of here!" Slammer shouted above the noise. He scrambled to the back of the van and opened the doors. The raging wind thundered into the van.

"Slammer! No!" Razz cried. "Stay inside!"

But it was too late. Slammer was gone. Then he appeared in front of the van, running down the gravel shoulder of the exit ramp. The wind ripped at his clothes, and chunks of wood and other junk spun around him. Then something hit him in the legs and he fell, hard. He rolled, pushed by the wind, and smashed up against a white guardrail post. Through the swirling dust Allie saw him wrap his arms around the post. But the wind plucked him away like a doll. He was picked up and thrown at the van. Slammer's body banged against the windshield, leaving a big red star of blood on the glass before it disappeared.

"Get *down,* Allie!" Razz yelled again.

But she couldn't. She was in a trance. She felt like she was going to vomit as Slammer's blood ran down the windshield. The van rocked in the powerful wind. Then, as the center of the whirlwind came toward the van, it turned and went down Essa Road! The black finger passed through an intersection, scattering cars. It began to climb the hill, ripping trees from the ground and chewing them up. It hit the Holiday Inn. The big picture window blew out and millions of bits of glass climbed into the cloud.

The finger scratched its way up the hill and began blowing the houses on the edge of the hill to pieces. Roofs lifted into the air, spun and fell away. Walls blew out and splintered to bits.

Allie watched the whirlwind disappear over the hill.

Then she began to scream, over and over.

Her parents' house was in that neighborhood.

EMMAUS HIGH SCHOOL LIBRARY
EMMAUS, PA 18049

Chapter Six

Razz had to shake Allie to get her to stop screaming. He slumped back into his seat, talking as if he was in a daze. "I guess… I guess we should go see if Slammer is… alive…"

Allie squeezed her eyes shut, trying to get her head straight. Was it a nightmare? Had she really seen a tornado snatch Slammer up into the sky and then rip the houses on the hill to bits? When she opened her eyes, the smear of blood on the windshield gave her the answer.

Razz kept trying to start the van. The motor groaned and coughed, but that was all. So they climbed out and walked slowly around to the back of the van. There was no wind now, and the sun seemed to smile from the clear sky as if everything had been a joke. It was dead quiet.

Razz pulled himself up onto the bumper of the van, then to the roof. He peered into the distance, turning slowly as he scanned the fields beside the highway. Slammer was nowhere to be seen. Razz lowered himself to the ground again.

"He's gone," said Razz, his voice quiet. "How could he just disappear?"

Allie shuddered when she thought of it. Slammer's broken body falling out of the whirlwind, landing in a field —or maybe someone's yard.

Then her mind began to wake up. "Razz! Our parents!"

Razz looked at her. "No way, Brainy. My place is miles from here, in the other direction. But—"

Allie felt her heart pounding with fear. "We've got to get to my house, to see if it's...Let's go!"

They began to run down the exit ramp to Essa Road. They soon reached the intersection. There were several overturned cars scattered around. Smoke poured from a pickup truck. A man with his shirt torn to ribbons stood watching it, shaking his head. A few people wandered around as if they were lost. An old man knelt in the middle of the road beside a woman in a pink dress. "Sara," he was saying as he shook her. "Sara, Sara."

"Maybe we should stop and help," Razz suggested.

"No, please," Allie answered. "Let's keep going."

At the corner of Fairview they stopped and looked up the hill at the blasted houses. The most direct route to Allie's house was up the hill and through the yards. But Razz and Allie turned and followed the road. They turned left onto Little Avenue, stepping over huge branches and chunks of debris.

When they got to the top of the hill, near their school, it was as if they had stepped into a science-fiction movie. All around them were the remains of smashed houses. Allie could see into living rooms and bedrooms because walls had blown away. Front lawns were strewn with chunks of wood, fallen trees, broken furniture.

In a daze, they walked down Marshall Street. Around them, voices called kids' names that Allie recognized. People wandered around their yards, staring at places where houses once had been.

"Looks like a war zone," whispered Razz. "Like the city was bombed."

At the corner of Allie's street, they saw her neighbor's dog, Scotty, lying in the middle of the road, his bloody tongue hanging out. A chain was hooked to his collar. At the other end of the chain was the front wall of a doghouse. They walked around the dog. Further down the street Allie saw a car lying on its side in the Dillons' garage. But the walls and the roof of the garage weren't there anymore.

They continued down the street. Then Allie stopped. "Oh, no," she moaned. "No, no, no!"

Where her house had been, only part of a sidewall remained. She could see the stove and the fridge, sitting on a bare floor in the kitchen. Everything else was gone. The big maple tree had been ripped out of the ground. It lay across the yard, its leaves stripped off, and its huge roots sticking up.

Allie put her hands over her eyes. She thought she must be going crazy! She felt Razz put his arm around her.

Allie broke free and began to run. She stumbled across her front lawn and climbed up a pile of loose bricks onto the floor of what used to be her house. It was easy to see that her parents weren't there.

"The basement!" Razz exclaimed. "Maybe they hid there!"

Allie ran to the steps that led to the basement and flung aside half a living-room couch. She went down the stairs, stepping over bricks and pieces of board. The basement was empty.

She slowly climbed the stairs into the sunlight.

"Maybe we should look around the yard," Razz said, "in case..."

He hopped off the floor and onto the grass of the backyard. It was strewn with smashed branches and pieces of other people's houses. Allie followed him.

In the distance they heard sirens, lots of them. Razz and Allie searched the small yard and found nothing. Allie sighed with relief.

"Maybe they weren't at home when the tornado hit," she said hopefully. "Yeah, that's right! Today is Monday, so Dad would be at work and Mom would be..."

Her voice trailed off. Her mom would be at home, she knew.

Razz seemed to read her mind. "She could have been out shopping or something, Brainy. I know it's hard, but try not to worry until we know for sure."

He bent over and picked something up. "This yours?" he asked. He handed Allie a small portable radio.

"No."

Allie snapped it on. It was working. She tuned it to the local station.

"Tornado" was the first word she heard. The announcer was in a panic, talking fast about the storm and the damage. So far, four deaths had been reported.

"Residents whose houses have been damaged or destroyed are urged not to try to enter their homes. Emergency centers are being set up in the following places."

One of the places he mentioned was the public school four blocks from Allie's house.

"Let's go," Allie said. "Maybe Mom and Dad are there."

"Okay, Brainy, let's go."

They walked around the house and back toward the street. At the corner of the front yard, Allie saw a piece of white paper caught in the stripped branches of the hedge. She thought of the note she had left for her mom and dad. She remembered the four red circles. She remembered writing "You'll be better off without me."

Allie began to cry.

Chapter Seven

Razz and Allie hurried down the street toward the school where the emergency center was set up.

Allie whacked her fist against the side of her leg as she walked. *I never should have run away*, she thought. *What did it solve? Nothing, that's what. Now the four red circles don't seem to be so important. Not even the one on the calendar.*

Allie looked once more at the smashed houses all along the street. The piles of brick and boards once were houses where her neighbors used to live. *Nothing could be as bad as this*, she thought.

Razz kicked a big batt of pink fiberglass insulation out of their way. The stuff was littered all over the streets and lawns. He looked at Allie.

"Come on, Brainy, don't cry. Everything will be all right. You'll see. Just hang in there until we get to the school, okay? I'm sure we'll find them and they'll be safe."

"I hope so, Razz," she said, wiping the tears away with the back of her hand. The sound of his voice calmed her a little.

They were turning the corner onto St. John Street when they heard someone shout. "Her! Her! Look, she could do it!"

Razz and Allie stopped. There were five people standing beside the foundation of a house. The house was gone, but there was a huge jumble of boards and smashed furniture piled there, like giant matchsticks. As Allie looked at the pile, the first thing she thought was *Pick-up Sticks*. It was a game she used to play when she was a little kid.

A tall, thin man rushed up to them. "Please help us!" he shouted, grabbing Allie by the arm. "Our baby...you've got to help."

He wrenched Allie's arm, and she pulled away, frightened.

"Hey, take it easy, man," said Razz.

The man tried to grab Allie again. She saw terror in his twisted face and shrank back.

"Please!" he cried again. "You've got to help."

Another man had joined them. He spoke more calmly. "My friend's baby is trapped in the cellar of his house," he explained, pointing to where the three people stood looking under the pile of lumber that used to be a house. "We've got to get her out before all that junk collapses. If that happens, the baby will be—"

He looked at his friend, then back to Allie and Razz. "Will you help?"

"Why don't you do it?" Razz asked. "There are three men, counting you two."

"Because there's no way in except a little opening." He took Razz's arm and led him toward the others as he spoke. Allie and the father followed. "None of us can fit into it," he went on.

A short, plump woman was crying hysterically, moaning, "My baby, my baby," again and again. Her dress was ripped and tears made white streaks in the dirt on her face. She stared into the mass of jumbled lumber. Allie could hear a baby wailing from somewhere in the mess.

The father pointed to the cellar window. Allie looked in and she could see right away what the man meant. There was a small opening there. A person her size could probably squeeze through the gap and get into the basement.

"Maybe it would be better to wait until the fire department or someone with equipment could get here," Razz said.

"Are you kidding?" the father answered, his voice angry. "Have you seen the streets? They're clogged with trees and hunks of houses. It'll be hours before anyone can get through."

Just as he spoke, the huge mass of twisted and jumbled lumber shifted, groaning and creaking as it settled. The mother shrieked and cried even louder.

"John, do something! She'll die in there!"

Allie didn't know what to do. She peered in through the window, then scanned the faces of the people.

"Don't do it, Brainy," warned Razz. "You'll never get out again."

Allie was scared. *Razz is right*, she thought.

She said, "I don't think—"

"Oh, no," said one of the other men. "Look!"

From the front corner of the house, a wisp of black smoke curled up into the still air.

The mother shrieked again. The other woman and man began talking at the same time. The father looked over at the smoke.

"The fireplace! I had a fire on in the family room when the tornado hit. It must be spreading!"

Allie was on her knees at the cellar window before she knew what she was doing.

"Brainy, no!" Razz yelled.

Allie didn't see the father shove Razz roughly out of the way. She felt someone grab her ankles.

"I'll lower you down," said the other man. "Gently now."

He let her slide slowly into the basement until her hands touched the carpeted floor.

"Okay, let go," she said over her shoulder.

Allie fell into a heap. She got onto her hands and knees and looked around. It was dark and gloomy. The basement ceiling had caved in, leaving only a narrow crawl space around the outer walls of the house. Allie couldn't see the baby's crib in the far corner, but she could hear the crying. As she started to crawl along the wall, a wisp of smoke floated toward her.

She reached the far wall of the house easily, scraping her back on the broken boards a few times. She turned left and headed for the corner where the crib was. When she got there, she knew things were going to be tough. When the ceiling had collapsed, it had pinned the crib against the wall. Now the crib was trapped in a cage of broken lumber.

The baby wore a white cloth diaper and a tiny white T-shirt with pink elephants on it. She was blonde, with curly hair. She was crying softly.

Allie couldn't see a way to lift her out. Gently she pulled at the wooden bars of the crib. The boards above groaned and shifted. *I can't lower the side*, she thought, *or the whole mess will fall in on us*.

Allie stopped to think. She was surprised at how calm she felt. Crawling along the wall, she had been terrified. She was still scared, but now she could think clearly. She smelled smoke again—stronger this time. *I'd better do something soon*, she thought.

Allie then noticed that the mattress rested on a frame with springs, and the frame was hung onto the crib with hooks. The hooks fit onto metal prongs attached to the crib, so that the mattress could be raised or lowered.

Taking a deep breath, Allie decided what to do. She slid under the crib and reached up to unhook the bedspring at one corner. The mattress was heavy. She had to heave upwards with all her strength and slip the hook off the prong. It worked. The mattress sagged suddenly at one corner, startling the baby. *Poor little kid*, thought Allie as the baby began to wail louder. Allie slid to the other corner, heaved up with all her might and unhooked the bedspring, which then dropped on top of her.

Carefully, she worked her way out from under the heavy mattress. The squalling baby began to slide toward the floor and Allie easily reached over and pulled her out.

She held the tiny girl in her arms, softly talking to her. The baby grew quiet. *How am I going to carry her out?* thought Allie. *I can't crawl holding her.* She looked around and found an answer.

Taking a blanket from the crib, she folded it several times to make it soft, lay the baby on it and began to crawl backward, gently pulling the baby along behind her. As she dragged, the baby began to giggle and kick her feet.

Allie got to the corner of the basement just as the pile of lumber shrieked and groaned. She snatched up the baby and held it to her as the floor collapsed further with a rumble and crash, sending clouds of dust over them. Allie moaned. She was sure she was going to die.

Outside, she could hear voices yelling. Razz's voice was loudest. "Allie! Allie!" he shouted. She could hear the fear in his voice.

"I'm okay," she yelled. She began to crawl again, very slowly, dragging the baby girl, inching backward on her hands and knees.

She felt something stab into her back. Behind her, the boards had collapsed to within a foot of the carpet, and a long spike projected down. She lay the baby down again and lowered herself to her stomach. Inching backward, she slid carefully under the nail. But she couldn't get flat enough. The nail dug into her, scoring a sharp, painful line along her back and catching on her bra strap. She struggled and felt the nail let go, then inched backward again. Then she stopped and carefully dragged the baby under the nail.

The smoke was really bad now. Allie and the baby began to cough.

"There she is!" the father shouted. "Come on, kid, you're almost home."

Allie tried to move more quickly. The baby was coughing and wailing, her nose running. She was twisting and struggling to get away from the smoke.

Finally, Allie was below the window. She got to her knees and pulled the baby to her. Lifting the little girl into her arms, Allie wrapped her in the blanket, covering her head. The baby screamed in protest.

"Just a little longer," Allie crooned to her. She turned and lifted the baby up to the waiting arms that stuck through the opening at the window, just as the black smoke boiled around her.

Allie couldn't see. The smoke choked her and she began to cough and retch. Her lungs burned and she felt as if the air was being squeezed out of her. She could hear the fire now, crackling and roaring. Trying to stand, she bashed her head on a board and fell down again. She got to her knees, fighting for breath, and slid her hands up the cement wall, feeling for the opening. Then strong hands grabbed hers and began to pull. The boards around her groaned and collapsed with a cracking roar as Allie was dragged upward.

She was out. She lay on the grass in the sunlight, gasping.

Allie struggled and sat up, trying to get her breath. Around her, voices cried and rattled. But this time the voices were relieved and happy.

"You okay, Brainy?" Razz's voice sounded wonderful.

"Yeah," Allie gasped. "I think so."

Razz helped Allie to her feet. The adults surrounded her, touching her, telling her how brave she was. Allie didn't feel brave—just embarrassed and sore. The mother, holding the baby tightly, thanked Allie again and again, talking through her tears. They made Allie tell them her name. And that made Allie remember her own family.

She said to Razz, "Let's get going."

Chapter Eight

Allie and Razz were back on the street, hurrying to the school. The air was warm and the sun shone brightly.

They had to keep going around things or stepping over things. A crushed baby carriage, tree limbs, a TV set, smashed couches. Allie was terrified that she would see a dead body in the road.

Sirens screamed in the distance. People yelled constantly. They shouted names and called out orders to each other.

Finally Allie and Razz reached the elementary school that was serving as an emergency shelter. Many of the windows had been blown out, but Allie could tell that the whirlwind had not hit directly. Some of the houses around it were still okay. They had no windows now, and some had a lot of shingles missing, but they were all right compared to Allie's house.

Allie and Razz went in the front door of the school, their feet grinding on broken glass. People were moving back and forth quickly through the dark hall. There were cops, firemen and people in other uniforms. But these people weren't like the ones on the street. They all seemed to have a purpose.

Allie and Razz went to the main office. A fat woman in a cop uniform was talking quickly into a walkie-talkie. The cigarette in the corner of her mouth bounced up and down as she talked. When she said, "Over!" Allie told her she wanted to find her parents.

"What's your name?" the woman asked.

Allie told her. The woman looked at a clipboard that had a lot of dog-eared sheets of paper clipped to it.

"I have nobody of that name working here," she said. "But we've only been set up for ten minutes, so we might hear something. We've just started to make up a lost-and-found list. So if your parents are looking for you, I can tell them you're okay."

The walkie-talkie crackled. The woman held it to her ear for a minute, then the cigarette began to bounce again. "Okay, make sure the gas, electricity and water are turned off for the entire area. We already have two gas fires reported.

We got one clear route to the hospital, along Elm, then west on Ranch Avenue. When does the army get here?"

The walkie-talkie crackled some more, then the woman said, "Over."

Razz asked, "Are you calling in the army?"

"Yeah," the woman answered, "the base is pretty close and we need lots of manpower to close the area off, search for injured people, prevent looters— all that."

"Looters?" Allie replied. "What kind of creep would do that?"

"You'd be surprised," was all she said.

People ran in and out of the office, firing questions at the woman or giving her reports. She was the only calm person in the school, it seemed.

When the office was empty of people again, she said to Allie, "Was your house damaged?"

"It's gone!" Allie replied. She began to cry again. She felt Razz's arm around her.

"Do you know where the gym is?"

"Yes."

"Go there. We're putting up a huge poster on the wall. Soon as we get information on people—where they are and how they are—we'll post it. Now, you live nearby, right?"

Allie said yes again.

"Okay, then you can be a big help because you know some of the people around here. We're going to need lots of help in the next couple of days, Allie. Lots of it. Will you help us?"

"Of course," Allie said.

"Good. Now, off you go. And," the woman added as the walkie-talkie crackled at her, "try not to worry. Your parents are likely okay. It just may take a while to find that out."

Allie turned to go but Razz stayed put. He told the woman about Slammer.

She shook her head and made a note on her clipboard.

"Was he a friend of yours?"

Razz looked at Allie. "Sort of," he answered. "We don't know his real name."

"All right, we'll keep an eye out for his...for him."

Razz nodded. "Um, do you need anyone to do some driving?" he asked.

The woman looked up from the clipboard. She lit another cigarette from the butt of the last one. "Well, probably we'll need that, yeah."

"I've got a van. Maybe I can help," he said.

"Sure. Is it here?"

"No, but I think I can get it here in a little while."

"Great. Come on back in when you can."

Razz turned to Allie. "Will you be okay, Brainy?"

"Sure, Razz."

When they were out in the dark, busy hall, Razz added, "I'd...I don't know...I'd sort of feel better if I could do something, you know? Like you did back there at the house."

Allie went to the gym. There were about twenty people there, setting up tables, talking into walkie-talkies, spreading mats on the floor. She saw grouchy old Mr. Beekman, who had chased her out of his backyard a million times when she was little. He was wrapping a bandage on Mrs. Pearce's arm. She lived two doors from Allie and right now she looked a little rough.

Allie went over to a guy in a fireman's uniform.

"Can I help?" she asked.

"You know how to use one of these?" he asked, holding up a walkie-talkie.

"No."

The fireman showed her.

"We're working on a list of missing persons," he said. "Any news you get from the other end," he held up the walkie-talkie, "you make note of it. Mostly, you'll be putting names on this list, but after awhile, you'll get news, from the hospital, from the streets, that someone has been found. You put them on this list. Got it?"

"Got it," Allie said.

"Someone will collect your sheets and put the dope on the big posters over there." He pointed to the wall across the gym from Allie. One huge poster was headed MISSING, the other, FOUND.

Allie sat down behind the table and pulled the stack of sheets toward her. On the top of the first sheet she wrote the names of her parents.

Chapter Nine

Allie sat behind the table for the rest
of the day. She was very busy. She got
calls from the hospital, the police station,
the radio station, and from the streets.
The list on the big poster headed
MISSING grew and grew, and they had
to start another one. Her parents' names
were still on the top of the list.

No matter how busy she was, she couldn't stop thinking about her parents. Her imagination ran wild at times. She pictured them crushed by a fallen wall or sucked up into the black finger-cloud like Slammer. When those thoughts grabbed hold of her mind, she got scared and cried again.

But she was still able to do something useful. It didn't take Allie long to get used to talking into the walkie-talkie. It reminded her of all the war movies and cop movies she had seen. She got to recognize the voices on the other end. The hospital voice was a woman. The voice from her neighborhood was a guy. She could tell he wasn't very old. He sounded a little like one of the guys at the skateboarding meet who had wanted Razz to autograph his new skateboard.

After it got dark, Allie had to work with a big flashlight. The gym was lit with big gas camping lanterns. It was a little creepy.

Later, Allie asked someone to take over while she went to the washroom. It was dark in the halls of the school too, and lanterns lighted them. It was eerie. Shadows moved along the walls and groans came out of the darkness. The halls were full of people. Some lay on mats, some sat against the wall, in a daze. A lot of them were injured, waiting for rides to the hospital. Some were getting fixed up by the dozens of nurses and St. John Ambulance workers. Kids cried.

She took a walk past the office. The same woman was there in the same place, talking into the walkie-talkie. She looked very tired. The hall by the office seemed full of uniformed men and women—cops, army, gas company, electric company, medics. It was like everyone in town was gathered in this one building.

A few hours later, the lights came on in the gym and Allie snapped off the flashlight she had been using. She was taking down a name on the FOUND list when she looked up and saw Razz standing in front of the table.

He looked awful. His yellow silk T-shirt was torn and bloody. He had scrapes all over his arms. His face was dirty and tired looking. But he was smiling.

"Hey, Brainy, looks like you're an important person around here."

"Not me. I just answer the radio."

Razz tossed a chunk of chocolate cake wrapped in plastic to her. "Hungry?"

"Yeah, thanks." Allie unwrapped the package and bit into the cake. It tasted wonderful.

"Sorry I took so long," Razz went on. He fished a couple of red twisters out of his pocket and began to munch. "I've been hauling passengers to the hospital.

The ones who aren't too badly hurt. They sent me over here to pick up a load, so I thought I'd come and see how you're doing. I guess you haven't heard."

"Heard what?" Allie was too tired to fill in the blanks.

"Your parents are at the hospital."

"Really? Are they okay?"

"Well, your mom got pretty banged up. Nothing real serious, though. Your dad is fine. He was at work when the tornado hit—and your mom was shopping. She was hurt when the mall got hit. I saw them. I told them you were okay."

Allie said nothing for a minute.

"Razz," she said at last, "can you take me over there?"

"Sure, Brainy. No probs. Let's go."

"Wait a second. I gotta find someone to replace me first."

Before she left the table, Allie wrote her parents' names on the FOUND list.

Chapter Ten

The hospital was a madhouse. The emergency ward, the halls, the rooms were packed with beds and cots and worried people. Nurses slipped back and forth quickly through the noisy halls. Every few seconds a doctor's name was called over a loudspeaker.

Razz led Allie to a big ward on the second floor. "I'll leave you here, Brainy," he said. "Gotta get back to work. Will you be okay?"

"Yeah, no probs, Razz. See you later."

I wish I felt as brave as I sound, Allie thought. She wanted to go back with Razz. She didn't want to see the Hurt Look her father would give her and the I Told You So Look that would come to her mother's face as soon as Allie walked in. But she knew she had to stay.

She took a breath and walked into the crowded ward.

She saw her mother at the far end of the room, propped up on a bed. One leg was in a thick white cast that was attached to a rack over the bed. One of her arms was in a cast too. Allie's father stood beside the bed.

"Hi, Mom. Hi, Dad," she said as she got to the bed.

Allie's father spun around. He grabbed her and held her tighter than he had ever done. He said nothing. He held her for a long time.

"Allie!" her mother cried, her voice starting to wind up. "Where have you been? If I could get out of this bed I'd give you a darn good slap!" Then she calmed down and asked, "Are you all right?"

"Sure, Mom. I'm fine. What about you?"

"Oh, I'm all right, now. Where were you? We were worried sick. We even called the police."

Allie looked at her mother. Her mother's blonde hair was a mess. She had a purple bruise around her left eye. She looked like she'd been through a war. Allie's father didn't look so hot either. His suit was dirty and wrinkled and there was an angry red scratch across his forehead.

"I left you a note, Mom. I ran away."

"What on earth *for?*" her mother almost shrieked.

"Maybe we should talk about this some other time," her father said. "This isn't the right—"

"*No*! You're always avoiding things," her mother cut in angrily.

"I *don't* always avoid things! You're the one— "

Allie clapped her hands over her ears and shut her eyes.

"*Stop*! Stop arguing!" she shouted.

She opened her eyes again. Her father looked embarrassed. Her mother hung her head and picked at the bandage on her leg.

"Allie, what was it?" she asked softly.

Allie looked into her mother's bruised face, then at her father. She thought about why she had run away—the fighting between her parents, the four red circles. Three on her report card. One on her calendar.

Should I tell them? she thought. *How much should I tell them? Will it do any good*?

Then Allie realized they were going to find out anyway. She took a deep breath and started talking.

She told them everything—about the three subjects she failed, about Jack and how she might be pregnant, about the skateboard meet and about Slammer's death in the whirlwind. When she was finished, she was crying. And she felt worthless.

Allie's mother and father were silent for a minute. They looked shocked. But they didn't yell at her.

Her mother said, "Are you sure?"

Allie knew what she meant. "Yeah, pretty sure, Mom. I'm way overdue."

Allie's father ran his fingers through his thin hair. "I guess we shouldn't think of you as our little girl anymore," he said quietly. "You've been through a lot. Are you and Jack—"

"Dad, I'm through with him," she cut in. "I don't even want him to know. He's not important anymore."

He gave her a strange look. "No, I guess he isn't," he agreed.

Allie's mother said, "Come here, Allie."

Allie stepped closer to the bed, half expecting the shrieks to start. But her mother took her hand and held it. Her face looked serious and worried.

"You forgot to tell us a few things, didn't you, dear?"

What did she mean, Allie thought. "Honest, Mom, I've told you everything. Honest."

"You didn't tell us you saved that baby's life. You didn't tell us how you helped out at the school. Razz told us all about it."

"Mom, that doesn't mean anything," said Allie.

"Of course it means something," her mother said. "It means a lot. We're proud of you, Allie. You're a very brave kid. And you're a very *good* kid."

Allie looked at her father. He was smiling. He pointed to the window.

"Look," was all he said.

Allie let go of her mother's hand and stepped over to the window beside the bed. She looked out across the sunny neighborhood. She could see the scar-like path the tornado had left as it chewed up trees and smashed houses. It changed people's lives forever. She remembered what Razz had said, that it looked as if the neighborhood had been bombed.

Then she began to pay attention to the small groups of people. Already they were cleaning up the streets, moving furniture out of houses to waiting trucks, starting over. In the distance she saw a tiny figure on a roof, swinging a hammer.

Her father's voice came from behind her. "I guess we—the three of us— I guess we've got some things to work out. We've got some rebuilding to do."

Allie turned to see he was looking at her mother.

Her mother nodded. "Yes," she whispered. "Yes, you're right."

"Mom, Dad, we can do it together, can't we?"

Allie's mother and father spoke at the same time, "We can try."

Author's Note

There are lots of words to describe the atmosphere on that final day of May—brooding, ominous, foreboding— but I'd choose *weird*. The day before, Thursday, had been stormy, with thunder and downpours and damaging winds. Friday dawned hot and humid and stayed that way. When I walked through Innisdale Secondary School's parking lot at 4:30 PM, the air was heavy and clammy. The sky was dark gray, the clouds low. On the towering maples in front of the school, not a leaf stirred. The birds were strangely silent.

When I drove down the hill on Fairview Avenue it had grown so dark it was like nighttime. In the northwest, the sky was an ugly purple with a yellow tinge, like a bruise. I turned onto Highway 400 and headed north, passing through a few showers on my way home. I put a rock 'n' roll tape on the deck to brighten the mood.

When I got home, I turned on the radio to hear the news. Two words struck me: Barrie Tornado. I had missed being swept up in the whirlwind by twenty-five minutes. On that afternoon, fourteen tornadoes ripped through southern Ontario, killing twelve people, injuring dozens of others and causing about $100 million in property damage. The largest tornado left a path of destruction 90 kilometers long—much greater than the average. The Barrie Tornado was really five separate tornadoes that slammed into the town at 5:00 PM, May 31, 1985.

This novel is based on the tornado and its aftermath. With many other teachers, I was part of the clean-up crews that set to work immediately to bring order back to the community. Thousands of people helped. *Death Wind* is dedicated to them, and to the many who suffered from the storm.

—*William Bell*

William Bell is an award-winning author of more than a dozen books for young adults. Born in Toronto, Ontario, in 1945, he has been a high school English teacher and department head, and an instructor at the Harbin University of Science and Technology, the Foreign Affairs College in Beijing and the University of British Columbia. He lives in Ontario.

orca soundings

The following is an excerpt from
another exciting Orca Soundings novel,
Riley Park by Diane Tullson.

9781554691234 $9.95 PB
9781554691241 $16.95 LIB

CORBIN PLAYS HOCKEY AND IS KNOWN

as a scrapper on and off the ice. Fighting makes
him feel strong. His friend, Darius, is popular,
and his reckless risk-taking makes Corbin feel
alive. But at a party in Riley Park, Darius crosses
a line with a girl both boys like, and later Darius
and Corbin are attacked. Darius is killed, and
Corbin is seriously injured. Left with a clouded
memory and a weakened body, Corbin struggles
to identify the assailants and fights against the
loss of his friend. Will he ever be able to give up
the fight and find strength in acceptance?

Chapter One

In the Safeway parking lot, I drop two flats of beer into the back of my car. I leave the hatch open and wait for Darius to arrive with the hotdog stuff. I notice a girl getting off the bus across the parking lot at the bus stop. I'd recognize her from a mile away: Rubee.

Rubee is wearing her Safeway shirt and she's walking fast, like maybe she's late for work. Her dark hair is loose on her shoulders.

Darius shows up and slings the grocery bags into the car, fitting them around the beer and my hockey bag.

As Rubee walks, she combs her hair back with her fingers and catches it into a thick ponytail.

Darius says, "She is so hot."

Darius is watching her too.

I say, "Hot, yes. But Rubee is beautiful."

Rubee is a senior like Darius and me, but she goes to a different school. I've never seen Rubee anywhere but here, at Safeway. We always choose Rubee's checkout line, even if hers is twice as long as the others. Rubee is worth the wait.

Darius says, "Weird that she took the bus. Her boyfriend always drops her off."

I've never seen her boyfriend, but Rubee wears a guy's ring on her thumb. Plus, a couple of months ago, she rejected

Darius when he asked her out. Go figure—he asked her if she'd like to spend the night with a wild man.

I say, "You've seen Rubee's boyfriend?"

Darius nods. "He has a nice car."

I glance at my Civic. One fender is a different color and the left taillight is covered with a red plastic bag.

I say, "Maybe it's her brother."

"No." Darius turns to me. "It was her boyfriend. But she took the bus today, so that means he isn't her boyfriend anymore."

"Maybe he had to work or something."

Darius says, "From the car he drives, he makes way more money than a regular job."

"You think he sells drugs or something?" I watch as Rubee enters the Safeway. "She wouldn't go out with a guy like that."

Darius looks at me. "And you would know?"

An excerpt from *Riley Park*

"Yes. She's too sweet."

He says, "Sweet girls fall the hardest."

I say, "How can you be sure they broke up?"

"Let's just run with it," Darius says. "You think she's too sweet for you?"

My face grows hot. "No."

"So go ask her out."

"No."

He laughs again, and I'm getting pissed off.

I say, "Not today. I'll ask her out sometime when I'm wearing my team jacket. A hockey jacket makes a busted nose look tough." Instead of ugly. "And I'll wear my ring, my junior hockey championship ring."

Darius says, "If you don't ask her out right now, I will."

My hands curl into fists. "Like she'd go out with you, Wildman."

He shrugs. "Only one way to find out." He slams down the hatch on my car and strides toward the store.

I catch up with him. "We've got everything we need. Let's go."

But he's in the store and in Rubee's line.

Ahead of us, an old woman in sweatpants smacks coins onto the counter. She is ranting to Rubee about an expired coupon. She doesn't have much on the conveyor: bananas, toilet paper—the cheap stuff—and some liquid meal replacement old people drink. The cans of meal replacement have a red clearance sticker. They must be close to the best-before date. Maybe they've expired.

Rubee speaks quietly to the woman as she pushes several coins back to her. The woman grins, gathers the coins, grabs her bag of groceries and scuttles out of the store. The guy in front of us shovels the rest of his stuff onto the conveyor. Rubee counts the old woman's coins into the cash drawer. She looks up and sees me. She smiles.

I look at her hand. She's not wearing the ring.

I watch her scan the guy's groceries. She's wearing a black cord bracelet with a round red stone. The stone slides back and forth on her wrist as she works. But she's not wearing the ring. She smiled at me, she's not wearing the ring and we're standing in her line with nothing to buy.

I grab a pack of gum and toss it in a shopping basket.

Darius laughs. "Corbin, if you're asking her out, you'll need more time than it takes to ring in one pack of gum." He turns and snags a half-filled cart someone has left unattended. He pushes the cart into Rubee's line.

I say to him, "I'm not asking her out. I'm not ready. If she says no, I'll lose my once-in-a-lifetime chance." I peer into the cart. "Nice. You were right out of Huggies."

Behind us, a woman says, "Now where did I leave my cart?"

Darius says, "Once in a lifetime? You're asking her out, not proposing."

I pull a package out of the pile of groceries in the cart. "And animal crackers."

The woman's voice is louder now. "I swear, I left my cart right here."

Rubee looks up then, sees the woman. She glances at our cart and rolls her eyes. She picks up the security phone.

Darius says, "Oops, I seem to have someone else's cart." And he leaves it there. Just abandons the cart in the line. He walks by me and past the guy ahead of us until he's standing in front of Rubee. Rubee puts the phone down.

I elbow my way past the guy so that I'm beside Darius. I struggle to meet her eyes. "Uh, sorry about the, uh, cart."

Darius just stands there. Finally he says to me, "Anything else?"

I glance at Rubee. She looks like she's waiting for me to say something. Her eyes have little gold flecks. I feel my cheeks turn bright red. I hand her the pack of gum.

She smiles. "Just the gum? No diapers?"

I shake my head and hand her the money.

Darius sighs. He says to me, "Are you done?"

I look at my shoes.

"I'll take that as a yes." He turns to Rubee. "Riley Park, tonight. I'm saving myself for you."

She looks at him and crosses her arms. "Unlikely," she says, "on both counts."

"We'll go swimming."

"You might, but you'll freeze."

"I'm a wild man." Darius smiles at her. "I'll bring blankets."

It's not like Darius is super attractive. He's built, but he's not that tall. He spends a fortune on his hair. Maybe that's why the girls go for him. Darius reaches into a pail of plastic-wrapped flower bouquets by the check stand. He selects an arrangement of red and white roses. Water from the bouquet drips on the counter. He presents the flowers to Rubee. "These are for you," he says. "A token of my love."

Rubee takes the flowers and smiles.

Darius says, "Riley Park. Tonight. Nothing complicated, Rubee. You're your own woman. No one telling you what to do—you're in control. Come to the party if you want, bring some friends, have a few laughs, or don't. It's totally up to you."

The guy with the groceries tells us to piss off and get out of the line.

Darius ignores him. "Later, I hope," Darius says to Rubee, and he blows her a kiss.

orca soundings

The following is an excerpt from
another exciting Orca Soundings novel,
Running the Risk by Lesley Choyce.

9781554690251 $9.95 PB
9781554690268 $16.95 LIB

SEAN IS ATTRACTED TO DANGER.

After being the victim of an armed robbery, Sean
should be terrified but he isn't. He finds he likes
the rush that comes from danger and tries to
recreate the feeling. But when his risktaking leads
him to some of the worst parts of town and he
finds himself face-to-face with the original armed
robbers, he finds he must do the right thing.

Chapter One

The gunmen arrived at Burger Heaven shortly after midnight on Friday. I was on the frontline, taking orders along with Lacey and Cam. It was like a dream at first. The place had been quiet except for some workmen laughing over their French fries, and a couple of slightly drunk kids from school goofing around at a table by the windows.

And then the door opened and two guys with ski masks on walked in nervously. One walked straight to me. The other went to Lacey. As they approached, the guns came up. Lacey, Cam and I froze. The room suddenly went dead quiet except for the sound of hamburgers sizzling in the back and the buzz of the overhead fluorescent lights. I'd never even noticed the hum of the fluorescent lights before.

The guy with the gun pointed at Lacey spoke first. "Open it, girl."

Lacey froze.

"I said open it."

The guy with the gun on me said nothing. I was looking at Lacey. And then at Cam. There was a panic button on the floor beneath each register. A silent alarm. You triggered it and the cops would know we were in trouble. I saw Cam looking down at the floor.

But something told me that right here, right now, hitting that button would be the wrong thing to do. These two guys were nervous. I was looking my gunman right in the eyes. I knew there was something there. These guys were whacked on something. Anything could make them freak. The guns were real. Everything was real.

And that's when it kicked in.

This feeling of calm.

"Be cool," I said to the guy pointing the gun at Lacey. Then I looked at the guy with the gun on me. I stared straight into his eyes, and then I looked at the barrel of the gun like it was no big deal.

"I'm going to push this key and the drawer will open," I said. "Okay?"

My gunman nodded. I pushed the key, and the drawer opened. I saw one of the workmen get up. At first I thought he was going to try to do something. And I didn't want that.

But I was wrong. First he and then his buddy got up and slipped out the front door. Lacey's gunman turned and aimed in their direction. He pulled the trigger and the shot was deafening. "Shit," was all he said. The bullet must have hit the ceiling because no glass shattered. He turned back quickly and pushed the gun into Lacey's face.

"Here," I said, cleaning all the bills out of my register and handing them across the counter. "Now I'll get you the rest," I said.

"Yeah," my gunman said.

I walked to Lacey and made sure it was obvious what I was doing. I hit the key, the drawer opened and I offered over more bills.

Then I walked over to Cam's station and did the same. It was only money.

Nothing to die for, that's for sure. It was all clear as day in my head.

The two gunmen stuffed the money into their coat pockets, turned and ran. As soon as they were out the door and away from the parking lot, I hit the silent alarm.

Lacey began to cry and Cam said the stupidest thing in the world. "Why'd you give them the money?"

"You all right, Lacey?" I asked.

"No, Sean," she said, "I'm not all right."

"What were you thinking?" Cam asked. Somehow he wasn't getting it.

The kids at the table were standing up now. "I don't freaking believe it," one of them said and then puked on the floor.

Riley and Jeanette, who'd been listening from the food-prep area, came up to the counter now.

"Is everyone all right?" Riley asked.

"Yeah, we're all alive anyway," I said.

"Did you see what this jerk did?" Cam said, pointing at me.

"Yeah," Jeanette said. "I saw what he did. He saved you from getting killed."

Cam looked mad. He looked at me like it was all my fault.

The kids at the table out front were helping their buddy who had just barfed on the floor get himself together. Then they headed for the door. I probably should have asked them to stay until the cops came, but I didn't. I understood they wanted to get the hell out of here. I knew who they were, so I didn't bother to ask them to stay. The police could find them for information if they needed to.

Jeanette was holding Lacey.

Cam was blathering. "This isn't worth it," he said. "I'm quitting this stupid job. Now." He walked around the counter and kicked over a chair. Then he left. I didn't ask him to stay either.

When the police arrived, two officers in bulletproof vests pushed open the glass door and walked in, guns raised. I watched their eyes as they looked at us and then scanned Burger Heaven. I noticed the buzz of the lights again.

"They're gone," I said.

The guns came down and the cops moved forward.

"Anyone hurt?" one of them asked. Two more policemen came in the door.

"No," I said. "I think we're okay."

"Do you know which way they went?"

I shook my head no.

One of the policemen saw the bullet hole in the ceiling. "You guys had a close call," he said. "That wasn't a cap gun."

It was about then that I noticed something about the way I was feeling.

My heart was still pumping so loud I could hear it in my ears, and my breathing was a bit ragged.

But the weird part was that I was feeling great. And I'd been feeling this way from the moment the robber put the gun up to my face.

Titles in the Series

orca soundings